P9-CMY-524

# SLIM AND NONE

ALSO BY DAN JENKINS

NOVELS

*The Money-Whipped Steer-Job Three-Jack Give-Up Artist*
*Rude Behavior*
*You Gotta Play Hurt*
*Fast Copy*
*Life Its Ownself*
*Baja Oklahoma*
*Limo* (with Bud Shrake)
*Dead Solid Perfect*
*Semi-Tough*

NONFICTION

*I'll Tell You One Thing*
*Fairways and Greens*
*Bubba Talks*
*You Call It Sports but I Say It's a Jungle Out There*
*Saturday's America*
*The Dogged Victims of Inexorable Fate*
*The Best 18 Golf Holes in America*

DAN JENKINS

# SLIM AND NONE

A NOVEL

DOUBLEDAY

NEW YORK • LONDON • TORONTO • SYDNEY • AUCKLAND

PUBLISHED BY DOUBLEDAY
a division of Random House, Inc.

DOUBLEDAY and the portrayal of an anchor with a dolphin
are registered trademarks of Random House, Inc.

While all of the incidents in this book are true,
some of the names and personal characteristics of the individuals
involved have been changed in order to protect their privacy.
Any resulting resemblance to persons living or dead
is entirely coincidental and unintentional.

Book design by Fritz Metsch

Library of Congress Cataloging-in-Publication Data
Jenkins, Dan.
Slim and none : a novel / Dan Jenkins.—1st ed.
p. cm.
1. Golfers—Fiction. 2. Golf—Tournaments—Fiction. 3. Golf stories.
I. Title.
PS3560.E48S58 2005
813'.54—dc22 2004058561

ISBN 0-385-50852-2



PRINTED IN THE UNITED STATES OF AMERICA

May 2005

First Edition

1 3 5 7 9 10 8 6 4 2

*For my four treasures:*
*June Jenkins, Sally Jenkins,*
*Marty Jenkins, Danny Jenkins*

*Thanks for making my trip*
*on this planet a pure joy, and*
*for keeping in mind that everything*
*that happens to you in life is*
*not necessarily funny, but most*
*of it sort of is.*

I regard golf as an exercise in Scottish pointlessness designed for people who aren't strong enough to throw telephone poles at each other.

—FLORENCE KING,
columnist lady

# PART ONE

# THE MAGNOLIA JOINT

# 1

It had to be the first bare navel on the Masters veranda. Luckily it came with a shapely adorable. Could have been a bulker. All in all, she was your basic tri-state crime-spree gorgeous. Make you try to eat corn through a chain-link fence, as Cary Grant or Fred Astaire used to say, or maybe it was Grady Don Maples.

Picture this: a long-haired brunette babe poured into a pair of low-hanging stretch jeans looking like the same thing as one of those half-time college showgirls. She stood between the two big trees on the veranda. Her tummy was flat as a West Texas fairway, and she was wearing the minimum legal requirement of a white knit top. This helped her display two tickets that would easily gain her admittance to the hospitality tent at any golf tournament she'd wish to attend.

I should add that she also wore a clubhouse badge for the Masters.

"Screen-saver," Jerry Grimes said alertly.

"Fire in both engines," Grady Don said.

"Riders up," I said.

I don't know that there'd been too many sights at Augusta to equal that one. Usually the veranda was a gathering of geezers in their green jackets, scads of privileged folks sitting at tables under bright umbrellas, scattered groups of serious business execs looking worried about something, and assorted media intellectuals shopping around for scoops and scandals.

As a rule, the serious business execs would be talking to each other, their hands clasped behind their backs while they rocked back and forth in their FootJoys. They could be equipment salesmen, they could be the dapper officials of various golf organizations, or they could be powerful sports agents, but if they were powerful sports agents their eyes would be darting this way and that, and they'd have a tendency to bite their nails.

Assorted wives of Tour pros frequently emerged from indoors—two lookers, say, and one bulker. They would have dined upstairs on the balcony, where they'd discussed maladies, child-rearing, exercise classes, difficult mothers-in-law, catalog orders.

Players' wives have changed over the years. I wasn't around when they were all needlepoint ladies, but I'd been around long enough to see the lookers go from stately former yearbook favorites to Barbie dolls that could actually make noises like human beings talking.

We'd walked up on the roped-off veranda after our Tuesday practice round. I'd smiled at the two security guards who were stationed there to keep out the K mart shoppers. That's when we spotted the shapely screen-saver displaying her finest features.

She was obviously at the magnolia joint for the first time. If she was trying to arouse any of the gentlemen on the veranda, she was making a mistake. Most of the veranda gentlemen were on the high side of sixty and were more likely to be aroused by the report of a new oversized driver that would give them fifteen more yards.

Jerry Grimes said, "It's too bad that lovely thing happens to be the asshole's mother, Bobby Joe."

"That's no mother," I said. "I know what mothers look like. Mothers look like Betty Crocker."

"They do?"

"Cheerios."

"Mothers look like Cheerios?"

"Detergent . . . type of thing."

Grady Don Maples said, "I guess she don't crochet a lot, but she's still the asshole's mother."

"Which asshole?" I said. "I have choices."

"Scott Pritchard," Grady Don said. "That's old Gwendolyn Pritchard, it sure is. Scott's mom. Right there with her steel belly and her lung problem. Kill me first, Gwen."

"That's the child star's mother?"

I must have blurted it out. The dapper official of a golf organization glared at me. Guy in a dark blue blazer, white shirt, striped tie, red face. Looked like he knew for a fact that I ate with my hands.

Some hasty arithmetic was called for. Scott Pritchard was nineteen, our newest phenom on the Tour—there seemed to be one every year. He was six-three, muscled up, too handsome for his own good. He came out loaded with amateur titles, an average driving distance of 324 yards, a satchel of contracts too heavy to lift, and you could add the blank stare of a young Beverly Hills valet parker. His age meant the mom must have been a tap-in under forty, but she could play younger, as evidenced by this penetrating veranda moment.

"Scott Pritchard's a big kid," I said. "He must get his size from the lumberjack who knocked her up."

"It could have been a tight end," Jerry said.

"Naw, tight ends don't get laid by adorables," Grady Don said. "I was a tight end in college. Might as well be a defensive tackle. Scrap around with the meece."

We were interrupted by a media celeb. It was Irv Klar, a sports columnist for the *Washington Post*, as in D.C. I'd first known Irv as an aggressive young guy working for a small paper in California. He'd wanted to do a book with me. Me being the first golfer he'd ever met. I'd dusted him off. But since then, while my back was turned, he'd become a big-shot columnist and a best-selling author.

Irv's first bestseller was *Speed Freaks: The Story of How the Nazis Invented Amphetamines to Win the '36 Olympics*.

When it came out I'd seen Irv at a tournament and said, "Irv, I thought Jesse Owens won the Berlin Olympics, and the Nazis invented speed to keep their troops awake."

"That too," he said.

I'd read almost all the way through the first chapter.

Irv Klar had written two other bestsellers since. With time, I could remember the titles. He was always working on a new book.

Irv was wearing baggy shorts, frayed sneakers, faded knit shirt, and an old Brooklyn Dodgers baseball cap, to prove he was a man with a sense of history.

"Hey, guys," he said. "Who's your pick this week? I'm taking a poll for the column."

"Ben Hogan," I said.

"Ben Hogan?" Irv frowned. "Ben Hogan's dead."

"You're shitting me."

"You don't want to pick somebody serious?"

I said, "I'll stick with Hogan. Dead, he's already got me four back."

Irv said, "What about you two? Grady Don . . . Jerry?"

Grady Don said, "I'll go with old dead Sam Snead."

Jerry said, "I'll take Jimmy Demaret. He's dead, too, isn't he?"

Irv had spunk. He said, "I thought y'all had to win something big before you got to be assholes?"

He walked away, shaking his head.

"It's on our list of things to do," I called after him.

We turned our attention back to the shapely, or I should say the chick-babe-mom, who was dolling up the veranda. She was now smoking a cigarette and accepting a drink from a waiter in a white jacket. The waiter had carried the drink on a tray from the outdoor bar that's under an overhang near the main clubhouse door.

"How come I haven't seen her before?" I asked.

"Because she didn't come out till Bay Hill," Jerry said. "You skipped Bay Hill and Doral, remember?"

"True," I said. "I stayed home to do something. Oh, I know what it was. Get divorced."

Gazing at the chick-babe-mom on the veranda I was reminded of the time I was taken prisoner by another showstopper in a pair of low-riding jeans and skimpy top. Only she'd been a blonde. But Alleene Simmons, my first wife, hadn't dressed like that on purpose. It had been required of her by the low-rent owner of the café-bar-singles-derelict joint where she'd been employed as the hostess when I met her. The bucktoothed owner, Bodobber Roberts, had long since gone indoors for bookmaking.

Bodobber's was mostly a hangout for gambling degenerates in those days. Guys in Fort Worth who'd bet on everything from ice hockey to bugs crawling up a wall to how many weekend traffic fatalities there'd be—city, county, state, nationwide.

Alleene won my heart the minute I walked in. Not only with her looks but with the first thing she said to me.

As she led me to a spot at the bar, I asked her what was good tonight, meaning what was good to eat. She said, "From everything I've heard, it's Oklahoma, give the six and a half."

Now at the magnolia joint, still looking at the babe, I said to my pals, "You know, your teen trash and your rock sluts flash skin like that, but a mature grownup woman ought to know better. I mean, she could have asked somebody how to dress when you go to the Masters. She must be dumber than dirt."

"Yeah, maybe," Grady Don said. "Of course, as I recall, you don't fuck the dumb."

# 2

This was the year the former Cheryl Haney sent me to Downtown Dump City. She joined my heavy-hitting ex-wife lineup as old number 3, falling in there behind Alleene Simmons, old number 1, and Terri Adams, old number 2. I do believe Alleene is the only one of my wives I ever really liked.

Cheryl kicked me out of the $950,000 house she'd made me buy two blocks from the Colonial Country Club because she said that after three years of trying to make a marriage work with an asshole who didn't aspire to do anything with his life but hit a golf ball, it wasn't worth the effort.

I found out I'd missed the cut in my own home the day I came back from a California tournament and found the note that said, "You—out! And I'm putting a sign in the yard that says 'No More Shit-Brains Need Apply for Husband Duties Here.' Now, asshole. Adios your butt and your golf clubs down the road. I don't fuck for food anymore."

What happened was, Cheryl had turned about half socialite on me. She'd decided I didn't measure up to the kind of husband she ought to be seen with. Her a successful businesswoman now who hobnobbed with other Fort Worth rich ladies who shopped in Dallas and supported the symphony and got their hair done all the time. Never mind that those rich ladies had once worked as law firm receptionists and department store salesgirls and had only become socialites because they married rich guys.

I smooth-talked my way out of having to move immediately and our split wasn't finalized until another social occasion. It was the night Cheryl dragged me downtown to the Bass Hall again to hear the Fort Worth Symphony play music for animals romping through the forest.

Then afterward to the black-tie dinner party at the Fort Worth Club to discuss cellos with the city's culture lovers.

I was accused of humiliating and embarrassing her all evening by looking bored, yawning, and committing the sin of telling the conductor at the party how much I was in awe of his ability to read music while he waved his stick in the air.

I said I didn't see how anybody could read sheet music. Sheet music looked to me like my nine-iron and sand wedge trying to climb over fences.

"You're a disgusting fuckhead," Cheryl said, pushing me into a corner out of everybody's hearing. I countered by quoting from an old country song: "It wasn't God who made honky-tonk angels."

"You shit-heap!" she said viciously.

"Good," I said. "Fucks and shits. Now you sound like the chick I used to know . . . the one who swam across the Trinity to get out of her old neighborhood and let me introduce her to a better way of life."

Which was a cruel thing to say. I didn't judge people by their neighborhoods. Well, some people, maybe. But Terri Adams, old number 2, had come from the wealthiest side of town, the west side, and I discovered she'd sport-fucked every happy hour sumbitch in Tarrant County before she got around to me.

Cheryl was like a lot of mercenary chicks in this world. Chicks who thought that because they were born good-looking, they deserved to be rich, it was what God intended, and they were determined to become rich, even if it meant marrying a pot-bellied, bald-headed A-rab.

Cheryl took up golf, same as my other wives, although it was hardly because she liked the game as much as Alleene and Terri did. It was a social move, part of her plan. So, divot by divot, she golfed her way into the heart of every well-to-do male member at one of my country clubs, Mira Vista, which I came to learn was Spanish for Take Another Man's Wife to Lunch.

If I'd been as smart as any of those Mozart cellos I would have seen what was happening. Seen Cheryl slipping back into the life she knew before me—that of breaking up homes for sport and pleasure.

Now I was sure that if she ever hooked onto a damage-proof wealthy gentleman who owned a yacht and knew where Sag Harbor was, she'd fall deeply in love overnight and truly believe she'd won the ball game.

One of the last things she said to me was, "Just so there's no mistake about it, I'm keeping the house and the BMW."

"Naturally," I said, faking nonchalance. "Trinity River deal."

I must have hit a bull's-eye. I heard a medley of fucks and shits as I took my leave.

I was back living in a townhouse near the TCU campus. I was lonely, I confess—I'd had some good times with Cheryl when she wasn't giving me shit and spending with both hands—but I was happy to be unattached for the first time in a while. Which was evidently an attitude you could chalk up to being easily distracted by the Gwendolyn Pritchards of the world.

# 3

Where my profession was concerned, something of a more dire nature than loneliness was in the works. I'd turned forty-four.

Most people don't know it, but forty-four is not a good age for a pro if he's never won a major—a Masters, U.S. Open, British Open, or PGA—and I'd clean forgotten to do any of that in my eighteen years on the tour.

Winning a major is the only way a pro can prove he's succeeded in life. Prove he's not lower than a left-wing Hollywood midget, or a dick-nose Muslim fanatic roasting his camel dung dinner over the campfire, or, as Cheryl Haney once put it, referring to me, "a loser scum-pit shit-brain."

But win yourself a major and you're an overnight sophisticated genius celebrity. You're capable of curing diseases, finding homes for orphan babies, improving the economy, and solving all the problems of the Middle East—nobody gave a damn about Israel, as we know, until they put in bent greens.

While I haven't checked with Vegas on it, I'd say the odds on a pro winning a major after he's forty-four are about the same as they'd be on me ordering the line-caught octopus and rare loin of fallow deer with squash blossom mousse in a San Francisco restaurant.

Or even *dining* in a San Francisco restaurant that has tablecloths and napkin rings. Too risky. Might take a bite of free-range ballet dancer.

Of all the thousands of pros who've played this game at the highest level over the years—from the shepherd's crook up to now—it so happened that only seven players had won a major at the age of forty-four and over.

Only seven. You could punch that number upside the head and it wouldn't budge.

I'd been talking about this since my birthday on Sunday and all day long on the golf course that Tuesday. Jerry Grimes and Grady Don Maples may well have gotten tired of hearing about it.

Julius Boros is still the oldest player to do it. Boros was forty-eight when he won the PGA in '68 at Pecan Valley in San Antonio. Boros won by one shot over Arnold Palmer and Bob Charles when he got up and down for a par from forty yards off the final green.

I'd heard it was so hot and humid in San Antonio that week the Alamo almost melted into a Taco Bell.

Jack Nicklaus was forty-six when he shot that 65 in the last round and won his sixth Masters in '86. Reached in and snatched it away from Greg Norman and Tom Kite. They finished one back.

That was some scene, Jack striding up the last fairway, coming out of nowhere to grab his twentieth major. Everybody standing, applauding, not a dry eye in the gallery. Jack hadn't won a major since 1980 and most people thought he was all done, lift him on up.

I'd played in my second Masters that week. I was in the crowd on 18 when Jack came up. I wanted to see the historic event in person, and I shed a tear myself.

But not for Jack. The tear I shed was for the 79 I shot in the last round. I coughed up money on every hole. It was a Perle Mesta deal. I threw a party on every one of those slick greens, and delivered myself from sixth place after fifty-four holes to forty-third.

Hale Irwin was the last guy to do it. Hale was forty-five when he won his third Open at Medinah in '90. That time he made the long putt on the last hole, did the victory lap around the green to the delight of TV, slapping palms, and then beat poor old Mike Donald in the playoff.

I played in that Open, too, but I don't remember much about it. It's hard to remember anything about a tournament when your swing disappears for no reason and you finish in a tie for last, or sixty-first, whichever you prefer.

I do remember the goofy Medinah clubhouse. It was either built to look like a temple for Shriners or the architect designed it after he put on a fez and hit every bar on Rush Street.

Chicago is where a lot of peculiar stuff happens. Another forty-five-year-old won a major there, the '61 PGA at Olympia Fields. Jerry Barber sank putts from three area codes on the last three holes to tie Don January. It was a daylight robbery. Then he robbed January again in the playoff when he sank putts from two more area codes. A robbery may have been appropriate. Olympia Fields was where Al Capone once played golf.

Jerry Grimes said, "I read somewhere that a gangster named Machine Gun Jack McGurn used to play at Olympia Fields, too. He was one of Capone's buddies. Great name."

"He should have been there to machine-gun Jerry Barber," I said.

"You hold it against a man for making putts?" Jerry said.

"Only for the rest of his life."

Then I came to the forty-four-year-olds.

Harry Vardon was forty-four when he won his last British Open, at Prestwick in 1914, the last of his six. Roberto de Vicenzo was forty-four when he won the British Open at Hoylake, in '67. And Lee Trevino was forty-four when he won the PGA at Shoal Creek in '84.

"What about Vardon in Toledo?" I said. We were somewhere on the back nine waiting for a group of slow-playing plumb bobbers to plumb-bob their asses out of the way.

"Sumbitch had a grip," Grady Don said. "Vardon."

Jerry rewarded him with a chuckle.

I said there was no doubt Harry Vardon should have been the oldest man to win a major. He should have won the U.S. Open in 1920 at Inverness when he was fifty years old. Think about that, I said. A fifty-year-old man. He had a mortal lock on that Open, too.

"What happened to him?" Grady Don said. "His pipe catch his tweed coat on fire?"

I explained how even though Vardon missed a one-foot putt on the first hole the last day—a *one-foot putt*—he went on and shot his way into a four-stroke lead with only seven holes to play. But at the 13th he missed a two-foot putt—a *two-foot putt*—and he three-putted the next three holes in a row, and double-bogeyed the 17th when he hit a ball into the water, and despite all that he *still* finished only one stroke back of the guy who won, Ted Ray, another Englishman.

"Tell me Vardon shouldn't have won that Open," I said.

"You won't hear it from me," Grady Don said.

"My lips are sealed," Jerry said.

Grady Don said, "I don't see what's so bad about forty-four, Bobby

Joe. It's better than twenty-four. When you're twenty-four you don't own shit, you can't afford shit, and you can't see how you're ever gonna own shit, do shit, or amount to shit."

I said, "All I know is, I'm forty-four and if I don't win a major this year I'll only have two chances left."

Nobody had to say it. We all knew what those two chances were.

Slim and none.

# 4

There are no good opening lines left—they've all been used up by married guys in singles bars.

Honey, I hope you're not gonna hold it against me because I was born rich.

Excuse me, sweetheart, but my buddy and I were just talking about how much you look like Rebecca—that's my wife who died a year ago.

Hi, my name's Bond . . . James Bond.

Hi, my name's Kent . . . Clark Kent.

Darling, you can't be this beautiful and not have a valid passport.

Baby doll, I'll bet your armpits taste like apple juice.

You and me, angel pie . . . want to form the perfect race?

You throw all those out now.

Which was why, when I went over to Gwendolyn Pritchard on the veranda, I merely said, "If your name is Amber, I know you're not married—there's never been a wife named Amber."

"*What?*"

Attention, irritable-squint collectors. Found one.

"It's true," I said. "There are no wives named Amber."

"Gee, that's interesting," she said.

"Ashley sometimes. Never Amber."

"Do you mind?" She turned away.

Undaunted, I moved around to confront her. "Your wives are basically Mary Margaret . . . Ruth Ann . . . Dorothy Sue . . . Betty Jean. There *are* occasions where you might run into—"

"It's not working," she said.

"It's not?"

"Nope."

"You sure?"

"I'm positive. Trust me on this."

I wanted to tell her I hadn't seen lavender eyes on a brunette since Elizabeth Taylor, but she was looking through me or around me. I never could do that. When I looked at somebody in the face, I usually saw their face.

She sipped her tall drink and smoked her long cigarette while I dealt with the problem of trying not to be too keenly aware of her body. It was good I didn't see any jewelry stuck in her navel, and it was only mildly terrifying that up close her lung problem had become more severe.

I glanced at Jerry and Grady Don. They were twenty yards away, trying to act like they weren't watching us. Trying to act like they were listening to the equipment salesman. The equipment salesman was babbling at them nonstop, taking the dimple pattern on his new golf ball—the 401-K, Airborne Express, I-95—to a new scientific level, I assumed.

Under the other big tree on the veranda, a three-man Japanese TV crew was setting up to interview a Jap contestant. The contestant was holding a putter in his hand and glancing around, changing stances, looking impatiently inscrutable, like he hoped the interview would be over pretty quick so he could go inscrut the putting green.

I don't honestly know what they talk about on Japanese TV, but I do know the difference between the TV wizards in the United States and the ones in Great Britain.

Hit a bad shot in America and every announcer but Johnny Miller will throw you a softball. Say something like, "That's not exactly what he had in mind."

But hit a bad shot overseas and the Brit on the mike will say, "Ah, there's old Aunt Martha, trying to play golf again."

Off to the side were two geezers in green jackets. Augusta members. They were peering with puzzlement at the Japanese TV crew.

"See those two gents over there?" I said to the chick-babe-mom.

She scanned the crowd.

"Over there," I said with a nod. "The green jackets staring at the Yamamotos. They look like they're wondering who dumped the fucking stir-fry on their veranda."

One of the things I'd learned as I traveled life's weary path was that a man could say fuck in front of a lady dressed as sexily as Gwendolyn Pritchard was and she wouldn't be offended.

"This the restart?" she said.

Quick lady.

I liked quick ladies. Most guys don't. Most guys don't like ladies who talk at all. That's because the ladies most guys know like to talk about drapes, furniture, hardwood floors, children, and relationships. That book about men coming from Mars and women coming from Venus could have been called *Men Are from Carpet, Women Are from Hardwood Floors*.

"You can call it a restart," I said to Gwendolyn. "Nice day."

"Yes, it is."

"Handy for your outfit. Which I admire very much."

"Thank you."

"What comes with it, I mean."

"I *know* what you mean."

"Any other day here, you couldn't dress like that. The thing about the Masters, the weather's different every day. You can usually count on one day hot, one day cold, one day windy, one day of rain."

"Amazing," she said.

"I suppose it is, when you stop to think about it."

"No, I mean here I am talking to a meteorologist, and all along I thought you were Bobby Joe Grooves."

# 5

It's difficult not to look pleased when somebody recognizes you. Even knows your name. I tried not to act too surprised. Me, a lowly twenty-third on the money list. One of the guys walking around with no majors. "In other news," as some golf writers refer to us.

She said, "I follow golf rather closely. I'm Gwendolyn Pritchard."

She dropped her cigarette on the ground, stepped on it, and extended her hand for a formal intro.

As I took her hand a black kid in white coveralls and green cap appeared instantly with a plastic trash bag and a pointed stick and plucked the cigarette butt off the elegant lawn.

I said, "You might as well drop that on the carpet in the clubhouse. Don't you know this place is a cathedral?"

"I *am* aware it's the 'cathedral of pines,' but I could have sworn we were outdoors."

"Easy enough to field-strip your smokes when you're out on the course, or even standing here. We like to keep it pristine."

"You're a member?"

"Grizzled veteran. It's a curious thing. Come here a few years and you develop a pride of ownership, even though you're only a guest."

"You've seen my son play? You've watched Scotty?"

"You know, I just heard you were Scott Pritchard's mother. Grady Don Maples and Jerry Grimes over there . . . they told me. I was sure they must have meant you were his sister."

"Uh-huh."

"But you win 'Low Mom.' The trophy's being engraved."

"What do you think of Scotty's game?"

I said I was aware of how well he'd done as an amateur. I'd only seen him on TV, and on the practice tee this week, but I was impressed with his action, the way he went at it. I said he was a sweet-swinging lad, and Jesus Christ, he was long.

"I mean *long*," I said. "I don't cook chili that long. Listen, why don't we go sit at a table under an umbrella and talk golf? I'll have a beer and you can smoke with an ashtray?"

"Why not?" She started toward the tables.

As we threaded our way across the veranda, I said, "I have an in-depth question. Is there no Mr. Pritchard in town this week?"

"Good catch," she said.

"Even in your life . . . presently . . . ?"

"You got it."

Another thing I'd learned as I traveled life's weary path was that it wasn't remotely possible for a woman dressed in public like Gwendolyn was to have a husband in town with her.

"Marital discord strikes again," I said.

"Marital discord has legs."

"You're separated or you went all the way with Tammy Wynette?"

"I Tammy'd out. Two years ago."

"You sluffed him or he sluffed you?"

"I was the sluffee."

"The guy must be crazy," I said. "Where is the demented Mr. Pritchard these days?"

"He's in Beverly Hills with Lolita, of course."

It was no strain for me to envision Lolita.

"Younger than you?" I said.

"Only by fifteen years."

"Blonde?"

"Uh-huh." That answer had a melody to it. "I kept the house in La Costa."

"*La Costa?* You're too young to live at La Costa," I said brilliantly.

"Spent some time there, have you?"

"I've been roughed up by the gold lamé out there, yeah."

"I'll bet you have."

"What was in it, I mean."

"I *know* what you mean . . . Rick and I grew up in Encinitas. We both went to SC."

"Southern Cal?"

"Is there another SC? I was a cheerleader. Yep. I was Gwendolyn Gayle Turner, cheerleader for the cardinal and gold."

"Gwendolyn Gayle Turner is a Miss America name if I've ever heard one. Were you in the contest?"

She shook her head. "I couldn't sing 'On a Clear Day.' Cheerleaders were a normal size in my time—they didn't have to do Mary Lou Rettons. I don't apologize for being one. It was a big deal and gobs of fun. Rick was a fullback. He carried the ball some, but blocked mostly. We went to the Rose Bowl one year. Beat Ohio State. It was my favorite day in the whole world till Scotty won the Amateur at Oakmont. Scotty's size comes from his dad. After college Rick took over his father's signboard business. I got pregnant. Rick's been very generous. He'd give me anything I asked for. Guilt, right? I don't have to work, but I enjoy it. I have this shop in Del Mar with a co-owner. My friend Sandy Knox. Sandy's husband dumped her . . . to marry her tennis partner. Is that California enough for you?"

Gwendolyn explained that the ladies of La Jolla, Del Mar, Rancho Santa Fe were always looking for places to spend their husbands' money.

I said, "A college buddy of mine was married to a La Jolla lady one time. He said when La Jolla ladies discuss a maitre d', they're talking about the one in Zurich."

"Those are my customers."

"Gwendolyn, I have to confess. All my life I've lusted after Southern Cal cheerleaders. I finally know one but she's not a blonde—"

"Poor baby."

"I was going to say it doesn't hurt that much."

"I put the first golf club in Scotty's hand when he was five, I'm proud to say. That's when we moved to La Costa—so Scotty would have a golf course to grow up on. I like to think golf kept him from becoming a surf captain or a weed grower—there's a lot of that where I live. Rick and I spent our lives going to junior golf tournaments. Up and down the coast, all over the country. I thought it was fun. Rick acted like he thought it was fun, too, until one day he decided Lolita was more fun."

"Her name can't be Lolita."

"It's Ashley. I can't *believe* you said Ashley when you came over and hit on me."

"That wasn't a hit. You can't call that a hit. I didn't slap you around with my money clip . . . offer you a round-trip ticket to St. Croix."

"Your wife must not be with you this week, Bobby Joe Grooves—and don't tell me she died tragically a year ago."

I confessed that I *had* been married—and more than twice. How else would I know how to write poetry and overhaul a diesel truck at the same time? One wife was a good person, I said. Still is. The other two, it was a toss-up as to which credit card they liked to test-drive the best. Some days it was Amex, some days it was Visa. I said my most recent wife, Cheryl, instead of dying, had chosen to divorce me and seek out someone who liked seated dinners more than I did.

"You were married to a socialite?"

"Socialite is what she's aiming for."

"How far does she have to go?"

"She still has some trailer park to shake off."

"I see."

"Gwendolyn, all this means is, I'm a lonely single guy. I'm at the Magnolia Inn, and have no dinner plans. Where are you staying?"

"You're staying at the Magnolia Inn?" she said brightly. "*I'm* staying at the Magnolia Inn."

I said, "Further proof that fate don't have a head."

She repeated it. " 'Fate don't have a head'?"

"Fate's a funny old boy. You never know which way he's apt to turn."

"I'm keeping that for my own," she grinned. "Fate don't have a head."

If I'd put the over-under at ten minutes on Grady Don and Jerry coming up to our table, I'd have bet the under—and won. They were now standing there, looking down at us.

"We're going over to the practice joint," Jerry said.

"I'll be there in a while," I said. "Tell Mitch if you see him."

Roy Mitchell was my caddy. He'd been with me for ten years. There were those who thought he looked like a shorter version of Michael Jordan, but he'd looked like that before people knew who Michael Jordan was or what Michael Jordan looked like.

"You know these guys?" I said to Gwendolyn. "Good pals of mine. Grady Don Maples . . . Jerry Grimes."

"I know who they are," she said.

"How you, Gwen?" Jerry said.

"Good, thank you, Jerry," she said. "You played awfully well at Bay Hill on Sunday. You were in the group ahead of Scotty."

Jerry said, "I didn't know you were in my gallery—I would have dressed better."

Gwen laughed.

"Any of that hurt?" Grady Don asked her.

"I'm sorry—?" she said.

"Looks like them togs might be putting a strain on some of your exquisites."

I explained to Gwen that Grady Don couldn't very well help it, he was a born sophisticate.

Jerry said, "Gwen, I played a practice round with Scott at Bay Hill. Damn, he's long. Rock bands don't ride in limos that long."

Gwen smiled.

Grady Don said, "Shit, NBA players don't have dicks that long."

Gwendolyn glanced around with alarm. She was wondering if anyone at the nearby tables might have been listening in. I looked around, too, and concluded that the people at the other tables were preoccupied with talk about the new tee on 17 and the current health of the dogwood and azaleas.

Grady Don nudged Jerry. "Let's bolt, pard. As Winston Churchill used to say, I have to go point old Percy at the porcelain."

Gwen looked around again to check for overheards.

Grady Don and Jerry sauntered off, but Jerry looked back. "We gonna eat dinner later, B.J.?"

I said, "I'll have my people talk to your people."

After a moment, Gwen said, "Tell me something—and be honest. Are you embarrassed at the way I'm dressed?"

"Do I act embarrassed?"

"You are, aren't you? For me, I mean."

"I'd say your outfit is a little advanced for the Confederacy."

"Great. Now I want to dig a hole and hide. I didn't think anything about it until Grady Don said that."

"OK, I admit it got my attention," I said. "But now that we've chatted I understand it's a basic California thing. Hot day, dress cool. Nothing else to it. No hard-ons intended."

"I wish I had a blanket," she said, wrapping her arms around herself.

We talked about golf a while longer—mostly about her son's golf. She spoke of how disappointed they both were when Scotty had been forced to decline his first invitation to the Masters when he reigned as the

U.S. Amateur champion. They'd been packed and ready to go two days ahead of time when he'd developed a terrible ear infection.

We discussed having a drink later in the hotel bar.

I said I'd meet her for a drink in the Magnolia Inn but only if she promised to wear clothes.

"I brought clothes," she said, smiling.

I said, "The reason I suggest clothes, if you drop too much skin on the local bubbas, they might not understand it, having not gone to the University of Southern California, and I'd be forced to defend your honor, and this would result in me getting my ass whipped."

She said she'd be the lady in the chic black pantsuit tonight.

Right then you could say I was feeling plenty OK about the week, but that's when I got a jolt I didn't see coming.

The jolt came when Gwendolyn Pritchard said she wasn't only excited about her son playing in the Masters this week, she was excited about Saturday, when she planned to join the other feminists who were coming to town for the big protest against the Augusta National Golf Club's all-male membership policy.

Whoo, boy.

I didn't say whoo, boy, but that cheery bit of news caused me to utter a sound that's generally known around my neighborhood as a killer sigh.

# 6

I called in sick for dinner with Grady Don and Jerry—they never wanted to go anywhere but Hooters anyhow. I also called in sick for drinks with Gwendolyn Pritchard, seeing as how she'd dropped that feminist protest shit on me.

It was a lie that I wasn't feeling like I'd be good company. Blamed it on a sinus deal. I couldn't think of anything better. A stomach type of situation might have scared her off for good—it would me—and I wasn't totally sure I wanted to lose sight of her.

I said I'd sentence myself to room-service soup tonight and watch a little cable. Catch up on the shows where people talk like people talk in real life. Say "fuck" and stuff.

She took the wave-off nicely, or pretended to, saying she was a little bushed herself. She suggested we reschedule for tomorrow night. She offered to make a dinner reservation for us on the hotel's outside terrace.

I said fine.

"I'll put the pantsuit on hold for another evening," she said.

With that, she wished me luck in the Masters Par-3 Tournament, which she was looking forward to watching, and hung up.

What I needed in the Par-3 Tournament was a new short game.

The next morning Grady Don and I played together and neither of us ever hit a shot within five feet of wonderful. Missed out on a chunk of crystal again.

It always amazed me that 4 million people swoop down from

somewhere to watch the Par-3 Tournament. It couldn't be less important, in the big scheme of things. But then I always have to remind myself that it's the one event where the fans can inch up close to their heroes.

The fans jam up around every green and tee and get to overhear the Tigers and Phils and the basic legends, the Jacks and Arnolds, say things like "I thought you had that one, pard," and they're thrilled to hear these real-life voices—they can almost reach out and touch the heroes. And they can't wait to go home with these tales and recite them to their golf-nut friends and their golf-nut family members.

"Hey, Aubrey. I heard Tiger say things last week. He said words. Like we do. Mickelson said words, too. I heard him!"

But thank the Lord these people exist or I'd have had to find a new line of work a long time ago.

I nearly backed out of dinner with Gwendolyn again on Wednesday night, but after letting it sit on a window sill a while I decided, oh, OK, maybe I could turn her around on the protest-feminist deal.

Failing that, I figured the time with Gwendolyn would be educational. She could catch me up on all the urgent social issues of the day. It was a cinch I'd be behind on all the urgent social issues of the day because I'd quit watching the news on network TV, not being a big fan of socialism, and I wasn't walking around with a pile of degrees in Communism from Berkeley and Harvard. I was just a simple patriot. And unlike your silly lefties, I wanted to see my country protected from the swarms of raving, subhuman assholes who want to kill us because they hate cheeseburgers, golf, football, soap and water, toilets that flush, the *Sports Illustrated* swimsuit issue, clothing stores, and women who don't smell like donkeys.

It would also be helpful, I'd mention, if we could delaminate all the dunce-cap university professors who want to "diversify" this and "globalize" that, provide air-conditioned condos and SUVs for illegal aliens, healthcare and satellite dishes for armed robbers and serial killers, and can't wait to blame the United States for all the bad shit that happens in the world. They could globalize this. That was my basic message.

I planned to get all that up front with Gwendolyn when she met me in the bar at the Magnolia Inn. If she wanted to know if all golf pros were as conservative as I was, I'd tell her most of them were, except more so, and if she wanted to know why, I'd tell her one reason was because we researched it a few years back and found out they didn't pay squat for prize money in the Che Guevara Invitational and the Beijing Classic.

# 7

The Magnolia Inn is in an old part of the city, not far from downtown, and not far from the Augusta National in another direction. It's in a sprawling neighborhood of southern mansions, many of them tucked away on side streets. Most towns have a similar neighborhood—an area of palaces built by cotton, cattle, oil, Coca-Cola. Huge old three- and four-story houses that have more lawns, trees, gardens, charm, and memories than closet space and bathrooms.

The five-floor hotel was a relic, like the homes around it, but it had been remodeled and modernized in terms of plumbing and electrical conveniences. The restaurant and bar on the second floor were cozy and there was an outside roofed-over terrace adjoining.

I made a point of going to the bar ahead of Gwendolyn to have a quiet drink and brood about my pairing. The pairings had been posted earlier on Wednesday. I was early Thursday, late Friday.

I didn't expect to find myself in a feature group with Tiger or Cheetah Farmer or any of the headliners, but neither did I expect to go off so early on Thursday, at 9:04 A.M., with a Belgian whose name I couldn't pronounce—Blisters, or something—and a rookie I'd never heard of.

Ace Haskell was the rookie. Guy named Ace. Guy calling himself Ace. Guy answering to Ace. In my humble opinion, the name didn't have a very substantial ring to it.

The idea of having a quiet drink was a pipedream, this being Masters week. I was immediately recognized and introduced to two fans of golf and Budweiser.

"Hey, it's Bobby Joe Grooves," one of them said.

"Hey, you're right," I said.

"I'm Blubber Doss. This is Hubbard Gilliam."

"How you guys doing?" I said nicely. Practice for outings.

Hubbard Gilliam said, "Aw, good as can be expected, I guess, considering there ain't near enough cunt on the perimeter."

He yelled at the bartender to bring me a drink and put it on his tab. I ordered a Beefeater martini on the rocks with four olives.

"Hell, I didn't know I was buyin' you dinner," Hubbard said.

I said I'd read where Ben Hogan enjoyed a cocktail or two every evening at a tournament. It helped him relax, pursue a good night's sleep.

Blubber Doss and Hubbard Gilliam were well-built guys and dressed neater than I would have expected most Blubbers and Hubbards to be dressed. They wore button-down short-sleeve dress shirts, nice slacks that fit, and polished loafers. Blubber must have been named for his gizzard lips rather than his waistline. Hubbard's thick brown hair, parted in the middle, was sprayed into place perfectly. He'd do as a poster boy for Frat Row.

Blubber said, "We're honored to be in your presence, Bobby Joe. I'm a four, Hubbard's a two. We're from Atlanta."

"Great city," I said, lying through my veins. Atlanta used to be a great city, but that was before it turned into the South's largest parking lot. It was only great now if you fancied traffic and concrete. But history had taught me that my health was best served if I humored strangers in bars.

"We played Palmetto today," Hubbard said. "Over in Aiken?"

"Fun course," I said. "Old-fashioned."

Hubbard said, "I'd have beat up on it pretty good, but I couldn't buy a putt, could I, Blubber?"

Blubber said, "You sure couldn't. But you didn't play bad for a guy with bad breath and a trick knee."

"He thinks he's a funny cocksucker sometimes," Hubbard said.

"We play at Rebel Creek in Atlanta," Blubber said.

"I don't believe I know Rebel Creek," I said.

"My daddy built it," Hubbard said. "All golf, no real estate. Great course, great club. No fags, no Jews, no nee-grows. We confine the membership to people who went to southern Ivy League schools."

"What might those be?" I said, trembling with curiosity.

"Aw, you know," Hubbard said. "W and L . . . UVA . . . Duke . . . Chapel Hill . . . Sewanee . . . Me and Blubber went to W and L."

As I dwelled on that information, thinking how fortunate Washington and Lee had been, Hubbard said, "Rebel Creek's good enough to hold the National Amateur, except they'd never let us have it since we don't have any fags, or Jews, or nee-grows in the club."

I said, "Why don't you invite some to join?"

Hubbard looked bewildered. "Who would they eat with?"

I chuckled, mainly because I was stuck for a response.

"Hey!" Blubber said. "You ought to know this, Bobby Joe, being a pro and all. Hubbard says Pine Valley is in Michigan. I say it's up east in one of them New Hampshirts. Me and him never played it but we're fixin' to. I say you need to play all the famous courses to complete your golf education, so to speak."

"Pine Valley's a great course," I said.

Blubber said, "That's what the bow-tie fucker said. Bow-tie fucker was in here a while ago drinkin' white wine, actin' like he was sorry for anybody who wasn't a member of Pine Valley, like he was."

Hubbard wasn't sure he wanted to believe it when I informed him that Pine Valley was in New Jersey.

"That's bullshit," Hubbard said. "I been to New Jersey on bidness with my daddy. There ain't nothin' up there but smokestacks and wops."

"It's kind of hidden," I said. "It's in the town of Clementon, but it's tucked away in a forest. I've played it a few times. I hate to tell you guys this, but the bow-tie fucker knew what he was talking about. Pine Valley is the best golf course in America."

"Man, you don't mean that," Hubbard said. "Better'n the Augusta National? That's more bullshit, is all that is."

Blubber said, "You can't call it bullshit, Hubbard. The man knows golf. Man plays the Tour!"

"Man can play with your mama's clump for all I care," Hubbard said. "It's still bullshit."

I said, "Augusta's great, don't get me wrong. Augusta has the greatest seven holes in golf, ten through sixteen. It has the greatest three holes in golf, eleven, twelve, and thirteen . . . although you have to consider eight, nine, and ten at Pebble. But Pine Valley has the greatest eighteen holes in golf. Every hole is distinctive, you remember it. Pine Valley is totally unique."

Hubbard elbowed Blubber. "Guess we better go play that sucker."

"It's not easy to get on," I said. "You have to know a member."

"Fuck," Hubbard said in a tone to indicate I'd made the idiotic statement of the decade. "We'll get on. My daddy'll money-whip their ass."

Blubber said, "Bobby Joe, what you think about that bitch gonna lead the protest this week?"

He was talking about Anne Marie Sprinkle, the rabble-rousing activist, always popping up on TV. Anne Marie Sprinkle was chairwoman of something called the National Assembly of Women Commandos.

I said the media had given Anne Marie Sprinkle far more publicity than she deserved. But all you had to do to get on TV or the front page today was holler real loud about one thing or another.

Hubbard Gilliam said, "I hear she's a academic doctor of something don't make a shit. She says she's bringing a thousand protestors. Somebody needs to butt-fuck Anne Marie Sprinkle."

I said, "Second chapter in the Hootie-Martha War."

Hubbard said, "Except we ain't got Hootie and Martha anymore. I figure Kisser can handle Anne Marie, though."

K. S. "Kisser" McConnell was the new Augusta National chairman, replacing the retired Hootie Johnson, and the busybody Martha Burk had found other causes to jack with.

"I've seen Anne Marie Sprinkle on TV," Blubber said. "She ain't no movie star."

Hubbard said, "Naw, she's about eighty pounds beyond movie star."

That made Blubber laugh.

"Aw, goddamn," Hubbard said, looking past me, slumping onto the bar rail, acting injured.

"Holy shit," Blubber said, gaping in the same direction, looking as injured as Hubbard from an invisible attack.

I turned to see Gwen Pritchard coming toward us.

She did look stunning enough to cripple somebody. Her long black hair falling softly around her shoulders. Her tan face and lavender eyes set off by her white blouse. She was wearing the black pantsuit, all right, but I'd forgotten to suggest that she might want to avoid the criminal cleavage.

"I see my business associate is here," I said to the guys, and quickly took Gwendolyn's arm to escort her to the outside terrace.

"Aw, help me, Jesus, help me."

I believe that's what I heard Hubbard Gilliam mumble painfully as I led the chick-babe-mom away.

# 8

The need for a second martini became pressing the moment we were seated at our table. That's because Gwendolyn said my killer sigh on Tuesday afternoon hadn't gone unnoticed, she fully understood the meaning behind it, and wanted to make something crystal clear to me about how she stood on the issue of the Augusta National's all-male membership.

"Discrimination is not a game," she said, her tone aimed at carving the words into the Sarazen Bridge on the 15th hole.

I was smiling before she said it, kept smiling as I flagged a waitress and ordered cocktails for us, and smiled on through my reply, which was:

"Brave men fought and died on Iwo Jima for your right to demonstrate against golf."

She said, "I would like to have a serious discussion about this, if that's possible, but—oh, here's Scotty. He wanted to stop by and meet you."

He stopped. I stood. We shook. The well-built Scotty made me feel in need of vitamins and a personal trainer. He was scrubbed up, Nike swooshed in his maroon form-fitting crewneck, diamond earring glistening, and his hair was scruff-styled like a young actor whose name I vowed not to remember in a movie I walked out of because nobody talked.

Scotty said he was off to meet two "bros" for a beer and pizza.

I asked what he thought of the course.

"No rough," he said. "I can't believe it. You hear about a place all your life but you get here and there's no rough. Geeaaah."

All his life. He was fucking nineteen.

"It has other difficulties," I said.

"That's what they say. So far, though, it looks like a putting track to me. Geeaaah, no rough at all."

"I find a good many sidehill lies myself," I said.

He looked confused.

"Uneven lies," I said. "Nothing level? Funny stances?"

"Oh, yeah, yeah, yeah. If you don't drive it far enough. You're on the senior tour now, huh?"

Mom laughed.

I said, "I'll have to wait a while longer for that mulligan."

He said, "Gotta roll. Good luck this week. Later, Mom."

She said, "Don't stay out late, honey. There's this thing called a major starting tomorrow."

"I'm all over it," he said, and was gone.

I said with some alarm, "You're not sharing a room, are you?"

"That's a rather sick question, don't you think?" the chick-babe-mom said. "Of course he has his own room. He also has his own home. In Florida . . . to avoid tax problems."

"I know Florida," I said. "I'd rather have a tax problem. Florida is home of the door-to-door reptile."

She smiled. "He has a two-bedroom townhouse in Windermere, near Orlando. He's a member at Isleworth."

"With Tiger, Shaq, and Cheetah. Shouldn't he have a nickname?"

I didn't tell Gwendolyn my first impression of her kid. That it wouldn't be much trouble for him to pass for an arrogant prick. But he was only nineteen and he played golf, which was the saver. Most teenagers today by and large are morons. Not capable of saying anything intelligent because they've grown up having to yell above their music, which sounds like two leaf blowers in combat. What's sad is that most teenagers today can hear the leaf blowers, but they can't hear Harry Connick Jr. doing "Sweet Georgia Brown." Now that I think about it, the only teenager I've ever heard say something interesting was Judy Garland—and she sang it in a movie.

Now Gwendolyn said, "Scotty's shy socially, but he's confident about his golf game. He doesn't think anything is impossible on the golf course."

"He has a world of talent," I said. "Who looks after his vast wealth?"

"His father. IMG made a strong proposal, but Rick is smart about finances. He said handling Scotty himself would be a no-brainer. Rick has started his own agency. He's looking around for other clients. He negotiated Scotty's deals with Nike, Titleist, American Express, Callaway, Dell, Porsche . . . all the foreign things."

I said, "Rick's smart to handle the kid himself. Let Dad be the thief. What does he take for himself, twenty percent? Thirty?"

"Thirty. IMG would have taken thirty."

"Man's office needs paper clips and pencils, and there's always the bottled water to think of."

She flicked an ash. "Scotty's financial setup is awesome. It's true what you may have read in the golf magazines."

"What might I have read?"

"Scotty was guaranteed fifteen million a year if he never made a cut."

"I wish Rick was my agent. But I'm not lugging around a National Amateur, two Westerns, and . . . didn't he win the NCAA too?"

"Yes. Last year. His only year at SC."

"Boy, he'll miss that degree someday—when he's trying to decide what country to buy."

"You know, I'm sorry he's missing the fun of college. I am."

"Yeah. The drugs, whiskey, parties, throwing up, car wrecks, getting chicks pregnant. Those were the days."

"You didn't like college?"

"I loved every minute of it."

"Scotty's never cared about anything but golf. It's too bad in a way. I suppose he's a monster I helped create. He does like girls and having a slick car to drive, but more than anything he likes hitting golf balls and winning tournaments."

"How often does Dad the Agent come around?"

"Not as often as I do. He drops in for a day or two here and there. I'm sure he'll be at the Open. We won't be sharing a room, in case you're interested."

The drinks arrived. Gwen lit a cigarette before she tasted her potato vodka and soda. I bit off half of a large green olive and washed it down with a sip of the martini. It seemed time for somebody to speak.

I volunteered. "Where did we leave off on the touchy subject?"

"I'm wondering if we can discuss it seriously."

"I remember you reciting Anne Marie Sprinkle's battle cry. 'Discrimination is not a game.' "

"It isn't."

"I appreciated you not yelling it out loud."

"I was taking pity."

"The Augusta National doesn't discriminate. Women have been playing the golf course as long as it's been a golf course."

"But women can't be members."

"They should be happy about it. They can play golf all they want and not have to put up with the cigars and the belching."

"I didn't realize how lucky they are."

"Man, it's a good thing Bobby Jones thought up the Masters or nobody would have heard of Anne Marie Sprinkle. This is the biggest thing that ever happened to her."

"She's fought for many good causes in her life."

"Well, she's on the wrong side of this one. The Augusta National is a private club. It can do what it pleases."

"It's not a private club."

"Yes it is."

"No it isn't."

"Yes it is."

"No it isn't."

"Yes it is."

"No it isn't. Not this week."

I was trying hard to hold my temper, not have to discount some of her exquisites.

I said, "It's a private club fifty-one weeks a year. What's so bad if one week a year it holds a Kentucky Derby . . . a Rose Bowl . . . a Masters? Jesus, what a terrible thing. One week a year the club holds one of the great sports events in the world, but all of a sudden it's a plague on mankind because some academic witch says it is—and a bunch of sportswriter and TV saps talk about it and build it into a big social issue. You know what we need? More wars and depressions. Give the activists and the media something serious to worry about."

My little speech didn't cause her to toy with the silverware or nervously light another cigarette to go with the one she was smoking. She sat there looking unmoved.

Then she said, "I love the Masters, Bobby Joe. I'm delighted to be here. I'm thrilled my son is playing in it. But this is a legitimate feminist issue. There are CEOs in the club whose companies sell products to women, and yet a woman can't join their club. There's something wrong with that."

"There are dozens of other all-male golf clubs in this country, but Anne Marie Sprinkle only wants to protest against the Augusta National. Why do you suppose that is?"

"Because it puts on a tournament that's available to the public—which means it's not a private club this week—and it has no female member."

"Wrong. Anne Marie Sprinkle wants to protest this week because the Masters is on national television. Has any activist ever protested anything anywhere if there wasn't a TV news crew around? No livin' way."

She was still looking at me calmly.

"I'll tell you something else," I said. "This wouldn't even be an issue if the club was in Massachusetts. But it's in the Deep South. That makes it an easy target for the libs. Anne Marie Sprinkle is so uninformed she's even said they can move the Masters to another town. Hey, I know. What about Hartford? I'm sorry, but Anne Marie Sprinkle is a horror movie—*Attack of the Fat Libs.* The worst thing is, she's trashing the Augusta National members in the media. She's accused them of being a bunch of decrepit old mush-mouth, tobacco-spitting Confederate generals who don't have anything to do but sit around the club and reminisce about all the great pussy back in Charleston."

"You're making another speech."

"Yeah, I am. Anne Marie Sprinkle is trying to be Joan of Dogwood, but she's so uninformed, she doesn't even know that some of the club's southern members are successful businessmen with a track record of working to integrate the South's banks, businesses, politics . . . and they've helped promote the careers of lots of women and minorities. That's just a damn fact. Christ, bad-mouthing southern white men is so old and tiresome, it's old and tiresome."

"Now you sound like a press release." Still smiling. "None of this would be a problem, you see, if the club would simply enter the twenty-first century and admit a lady member."

"Oh, I'm sure that would solve all the world's problems. You bet. Find a lady CEO of some investment company . . . woman in a ten-thousand-dollar designer suit . . . five-thousand-dollar haircut . . . fifty-thousand-dollar face job . . . invite her to join. That'll fix everything. Man, with that lady in the club there'll be no more wars, hunger, homeless, crime, discrimination. What else? No more disease, floods, fires. It'll be just one big happy globe—and the Masters did it, folks. There's a Lucille for you."

"A what?"

"Lucille. There used to be an old saying. Good deal, Lucille. Some of us have shortened it."

"Can we order dinner now?"

"I have a better idea for the Augusta National. Instead of the lady CEO, the club should cover more bases. Take in a howling, screeching, pro-choice, antiwar, anti-Christian, tree-hugging, veggie burger, crippled black lesbian. Perfect."

"Bobby Joe?" she said.

"What?"

"If you keep this up, I'm not going to sleep with you tonight."

# 9

This paperback novel got me. The kind you buy in an airport and intend to read on a flight but turn into a three-point shot by page 43 or a slam dunk by page 57.

Her creamy lips. Her warm tongue. He stroked her soft inner thigh. They explored each other's depths. The moist darkness of their depths. The darkness getting moister. Moister? She took him in her mouth. He took her in his mouth. How was that possible? Like this, that's how. Who ordered the combo? The raw lust seeped from their bodies. No dripping allowed. Seeping only. She guided him into her. He sighed as he entered her dark moist depth. She thrust her head back and squealed. He thrust his head back and groaned. Lot of thrusting going on.

That's about where I laughed out loud.

"Are you crazy?" she said, jerking away.

"I'm sorry," I said. "I didn't mean to laugh."

"What happened? Are you all right? Are you *injured*?"

"Nothing happened."

"*Something* did."

"It has nothing to do with you."

"The hell it doesn't."

"No, no. Really. It was . . . I swear on my mother's Bible . . . autographed by Jesus himself . . . it wasn't you. It was something silly."

"Something silly? I was something *silly* on your mind?"

"Not you. I started thinking about a novel."

"You're making love to me and thinking about a woman in a *novel*?"

"Not another woman, no. Something made me think about the way they write about sex in some books I've read. Sometimes it's so serious with the slurping and throbbing. It's like, you know . . . humorous."

"I'm humorous. I made you laugh. Terrific."

"That's not what happened."

"You didn't laugh?"

"I laughed, but—"

"Who do you think I am? One of those sad, desperate divorcées who need a vengeance fuck every now and then from an experienced, willing hand like yourself?"

"Come on, Gwen. You're making too big a deal out of it. You're incredible . . . fantastic . . . first-team all-world. That's what I was thinking. But out of nowhere this dumb thought jumped into my head and it made me laugh. I started thinking, 'He entered her . . . She guided him into her moist darkness . . .' That kind of thing."

She looked at me sadly. " '*He entered her*'?"

"Uh-huh."

" '*Her moist darkness*'?"

"Like that, yeah—you know—book shit."

"This is all so goddamn romantic, I need a cigarette."

She rolled over, gathering the sheet around her, grabbed a cigarette from her pack on the end table, and lit up.

I enjoyed her second-hand smoke. Most ex-smokers hate second-hand smoke. I like it. Second-hand smoke reminds me of the best friend I ever had.

I'd stopped smoking two years before while recovering from the mother of chest colds. I'd caught it on a flight. Probably from this guy next to me who was unquestionably using someone else's frequent-flyer points to sit in first class. This germ-flinging slug in sandals, jogging shorts, and a T-shirt. No wonder airlines are going broke. I seem to be the only guy who pays to fly anymore. Anyhow, it took me a month to shake the rot, and I never went back to smoking.

I'd been tempted to start again. Why not? Ben Hogan smoked every day of his life, won ten majors, and lived to be eighty-five. If Ben Hogan hadn't smoked, he'd never have cured his hook. That's what the Marlboros kept whispering to me.

I said to Gwendolyn in a weak voice, "I wish I knew what to say to you. I didn't mean to insult you . . . hurt your feelings."

"I know what to say to *you*," she said. "No wonder you've been married three fucking times."

# 10

Man with only two hours' sleep. Man who'd spent the night trying to get back on good terms with a woman he'd become extremely interested in. Man with one golf shoe on, one golf shoe in his hand, a sausage-and-egg biscuit from Mac's in his other hand, one bite gone. Man limping, hopping, struggling to make his 9:04 tee time in the first round of the Masters. Man looking more like he'd been by-god drunk last night than a man who'd overslept and was in a panic.

Fortunately there was this understanding with Mitch. If he hadn't heard from me and I didn't show up in the practice area within thirty minutes of my tee time, go to the putting green. If I didn't show up at the putting green within ten minutes of my tee time, go to the first tee. And if I never showed up on the first tee, go to the police.

I made it with two minutes to spare. Time enough to put my other golf shoe on. Time enough to inhale the rest of my sausage-and-egg biscuit. Time enough to shake hands with the Belgian—Karp Blisters? Kessters?—and with Ace Haskell, the wide-eyed rookie in the faded orange golf shirt.

This was after speeding to the club, doing a Dale Jr. thing into gate 3, the contestants' gate, which is next to Magnolia Drive, slamming the car into a parking place by the clubhouse that was reserved for Arnold Palmer, rushing into the locker room, snatching the golf shoes out of my locker, and hobbling across the veranda down to the first tee.

Mitch greeted me with, "I was fixin' to go to your hotel room . . . see if you was sleepin' so hard they drawed a line of chalk around the body."

Buoyed by Mitch's humor, I managed to scramble off the first tee without hitting a line-drive skank and killing somebody. I even parred No. 1 without any big adventures. The kind the Belgian dwarf and Ace

Haskell experienced. Ace rattled around in the trees, the Belgian buried himself in a bunker. Both made a triple.

It was after I turned the front with a light-running 34, two-under, that I let Mitch in on my secret.

"I'm so exhausted, I've got tempo," I said. "It's a Bobby Jones deal. Jones said you can't swing the club too slowly. OK, he was talking about hickory, but it still helps me. People forget Jones won all his majors with hickory. He retired before steel took over. The steel shaft was around, but nobody believed in it until Billy Burke won the '31 Open with steel."

Mitch said, "I'm glad you straighten that out for me. It's been preyin' on my mind."

"Hungover or exhausted," I said. "Those are the two things that keep me from swinging too fast."

"What we got goin' today?"

"Exhaustion."

"You make friends with whiskey last night?"

"I made friends with something stronger than whiskey."

"Sounds like a woman lady?"

"A too-much woman lady."

"You wear a raincoat?"

"No. We were in too big a hurry to think about taking precautions."

"Sure 'nough?"

I kept clubfacing it on the back nine. I steer-jobbed my way around Amen Corner, two-putted for birdies at the 13th and 15th after reaching both on my second, and found myself four-under as I stood on the 18th tee, needing par for 68.

My name was up on the scoreboards around the course, but I wasn't counting on being the first-day leader. There was already a crowd of celebs up there working on five-, six-, seven-under.

Tiger, Ernie, and Phil were among them. Celebs Grady Don Maples liked to refer to as Elvis, Madonna, and Britney, as in Elvis Woods, Madonna Els, and Britney Mickelson.

This was no insinuation that Ernie and Phil had become interior decorators. It was flattery. Grady Don felt they'd achieved a celebrity status that required only one name.

I looked at my wristwatch, saw it was only 2 P.M. I'd been on the course for five hours. Not bad for a major. I keep my watch in the golf bag for the simple reason that I like to know what time it is. However, there are those celebrity types, you may have noticed, who wear a leather-band wristwatch when they compete. The reason is, they're being paid. Soon as they leave the course they ditch those pieces of crap and put on their regular watches. Their headlight-size gold Rolexes and their solid gold hubcap-size Phillipe Toulouse-Lautrecs.

There was a long wait on the 18th tee. Couples and Duval up ahead were exploring the pines on the right and rulings were being discussed.

I had nothing better to do than stand there with Ace Haskell and the Belgian. After seventeen holes it was the first time we'd indulged in any conversation other than who was away or was that a seven or an eight?

They were both way over par, working on something in the 80s. Ace didn't act like he minded—he was enjoying the Masters experience for the first time. His wife, Jewel, was enjoying it too. He pointed Jewel out to me. She was standing among a half-dozen spectators behind the ropes, about thirty yards down from the tee markers. She was the short and wide person. The big fan of brownies and vanilla ice cream. She waved at us. I waved back.

In an effort to make conversation, I asked Ace how he got in the tournament, being a rookie and all.

"I drove," he said.

I almost choked on the bottle of water I was sipping. I said I meant how did he qualify for the invitation? Had he won something I didn't know about, like in Europe maybe? Asian Tour? World rankings? What?

"I don't know," he said. "The invitation come in the mail one day to Goldsboro, to where we live . . . to the mail box at our house."

I dropped the subject. We stood quietly for a moment, until Ace asked the Belgian a question.

"You ride a bicycle?"

The Belgian stared at him. "I am to do what?"

Ace said, "I was wondering if you ride a bike. You small and wiry . . . like them other Frenchmen who ride in the Tour de France. I've watched it on TV."

"I am from Belgium, not France."

Ace said, "Yeah, that's what I hear, but y'all are kind of pushed up against one another over there, aren't you? Maps I've seen, anyhow."

The Belgian patiently said, "Many cyclists of many different nationalities race in the Tour. Evidently you have not noticed this on your television. But it is the answer to your question that I am not a cyclist myself, nor have I ever been a cyclist."

"What's a cyclips?" Ace asked.

"The word is for you, cyclist—c-y-c-l-i-s-t, as in cycling, which is how the sport is known to those who understand it."

Ace said, "Well, I hope nobody raises too much hell if I keep on callin' it the Tour de France bicycle race."

I walked across the tee to stand next to Mitch, leaving the Belgian looking less patient than he had a moment earlier.

Excellent timing on my part. Up against the ropes looking at me was none other than Gwendolyn Pritchard.

"You're four-under," she said. "Great."

"Fate don't have a head," I explained.

We looked at each other for a moment.

"You OK?" I said. Probe deal. Meaning had she recovered from my behavior last evening?

She said, "Yep." Her eyes confirmed it, I thought.

Today she was wearing long, snug slacks, the kind you see on lady golfers, a pair of Nike sneakers, and a pastel blue shirt with the tail out and a turned-up white collar. Her hair was pulled up under a white baseball cap with the Masters logo on it.

"This is Roy Mitchell," I said, remembering that Mitch and Gwen hadn't met. "Mitch is my caddie, my swing guru, my sports psychologist—what else?"

"Nurse," Mitch said.

"Hi, Mitch." She smiled at him.

He smiled back.

She said, "I'll watch you hit and go catch up with Scotty. He should be coming to eight."

"How's he doing?"

"He was one under through six. I think he's doing great, but that's a mom for you. He looks upset with the greens."

"We on the tee," Mitch said.

Mitch offered me the three-wood, suggesting a steer-job.

"Gimme thc Show Dog," I said. He handed me the driver. The latest in the line of Bertha weapons. I teed up the ball, took my stance, waggled the club twice, three times, and with all systems go I took a big swing and put a full load of clubface on the ball.

I wouldn't say I was completely showing off for the lady, but the drive was perfect, a long fade around the dogleg and into the center of the fairway. I'd have only a short stick left to the green.

Gwen let out a little whoop and applauded. I acted like I'd expected no less of a tee shot, like it was the same drive I was accustomed to hitting my whole life.

"Good lick," Mitch said. "That ball got some hurt on it."

I smiled. "It's the equipment."

I bagged an easy par and checked and signed my card in the scorer's tent. When I left I was met by a young girl sportswriter.

She was in her late twenties, I estimated. She said they didn't want me in the press center for an interview. Most of the writers were out on the course following Tigers and Cheetahs—there wasn't anybody down there right now who'd want to ask me anything. She was the pool reporter today for the print media, she explained, which meant she was in charge of getting the birdies and bogeys on my 68, and a quote or two.

She was close to cute despite her outfit—she wore a retro Chicago Bears football jersey that drooped outside a pair of loose-fitting denims, and a red golf visor. Her brown hair was in a ponytail, and a press credential hung around her neck on a chain.

"I'm Ellen Wheeler," she said, shaking my hand. "*Houston Chronicle*."

"I haven't seen you around, Ellen. You must be new."

"I got the golf beat this year. I've been covering the NBA."

"Is that a good job?"

"If you like flying in blizzards at night. Fun."

"Think you might like golf better than pro basketball?"

"I already like golf better."

"Why's that?"

"I'll give you two reasons right away. You play in the daytime. You go better places."

"We do try to avoid night golf."

I gave Ellen Wheeler the birdies and bogeys and said my round was lacking in drama. The course was playing relatively easy today, no wind, no unfair pins.

She said, "They want me to ask everybody about the female protest coming up. Do you have a comment?"

I said, "Frankly, I don't understand it. I don't understand why anybody wants to disrupt an event where the athletes wear fewer tattoos, do-rags, and earrings than they do in any other sport."

"I'm not sharing *that* with anybody," she said grinning. "Thanks—and nice meeting you."

"My pleasure," I said.

That was my brush with the media on Thursday.

For the rest of the afternoon, when I wasn't hitting practice balls, working on my putting, or hanging around the contestants' lounge, I watched my 68 get laughed at.

The scoreboard told me Elvis shot a 65, Madonna and Britney shot 66s, and Cheetah Farmer and some guy I'd never heard of shot 67s.

In other words, I watched so many guys blow past me, I might as well have been a dead man lying by the side of the road.

# 11

My even-par 72 on Friday put me in a tie for eighth at 140, five behind Tiger-slash-Elvis, the leader. I was still in the hunt, but I needed help, like a couple of low rounds from my own game, and some oil leaks from the immortals up ahead. Grady Don saw it as no problem. "Hell, it's nothing old Harry Vardon couldn't handle," he said. "Just straighten your necktie, and give 'em a taste of the hickory."

My round wasn't exactly routine when you consider I was still paired with Ace Haskell and the Belgian dwarf—Blisters, Flackers, Flanders. I was forced to do a considerable amount of waiting while they took their exciting routes to the 80s again.

It got pretty thrilling for both of them down at Amen Corner.

The first bit of drama involved Ace Haskell. His seven-iron to the 12th barely cleared Rae's Creek, but it trickled back down into the water. However, the ball was visible. He could get at it if he wanted to try.

Ace studied the situation and decided to try to play the ball out of the pond with his wedge.

The crowd applauded as Ace took off his shoes, rolled up his pant legs, and stepped down into the pond. Crowds love a gamble—when somebody else is the gambler.

But something happened when Ace planted his feet. He sank into a black hole, is what he did. Clear over his head, out of sight. I didn't know the pond was that deep.

The crowd shrieked in horror when Ace submerged.

For a moment you could only see his white visor floating on the water, little ripples around it.

All of us rushed to the edge of the water and looked down to see where he was, see what we could do. From across Rae's Creek, over where the crowd was, we could hear Jewel—the short and wide Mrs. Haskell—screaming above the fans.

Mitch said later she may have been screaming at a worker in the concession stand for only giving her two pimento-cheese sandwiches when she'd paid for three.

Ace Haskell came up out of the creek before any of us were moved to jump in and try to rescue him.

There was a foolish grin on his face as he said, "Dang, I'm glad there wasn't no alligators in here, I'd have come up short again. Guess I better take an unplayable."

Next came the Belgian's drama. On the following hole, the par-5 dogleg left 13th, he hit a flaming hook into the pines, dogwood, azaleas, and underbrush on the left side of the fairway. The hook sailed far to the left of Rae's Creek as it runs along that side of the hole and eventually crosses in front of the 13th green.

I'm talking deep in there. Midnight in Augusta, Georgia.

Everybody looked for the ball. Blisters-Flanders himself finally found it. We took his word that it was, in fact, his ball. Then he went about the business of trying to play it out of the jungle.

Bad idea.

After fussing around with his stance and club selection, he took the club back to swing, but it never came down. At which point we began to hear noises. Whining, yelping, whimpering.

What it was, the Belgian and his golf club were caught—hung up—in vines, thorns, and stickers, and he couldn't pull himself loose.

Mitch and the other two caddies untangled him. You'd have thought he might have been grateful, but no. The Belgian turned into a rabid dog. He started swinging wildly at the ball with what I think was his eight-iron.

Tears ran down his cheeks. There were splotches of blood on his neck, arms, and shirt. But he kept swinging, moving the ball only three feet, two feet, hacking through the limbs, leaves, brush, flowers, vines.

There was no way to keep up with how many swipes he took at the ball. We let him settle for a 19 on the hole, but it may well have been twice that many.

I still remember the sound of it all.

"Grrrr-yuh!" he'd yell, taking a slash at the ball. "Eeeyiiih-yug!"

Grady Don was at 142, same as Scott Pritchard. They'd both shot a pair of 71s. Grade, as I sometimes call him, was happier about it than Scott, who stomped around the locker room, calling Augusta "a dumb zoo."

I asked Scott to have a drink and a snack with me. Thought I'd try to get to know him better, perhaps give him some tips on his demeanor. Like maybe around Augusta he shouldn't say such things in public as, "Shove an azalea bush up Bobby Jones's ass."

Scott said he'd give me a moment, but he couldn't sit long—he wanted to go to the range and work on "shaping" his short irons.

It didn't seem like that long ago that golfers only hit shots, they didn't "shape" them. I didn't shape anything. I didn't know how you could "shape" anything with the hot ball we were all using. Today's golf ball wasn't built for anything but distance. But maybe this was why Tiger Woods was Tiger Woods, and Scott Pritchard was Scott Pritchard, and I was the nonshaping Bobby Joe Grooves.

Not much was said as we ate club sandwiches and I sipped a beer and Scott drank two Sprites. It was while Scott's mouth was full of potato chips that he said, "Are you tapping my mom?"

It wasn't a question I was prepared for. But before I could say what did he mean by that, or could he repeat the question, he said, "It's OK with me if you are. She needs to be uncorked."

While I knew that the tapping and uncorking of women was a fairly commonplace occurrence in most parts of California, I guess I didn't know that most nineteen-year-old California kids assumed it applied to their moms as well, but this didn't mean I was going to confess over a club sandwich that I was tapping or uncorking his mother.

"Why would you say that?" I said, skillfully ducking the question.

Scott said, "You're a golfer. That's good. Ever since she dumped my dad she hasn't gone out much, and when she has gone out it's been with bankers and other jokers like that."

"Your mother is about the most beautiful woman I've ever seen, Scott. I've enjoyed having dinner with her. I assume you know what a great-looking lady your mom is."

"Yeah, I guess . . . if you like 'em old."

Some remarks require a momentary throat-clear and a look-off.

I returned to the present. "Has your mother been serious with any of the bankers or other jokers?"

"None that I know about. She never goes out with 'em more than once or twice. She says they always wind up being from SC or Stanford, and she's done that."

"She needs to move out of the Pac-10."

"What for?"

"Nothing. Not to pry, Scott, but were you aware that your mom and dad were having trouble in the marriage? Did you have any idea that your mom was gonna hit your dad O.B. two years ago? Divorce him?"

"Geeahh, I never paid much attention to what was going on around the house, as long as it didn't screw up my practice or my tournament schedule. My mom never let it interfere with that."

"You never noticed any trouble between them?"

"There sure could have been. I used to hear loud voices. You know what? I'll bet it had something to do with the fact that my dad likes strange ass better than just about anything in the world."

"He never got his share in high school, I guess."

"His share of what?"

Somehow or other, I got out of the conversation without the question coming up again about whether I'd tapped or uncorked the mom.

Our buddy Jerry Grimes shot 72–74 and missed the cut by one, which is the worst way to miss a cut. Nothing can make you hotter than missing the cut by one stinking shot. You think of all the places where you could have saved a stroke—if you hadn't been, in Jerry's words for himself, "a gutless, spineless, curled-up turd."

Jerry was in a mood to go home fast to Ponte Vedra, Florida, but not to Janeen, his wife. Janeen had never been to a golf tournament. Janeen refused to go anywhere. Janeen said travel was too dangerous. The last time I'd seen Janeen was during the Players two years ago, when she made Jerry rush her to St. Luke's Hospital for a brain tumor. I visited her shortly before she was released with what had been a mild headache. Jerry mainly wanted to get home to Maggie and Emma, his dogs.

Jerry made an elegant departure from Augusta.

Grady Don and I walked out to the parking lot with him. We watched him kick the door of his tan Toyota Sienna three times, sling his golf clubs in the back end, then go over and pick a handful of dogwood petals off a tree and put them in his pocket.

"What are those?" I said. "Souvenirs?"

He said, "They're to wipe my ass with when I stop to take a shit between here and home. A remembrance of this glorious week."

Missing a cut is never good for a man's disposition.

# 12

Grady Don and I met for breakfast Saturday morning at the IHOP. The one on Washington Road near the Augusta National's main gate. The IHOP that was only three hundred yards from the five acres of crabgrass and small oaks that had been designated by the sheriff's department as the official site for the protest sillies.

We got there early to grab a booth for our eggs over easy, sausage patties, hash browns, biscuits, and bowl of cream gravy to pour over them. Early was important because that particular IHOP, I'd been tipped off by Gwendolyn, had become the unofficial hospitality suite for the plethora of news people in town to cover the valiant protestors who were gearing up to follow Anne Marie Sprinkle to hell and back.

Grady Don and I were there because of our acute interest in American history. Although we'd be playing in the third round of the Masters later in the day, we wanted to be able to say we watched free speech in action.

I'd said to Gwen that while it had happened often enough in the privacy of the home, I wanted to observe it in person when women screamed at men about golf in public.

"That's almost amusing, Bobby Joe," she had said. "Really and truly . . . borderline humorous."

Grady Don and I talked about the tournament for a moment. How the leaderboard must make the fans happy. The scum was at a tolerable level.

Elvis was at nine under, one shot ahead of Madonna and Britney and Cheetah. Julius Claudius was in there at seven under, that being the nickname Grady Don had given Davis Love III in honor of the Roman numeral chasing after his name.

Three others were at six under. Two of them were Knut Thorssun, my old Swedish buddy, and Sergio Garcia, the nerve-ends Spaniard. They were known to Grady Don as "Mule Dick" and "Desi." The third was Stump Bowen, who didn't require a nickname. He'd been called Stump from childhood, apparently because of his withered arm.

Knut Thorssun had once been a friend. He was a no-clue Swede when he first came on the Tour. I befriended him, helped him find his ass with his other hand. I never could do much for his hair. It's still white-blond and hangs down to his shoulders. And I never could do much for the tight pants he wears—he still likes to show off his crotch bulge.

I did make the mistake of introducing him to Cynthia, a fun-loving stew friend. Plenty cute. They married and she became the mother of his two boys. Knut thought so much of Cynthia he fucked his way into a costly divorce, and she's now happily married to a close pal of mine, Buddy Stark. Buddy'd played the Tour for ten years, he'd always had an eye on Cynthia—he used to date her—and when she not only became available but rich after the divorce from Knut, Buddy left the Tour and went about capturing Cynthia's heart.

My friendship with Knut dissolved after he won two majors. With two majors to his credit, he got vaccinated with the asshole needle and decided I wasn't important enough to deserve his close friendship or even his occasional companionship at dinner.

Knut's best friend was always his dick, Bobo. He talked about Bobo as if Bobo was a person. Over the years I'd accidentally known the names of other dicks that belonged to guys. I'd heard references to a Wilbur, Sir James, Old George, Herschel, Tonto, and two Leroys, but I'd never known a Bobo until Knut Thorssun.

There were ladies who were acquainted with Bobo, I learned. Back when we were pals, Knut used to show me notes that chicks would write him. Notes that said, "Give my best to Bobo," and, "How is my friend Bobo?" and, "Please tell Bobo I miss him more than anything."

Grady Don has said we ought to write one of those Harry Potter children's books about it. Call it *Bobo the Mule Dick*. Get rich.

Since I'd been doing a disappearing act the past three nights, Grady Don grilled me about Gwendolyn.

What was she like? Where'd she come from? Was she interesting? Could she talk about anything but her kid? How many men had she killed?

I said she was a great American and a wonderful human being.

Grady Don said how great an American?

I said pretty darn great.

He said, "Is she General George S. Patton great? Babe Ruth great? Joe DiMaggio great?"

"You're close," I said.

He said, "Well, goddamn, is she Sam Baugh great? Red Grange great? Doak Walker? Who?"

I said, "Think of Secretariat with a sense of humor."

"Damn," he said enviously.

I watched him slice, chop, and stir his eggs over easy and pattie sausages into a hash. As he scooped it up, he said:

"So the two of you have just been a couple of shut-ins, eating in the room every night?"

"That's about it," I said.

Grinning, he added, "I expect you ordered dinner from room service, too, didn't you?"

"That's almost funny," I said. "Borderline humorous."

# 13

The first thing you saw at the protest site were the giraffes. Three guys on stilts in giraffe costumes. A sign dangled around the neck of one giraffe. It said: "Anne Marie Sprinkle Don't Bother Us, We're Above It All—Eat at Luther's Game Food Grill on Broad Street."

The giraffes towered over the four Elvis impersonators in their white jumpsuits and black wigs. The Elvises were standing with their arms interlocked singing a barbershop rendition of "Old Shep."

I had no trouble recalling "Old Shep." It was a sad song about a lovable dog that died. As a kid I used to cry when I'd hear it on the radio.

*"Old Shep he has gone*
*Where the good doggies go*
*No more will Old Shep roam.*
*But if dogs have a heaven,*
*There's one thing I know.*
*Old Shep has a wonderful home."*

When they finished the song, I asked an Elvis what the point was.

The Elvis said, "Shep is a euphemism for the world this protest woman wants to ruin."

" 'Euphemism,' " I said. "Elvis used that word a lot, I remember."

"Elvis loved golf," the impersonator said emphatically.

"Elvis *Presley* loved golf?" I said, wanting to make sure we were talking about the same person.

"Very much so," another jumpsuit said. "What do you think 'Are You

Lonesome Tonight?' is all about? It is obviously a song about his relationship with par."

Grady Don had heard enough.

He said, "Elvis loved golf? You people need to go back to the hospital. Elvis was too busy fucking to love golf. After that he was too *fat* to love golf. Then he was too dope-sick to love golf. That's all you need to know about Elvis Presley, other than the fact that he couldn't sing or play the guitar worth a shit."

One of the impersonators politely said, "There are many myths about the King that are patently untrue."

Whereupon they launched into a barbershop rendition of "Are You Lonesome Tonight?"

We listened for a moment and moved on to mingle with the T-shirt shoppers, media, TV technicians, and police.

Mildly curious, I led us over to the burned-out hippie with the scruffy beard and gnarled hair. A guy trapped in the Sixties. He wore filthy jeans and a grimy white T-shirt and held a hand-lettered sign that said "Golf Is Vile—It Ruins the Earth." He stood on a tree stump.

We were his only audience.

Grady Don said, "What's shakin', dude?"

The hippie burnout said, "I was going over my notes, like in my head—for the lecture I'll deliver later on, when the crowd's bigger."

Grady Don said, "Where you from?"

"I come here from Denny's—oh, uh, Austin, Texas."

He sat down on the tree stump—he did look tired—and said, "The theme of my talk is, like, you know, how golf destroys our land . . . our homes, farms, forests . . . natural resources. It displaces people, man. It serves no human need. Golf is a game for the privileged few. America needs to wake up to this terror before it's too late. Before we all get run over by all the rich people in their electric carts."

"Go for it," Grady Don said. "Golf's fucked me my whole life."

The morning paper had said Anne Marie Sprinkle would arrive at noon to speak to her followers. A pregame pep talk. We waited for that event by standing around near the donut-and-coffee stand under the shade trees near the deputy sheriff's car and the Ku Klux Klan table.

For a moment, we listened to Deputy Sheriff R. G. Hudgins, whose stomach suggested he hadn't missed too many breakfasts himself. He was addressing a group of people who were unhappy with the presence of the two men seated at the KKK table.

Quite possibly they were unhappy with the two men seated at the KKK table because they were wearing white pointed hoods and white bedsheets.

Also, there was this printed sign on a stake planted in the ground next to the table that said: "Our Team Color Is White."

The deputy sheriff was saying, "No, I can't do nothin' about them KKKs any more than I can about them giraffes or that hippie over there on the tree stump. That old boy, I don't know. The gates are down, the lights are flashing, but the train ain't comin'. I hope none of you has smelt him lately. It's a free country is what I'm sayin'. We've got our ground rules here. We established our rules yesterday when I met with the protest groups and made sure we was all singin' from the same page of the hymn book."

A man with a Masters media credential around his neck shouted a question. "How many protestors do you expect today?"

Deputy Sheriff R. G. Hudgins said, "Well, there's some here right now. About fifteen or twenty, I'd say. Yesterday they were talkin' about six thousand. I'm guessin' it'll be more like seventy-five or a hundred."

"I don't see them," the media guy said.

The deputy sheriff said, "Over at the big platform. Where you see them Apache Indians and Kodiak bears. Pocahontas over there is Ms. Sprinkle's spokesperson."

Everybody looked toward the platform.

Another media guy said, "Looks like we're not gonna see a lot of Catherine Zeta-Jones around here today."

Deputy Sheriff Hudgins said, "No, you ain't. Not unless she's turned into a Kodiak bear."

"Here she comes!" somebody shouted, pointing at the white stretch limo on Washington Road as it stopped at the vacant field.

Gwendolyn showed up at the same time. Carrying a cup of takeout coffee, she stepped out of a group of T-shirt shoppers.

She said, "Aren't you guys supposed to be hitting balls?"

I said, "Your tournament leaders have time on their hands. I don't go till two-thirty, as you may know. Grady Don goes a little ahead of me. We wanted to hear what Anne Marie has to say on this historic occasion."

"Nothing's going to happen today," Gwen said. "She's postponed the big march until tomorrow. She decided a protest during Sunday's final round would attract more attention to the cause."

"How do you know that?"

"I was here earlier. Her spokesperson told me."

"Pocahontas told you?" I said.

"Who?"

"Pocahontas. That's what the deputy sheriff calls the spokeslady."

"Does he really? God will punish him for that."

A woman I judged hefty enough to be Anne Marie Sprinkle now stood on the platform, flanked by two Kodiak bears and two business suits, and was starting to speak. We moved over to join the crowd.

Anne Marie Sprinkle wasn't wearing the whole town of Santa Fe, New Mexico—she left off the pottery. But elsewhere on her two-hundred-pound frame in her fringed buckskin dress there was enough silver and turquoise dangling and clanking that her name could have been Dances With Jewelry.

Anne Marie was a wide-body protestor. She reminded me of what I once heard a football coach say about an offensive lineman: "Some old boys don't move too good when their legs touch all the way to their knees." Her body got slightly narrower as it rose to the short black bangs on her head. She wore a pair of granny glasses from the Sixties. Grady Don said she looked like Cher's overfed aunt.

She preached a while about the Augusta National having all those members who were CEOs of companies that sold products to women, and what a disgrace it was, and what a tragedy it was for America and Western civilization that the club had no women members.

Among the hordes of media people in attendance, a guy yelled out, "What do you say to the people who call you a champagne socialist?"

She yelled back. "I say pop the corks and pass the stem glasses!"

Much laughter, whoops, applause.

Now she called out, "Who will be with me tomorrow when I march up to the front gate of that backward, bigoted, bonehead club and usher it into the twenty-first century?"

Cries rang through the oaks: "Me, me! Yeah, yeah! Go, go!"

I said to Gwen, "Backward, bigoted, and boneheaded?"

"You're enjoying this, aren't you?"

"Yes, I am. Very much."

A guy in front of us in the crowd instigated a dialog with the famed protest leader. I realized right away the guy was Hubbard Gilliam—and Blubber Doss was standing next to him.

"Make my dinner!" Hubbard shouted at Anne Marie Sprinkle.

"Wash my dishes!" she shouted back at him.

"Iron my shirts!" he yelled.

"Make my bed!" she yelled back.

"Bake my cake!"

"Sweep my floor!"

"Fry my bacon!"

"Take out my trash!"

"Do my laundry!"

"Clean my toilet!"

"Eat my cock!"

Deputy Sheriff R. G. Hudgins jumped forward.

"OK, that's it. That'll be enough of *that*." He grabbed Hubbard Gilliam and Blubber Doss by the back of their necks. "Ain't no sign here says 'Vulgar Language Allowed.' "

Hubbard said, "We're just having some fun here, sheriff."

Then he glanced over at me. "How you doin', Bobby Joe?"

Now Blubber Doss looked at me. "Hi, Bobby Joe."

I grinned back at them, but I couldn't help noticing that Gwendolyn and Grady Don were both staring at me with looks that said, "You *know* these two idiots?"

# 14

Irv Klar of the *Washington Post* said I'd make a good Sunday column. I was supposed to be flattered by that. After all, Irv Klar at this moment in history was among America's best-known sportswriters and best-selling authors. Never mind that Irv Klar—*Irving* on his book jackets—was also one of America's most irritating writers in his column and his books because he possessed that rare ability to be both arrogant and wrong at the same time, which was of no consequence to Irv.

He suggested we go upstairs in the clubhouse, sit on the balcony, have a drink, talk about my 67, how it threw me up there among the third-round leaders, but how I still didn't have a prayer of winning this Masters.

A little humor there from Irv.

I agreed to chat with him, having nothing better to do before my regularly scheduled room-service dinner with Gwen.

Irv had waited for me at the press center while I answered all the intense questions of the print guys. What was my game plan today? What would be my game plan tomorrow? What would I rely on the most—my woods, my irons, or my putter? If it was a two-club wind, which two clubs would I use?

Certain writers like to collect embarrassing questions asked by some of their lame brethren. I read this in a book by Jim Tom Pinch of *The Sports Magazine*, a writer who would be Irv Klar's idol if Irv ever bothered to read anybody else.

Among Jim Tom's collectibles:

Jack Nicklaus was in the interview area after he'd won the British Open at St. Andrews in '70, and a writer from Tennessee said, "Uh, Jack, we realize Arnold Palmer is your major adversary on the Tour, but golf aside for a moment, don't you agree with Arnie that we should be bombing Hanoi?"

At a Super Bowl press conference in '81 a writer from New Jersey frantically held up his hand to Jim Plunkett, the quarterback for the Oakland Raiders. It was well-known that Plunkett's mother had passed away and his father was blind, but that didn't keep the writer from saying, "Help me out here, Jim—is it dead father, blind mother, or dead mother, blind father?"

It was at a press conference for the '88 Super Bowl that a writer from Ohio asked the Washington Redskins' Doug Williams how long he'd been a black quarterback.

A Pittsburgh writer found himself covering World Cup soccer some years ago in Spain, and asked Diego Maradonna what month it was right now in Argentina.

Irv waited while I did quickie interviews with the local and cable TV personalities. It never takes long. You listen to the interviewer run off at the mouth, loving the sound of his or her own voice, then you get to say, "Sounds good, Lisa—nice chatting with you."

We sat at a table on the balcony and I ordered iced tea for us—from Alfred, my favorite clubhouse waiter—as Irv reached in his valise and handed me a copy of his latest bestseller.

"This is the first time I've seen you since the PGA in August," he said. "You may already have this, but here's an autographed copy. It came out last December. Good timing for hoops."

The book was *Murder Above the Rim: How Two Tall Africans, a Tall Croat, a Taller Russian, and the Tallest Egyptian Led the UConn Huskies to the NCAA Basketball Championship.*

"Thanks," I said. "I don't have it. I tried to buy it three or four times but it was always sold out."

He said, "I have two new ones coming in June and August. Golf and football. That's all I'll say. They should do well . . . Let's talk about the Masters."

I said, "Irv, I still have two chances to win this thing, you know."

"You do?"

"Slim and none."

"I can use that."

"I'm very pleased."

He scribbled on a yellow legal pad. "Somebody said you guys call this 'moving day.' Saturday. The day you want to move up on the scoreboard. Is that right? 'Moving day.' I like that."

"I heard it a long time ago. I've never called it moving day. To the best of my memory, I've always called it the third round."

"I'm using it."

"Irv, don't quote me saying 'moving day.' I'll have to kill you."

"I know how you shot the sixty-seven," he said. "You birdied the par-fives, holed a long putt on seventeen. That's it for the play-by-play. I have to file by nine o'clock."

"If you really want to know why it's impossible for me to win, I'll give you three reasons. Elvis Woods, Madonna Els, and Britney Mickelson."

"Elvis, Madonna, and Britney? Great. I love that."

He scribbled hurriedly on his pad.

I said, "That's what Grady Don calls them. They've got me by two strokes. The FBI might be able to catch one of them, maybe even two, but I doubt they could catch all three."

"I like that, too." Scribbling.

"I have an idea, Irv. Why don't I write the column and you play golf tomorrow?"

"You're how old now? Forty-three? Forty-four?"

"Forty-four—and counting."

He said, "I know you've been out here seventeen, eighteen years . . . won like twelve times. Your biggest win has to be the Players two years ago, doesn't it?"

"The cup wouldn't get out of my way."

"Do you think the Players will ever be a major?"

"Not now. Not since I've won it."

"I'm using that. You keep flirting with the majors. Looks like you'd break through sometime."

"It does, doesn't it? I tied for fifth here once. I've been third and fourth in the Open, third in the PGA, top ten in the British twice. I keep thinking that one of these days everybody else is gonna drop dead."

Irv said, "Who do you play bridge with now out here?"

"Nobody plays bridge anymore."

"Why not?"

"They don't know how or they're too rich, too busy."

"Busy doing what?"

"Oh, talking to their psychologists, their agents, their tax accountants. Sending their wives off sight-seeing so they can fuck the baby-sitters. You probably can't use that."

"Probably not. Your best friends are . . . ?"

"Mostly vagrants back home . . . from high school, college. Out here, Grady Don, Jerry Grimes . . . Buddy Stark, before he bailed."

"How's Buddy doing?"

"Buddy's in ecstasy. He's down on the farm in Ocala with Cynthia and her money. I say farm; it's more of a resort. She has an eight-bedroom lodge, a river, lake, horses, two tennis courts, swimming pool, regulation croquet court. They've even put in a nine-hole golf course—with bent greens and different sets of tees."

"I didn't know Cynthia did that good in her divorce from Knut."

"She won the Powerball lottery, is all."

"Cool," he said. "What's up with you and Knut Thorssun? You guys still speak?"

"We speak. We're friendly in public. He's finally graduated."

"What do you mean?"

"He's gone from being a studious asshole to just being silly."

"That's a hot chick he goes with. I read where they may get married. Have you met her?"

"I've met her. Her real name is Vashtine Ulberg. Her showbiz name is Snapper. Only Knut could fall in love with a Swedish rap star."

I'd have bet my stack against the existence of a Swedish rap star, but it lives. Grady Don bought some of her tapes so we could marvel at the artistry of her lyrics. The one we like the best is from her new hit single, "Horny Bitchy":

*"Ein wannen sluppen sockin fockin*
*Bitchy fretten fordik dickin*
*Eatim goodink vit der sockin*
*Fock me, fock me! Vant more fockin."*

We think you can hear the Irving Berlin influence mixed in with a touch of Cole Porter.

Irv Klar said, "Would it be indelicate of me to ask what happened with you and Cheryl, Bobby Joe? I ask as a friend. I liked Cheryl."

"I'll tell you about Cheryl," I said. "For a tricky-looking babe who was good fun at times, she could be a mean, angry, vindictive, greedy, lying, cheating bitch—and I'd say that even if I hadn't been married to her."

He laughed. "Sorry, Bobby Joe, but that's funny."

"Yeah, it was about two million funny on my end. I didn't fight with her in the divorce. I gave her everything she wanted. You could say our divorce was the genteel equivalent of the woman in the mobile home throwing all of her husband's clothes out on the gravel."

"I can use that," Irv said. "Can't I?"

I shrugged. He scribbled.

# 15

It's been the theory of coaches, teachers, and other authority figures dating back to—I don't know, Knute Rockne or somebody—that if you jack with a lady the night before a game, you'll be pussy-whipped when it comes crunch time on the scoreboard, and this is not a good thing. On the other hand, there's the more recent theory that if you have a new babe to show off for, you may be inspired to play out of your skin.

I was evidently in favor of the second theory.

After I ordered dinner for us in my hotel room Saturday night during a well-deserved timeout, I mentioned as much to Gwen, and she said, "You're showing off for me in more ways than one."

"I'm motivated," I said.

"So am I. Have you noticed?"

"I have."

"What does it mean?"

"I have no idea."

"Where are we headed, do you think?"

"I don't know that either."

"Does it matter?"

"Not yet."

She was smoking. I was enjoying it.

I said, "By the way, girl, has your obscenely wealthy son asked you how you're spending your nights this week?"

I thought it was about time I made such an inquiry.

"Nope." She sounded unconcerned.

"He's not curious?"

"He hasn't said anything."

"He doesn't ask how it's going with the escaped convict you've been seen with? He just stays focused on golf?"

"He asks me what I'm doing every night. I tell him I'm having dinner with friends. He says great. He goes out to eat with other players, comes home early, watches TV, talks to one of his girlfriends on long distance for a while, gets a good night's rest."

"Since he's a nineteen-year-old millionaire, I assume the babes are on him like gravy on grandpa."

"They are. But if they don't know who Phil Mickelson is, they don't last long. Which is a good thing for them, as I see it. A babe can only sit and stare at the ceiling for so long if the guy she's with doesn't talk about anything but golf, or think about anything but golf. It's not a babe's idea of romance."

"No, as I understand it, your babes have never been too interested in putting on the carpet."

When room service knocked on the door Gwen dashed into the bathroom. I made the waiter rich for bringing the Caesar salad for her, and the grilled-cheese sandwich with bacon and tomato for me.

I sounded the all-clear and Gwendolyn reappeared in one of my navy blue golf shirts and her white panty briefs, with a fresh cigarette.

Some men might have found that sight distracting enough to cause them to ignore their dinner, but I was more strong-willed than that.

As we ate dinner we discussed the leaderboard. The top 10 looked like this after fifty-four holes:

| | |
|---|---|
| Tiger Woods . . . . . . . . | 65-72-70–207 |
| Ernie Els . . . . . . . . . | 66-72-69–207 |
| Phil Mickelson . . . . . . . | 66-73-68–207 |
| Cheetah Farmer . . . . . . | 67-71-70–208 |
| Sergio Garcia . . . . . . . | 70-69-69–208 |
| Knut Thorssun . . . . . . . | 69-69-70–208 |
| Guy Yucca . . . . . . . . . | 71-66-72–209 |
| Bobby Joe Grooves . . . . . | 68-72-67–209 |
| Froggie Sommers . . . . . . | 67-74-68–209 |
| Dunn Matson . . . . . . . . | 70-69-72–211 |

There were four other players between the first ten and the two tied at three-under 213—who, as it happened, were Grady Don and Scott.

Gwen said, "Scotty's six strokes back. He'd have to shoot sixty-two or something tomorrow to have any chance."

"It's not the six strokes," I said. "It's the fourteen guys in front of him. It's impossible for all fourteen to fall in a ditch on the same day. Only one guy ever made a comeback like that. When Arnold Palmer won the Open at Cherry Hills, his sixty-five in the last round made up seven shots and passed fourteen guys. I hadn't been born yet in 1960, but I remember it well."

She said, "Tell me about Grady Don, your intellectual friend. Scotty's paired with him tomorrow."

I said, "First I want to know who you're following tomorrow, golfers or Anne Marie Sprinkle?"

"I'm going to the rally to hear the speeches. After that, I'll follow two guys I know who'll be playing golf. What about Grady Don?"

I said, "Aw, he's just a good old boy from Odessa, out there in West Texas—where an oil pump passes for a shade tree, and the plate lunches are bigger than footballs."

"My father was born in Ranger, Texas."

"No way?" I was shocked and delighted to hear it.

"Honest. My granddaddy was working in the Texas oil fields at the time. My grandmother used to talk about baking apricot fried pies and selling them to the roughnecks."

"Ranger was a famous boom town," I said. "There were lots of boom towns in Texas. The rowdiest must have been Burkburnett. There's an old movie, *Boom Town*, with Clark Gable and Spencer Tracy. They made it about Burkburnett. I knew there was something special about you. You're a semi-Texan."

"Even though I was born in California?"

"Minor deduction."

"My father moved to the Coast when he was a young man . . . for the same reason a hundred million other people did. Climate and opportunity. He was a traveling salesman. He sold furniture and carpet. He met my mother in LA, when she was nineteen and working at Paramount. They met in a Mexican restaurant on Melrose, near the studio."

"Your mother was a movie star?"

"She went to Hollywood to be a movie star, but she wound up in wardrobe. This was in the fifties, long before I came along."

"Your mom must have known all those Virginia Katherine McMaths."

"The Mack whats?"

"All those Hedy Lamarrs, Dorothy Lamours, Ginger Rogers. Their real names are always Virginia Katherine McMath. Actually, Ginger Rogers's real name *was* Virginia Katherine McMath. I know this because she grew up in Fort Worth. It's one of those small things we take pride in. She went to the same high school I did . . . but about fifty years earlier."

"My mother *did* know Ginger Rogers, and Hedy Lamarr, and Jimmy Stewart . . . Gary Cooper. Lots of stars. She thought they were nice. You were saying about Grady Don—?"

"Grady Don's younger than me," I said, "but we've been friends since he came on the Tour four years ago. We have TCU in common. TCU's our alma mater. He was a two-sport athlete. A tight end in football and captain of the golf team. Grady Don was a tight end when tight ends didn't have to weigh 275. He was a good football player. He was on the same bowl teams at TCU with Paregoric Sims, one of our All-America running backs."

"*Paregoric* Sims?" she said. "Nice nickname."

"It's his real name. His mama was taking her best shot at Patrick on the birth certificate."

"Bobby Joe, you're so politically correct, I can hardly stand it."

"It's Grady Don's influence. He's married to Monette, his college honey. They live in Southlake. That's a rich suburb with good access to the Dallas–Fort Worth airport. You can find some ungodly mansions in Southlake and it has a handmade little shopping village. Grady Don calls it Stepford Town."

"Grady Don has some wit about him."

I said, "Monette doesn't come out here much. They have a fourteen-year-old, Donny. He's into every sport known to mankind. She drives him to practice every day. Grady Don says Monette's major claim to fame at TCU was getting kicked out of Tri Delt for gaining too much weight. Like she went over 110 or something."

"That's awful."

"I agree, but he says she didn't take it too hard because her sorority sisters had stopped speaking to her anyhow. They found out her daddy in Houston was a veterinarian instead of a cardiologist."

Gwen said, "I think I like Monette. Grady Don still strikes me as being a trifle crude, if you don't mind me saying so."

"That's why he makes me laugh."

"You like crude, do you?"

"His kind of crude is funny. Grady Don is good-naturedly . . . totally . . . honestly crude—and not embarrassed by it."

"He's definitely not embarrassed by it."

"It's not all-out hilarious but lately he's been collecting colorful names for the female organ that was known in my carefree college days as the blissful chasm."

"I hate the c-word, if that's what you're talking about."

"Grady Don Maples doesn't bother with the c-word. He goes straight to fur taco."

"Crude."

"Lap moss."

"He's still a frat rat!"

"Wool."

"Oh, please."

"Texas pelt?"

"God."

"He used one I hadn't heard the other day. Hatchet wound."

" *'Hatchet wound'?*"

"Yeah."

"That's funny."

"Yeah."

# 16

Later in the evening, after I'd doctored the hatchet wound again, the good-luck phone call came from Buddy Stark and Cynthia.

They weren't calling from the resort in Ocala, Florida. They were calling from the oceanfront mansion in Sea Island, which I like a lot, where they were spending a week before driving up to spend a week in the mountaintop mansion in Highlands, North Carolina, which I like even more, before flying over to spend a week in Spain, which they could have.

Spain had tried to kill me twice—like Mexico.

Buddy said all the things golfers say to each other before a crucial round in a big-deal championship. Fairways and greens, pard. Take dead aim. Tempo, B.J., tempo.

"You want to be Viagra off the tee, Xanax on the greens," he said.

"I'll take it back slowly," I said.

Another reason they called was to share good news with somebody who'd appreciate it. The good news involved Cynthia's two sons by Knut Thorssun, Sven and Matt, who were once known coast to coast as "the unruly little shits." That was before a military academy in Virginia devoted five years to molding them into reasonably tolerable young adults. Now it seemed they'd been accepted by a small but very elite university—Mt. Gidley, in Vermont.

Thanks to their daddy's thoughtful donation of five million, Sven and Matt would be entering Mt. Gidley in the fall. It was one of those excellent universities in New England where for a tuition fee of only $50,000 a year the student is permitted to create his or her own four-year curriculum. Forget English, math, and history. That was old-fashioned.

Sven was going to spend four years studying the entertainment values of pharmaceutical opium, and Matt was going to spend four years studying various ways to overthrow governments and start revolutions in freedom-loving countries.

I said I couldn't be more impressed with Sven and Matt's progress—or with that of the academic world.

Cynthia came on the line to ask if the lady in the room with me was somebody she'd like to meet someday. I asked her why she thought there was a lady in my room. She said because she knew me well enough to know that if I didn't have company in the room, I'd be out on the town.

I said, "Is this the same party-going stew I used to know who was based in Dallas and flew for Delta when she wasn't a golf groupie?"

"It is I," she said, giggling.

She loved to say that. It was her favorite golfer's quote. Bernhard Langer had said it after he won his first Masters and a sportswriter asked him who was the most famous German golfer of all time.

I said, "Cynthia, honestly. A lady in my room? You only think things like that about men because you were married to the Swedish dolt. If Knut hadn't learned to play golf for a living, he'd have had to grow a mustache and work as the fuck god in porn flicks."

She said, "Damn, I wish I'd said that."

"I miss you guys."

"I miss you too. So . . . is this a keeper?"

"Who?"

"Don't gimme that *who*. The person listening to you right now. I hope she's a dynamite lady. You deserve it."

"Could be."

"Could be what? A keeper or a dynamite lady?"

"Both."

"Good. I hope I get to meet her someday. And B.J.—"

"Yes, dear?"

"Cheryl was a dirty leg. I'm sorry it took you so long to find it out."

"Me too," I said. "I could have had the title shot outdoors in the ballpark."

# 17

The whole ridiculous mess started while I was playing the 9th hole. Trying to, I should say.

I'll remember it vividly. Remember it the way people remember where they were and who they were with when momentous things occurred in the world or in their lives.

Things like, oh . . . 9/11, Pearl Harbor, JFK bites the dust . . . first wedding . . . first divorce . . . moon landing . . . the day the beloved high school won State in football . . . first car . . . first barbecue rib . . . first cheese enchilada . . . the day you finally broke 80 without cheating . . . the day the rich aunt took all the jewelry with her in the casket. Big stuff.

Looking back on it, you'd think the Masters officials and the law enforcement agencies would have been better prepared. But I suppose the last thing anybody considered was that Anne Marie Sprinkle would have secret agents on the inside.

This flat amazed me. The Masters is one of the toughest tickets in sports. It's dream the impossible dream, folks. And yet there must have been a hundred protestors on the course with legitimate Masters credentials. Who knows where the credentials came from—club members, ticket brokers, Don Corleone? All I know is, the protestors made themselves some mischief and created your basic turmoil.

I was overjoyed that Gwen Pritchard wasn't a part of the disruption. She'd gone to the rally and listened to the speeches and left, figuring that was the high-water mark for the protestors.

Which, as it turned out, was exactly what Anne Marie Sprinkle wanted everyone to think.

My day started off badly enough as it was. I was obliged to have breakfast in the clubhouse with Smokey Barwood, my agent. He'd flown in from the Coast, where he'd been involved with another important client during the week. The client was Trapeze Cobb, the Laker.

For several months Trapeze had been going through legal proceedings on two charges of rape. He was represented by a well-respected and good-looking criminal attorney, Rachel Stafford, who often appeared on Court TV, but it was a tough case. To recap: Trapeze had been invited by North Hollywood High to demonstrate to a class how rape could easily occur in today's society. Trapeze had misunderstood and demonstrated it too literally. With the students observing, he raped the redheaded teacher, an attractive thirty-five-year-old woman, by bending her over a chair. When he'd finished, he raped a sixteen-year-old blonde cheerleader on top of a desk. After many delays the case had finally gone to trial, and the jury had deliberated only thirty minutes before it found the NBA star not guilty.

Smokey confided that Trapeze Cobb was still angry about being put through the legal ordeal, a celebrity like himself. He'd said to the agent, "This judicious system better stop shittin' on me or I'm gonna change my name to Abboo Boogerhammett . . . be a terrorist motherfucker."

The quarterly tax returns Smokey Barwood brought for me to sign were no cause to be cheerful. I asked him how I could owe so much money. He said it was because I chose to live in a country that desired to have an army, navy, and air force.

I said OK, fine. I didn't mind paying my fair share of taxes for a strong national defense. Not as long as all the people on welfare could keep their country club memberships.

I was paired with Claude Steekley, which meant that if I found myself in urgent need of a dumb-ass, there was one handy.

Claude Steekley was a devout University of Texas grad—heir to the Crenshaw-Kite throne, he acted like—but that didn't excuse him for wearing a burnt-orange tuxedo in his wedding. His socialite bride, Pookie, wore a burnt-orange gown, and her bridesmaids wore burnt-orange dresses, and the groomsmen wore burnt-orange UT football jerseys bearing the numerals of past Longhorn gridiron heroes. Number 22 for Bobby Layne, number 60 for Tommy Nobis, number 20 for Earl Campbell—stop me before I kill more. When Pookie's big-shot oilman daddy was asked who gives this woman in the ceremony, he said,

"Her daddy, her mama, and the University of Texas Longhorns, national champions in baseball and women's basketball last year, and would have been in football if it hadn't been for two cheap holding calls. May God strike the Georgia Bulldogs dead and may the Eyes of Texas shine on this couple all they livelong days."

Talk of Claude and Pookie's burnt-orange wedding often entertained locker rooms on the tour. Locker-room rumor also had it that Pookie Steekley, socialite though she was, liked to fool around on occasion.

Claude and I heard the noise at the same time as we approached our drives on No. 9. Since the 9th hole comes back to the clubhouse, it was easy enough to hear the commotion from out on the street.

I envisioned Anne Marie Sprinkle and her faithful followers gathered at the gates of Magnolia Drive on Washington Road and yelling at the reception committee of Chairman Kisser McConnell, a gathering of other green jackets, and the state troopers who'd be there to protect them.

As the TV replays later confirmed, that was exactly the scene, with the activists chanting the predictable slogans: "Discrimination is not a game" . . . "Pigs play golf, women cook and clean" . . . "Georgia is a police state!"

Claude came over to me in the fairway.

"Can you believe this?" he said. "Those people don't realize this is our office and we're out here trying to make a living for our families."

I slumped. I don't know what pro said it first, but it was the same old remark that had been endearing us to the press for years. This was our office. There were golf writers who loved to hear this so they could remind us that we were playing a *game* for a living, for Christ sake, and for *somebody else's* money—and we didn't have to wear grease-repellent uniforms and crawl under shit.

From my own point of view, the most unfortunate thing about the disruption is that I was playing lights out. I had it all going—the tempo, rhythm, putter, attitude.

I was three under through 8. I birdied the second with a good sand shot out of the front bunker and a six-foot putt. I birdied the 3rd with a wedge and a ten-foot putt. My other birdie came at the 8th after a big drive, big two-iron, and short pitch to three feet. And there wasn't anything bizarre about the five pars I made. I was golfing my ball.

After doing all that, I was tied for the lead with Elvis and Madonna on the scoreboards. All you can tell yourself in a situation like that is, take it one shot at a time.

Claude Steekley and I stood at the bottom of the hill on the 9th fairway, where I was torn between a seven-iron and an eight-iron to the uphill green, the pin set middle-forward. Touchy deal. Long was Downtown Three-Putt City. Short was Spin Back Down the Fairway.

Talent, where be thou?

Back waiting on the 9th tee were Sergio Garcia and Knut Thorssun. Nearby, over on the 8th green, were Cheetah Farmer and Britney Mickelson. Down the 8th fairway was the last twosome on the course, Elvis Woods and Madonna Els.

Four groups ahead of me, somewhere on the 11th hole, were Grady Don and Scott. Meaning Gwendolyn Pritchard, enthusiastic golf fan, was scurrying back and forth between her son and the gentleman with whom she'd been having room-service dinner the past four nights.

Scott's name wasn't on the scoreboard, and it hadn't been there all day. This told me he was still having trouble with the old putter, and was probably cussing and crying about Augusta's speedy greens, and that Grady Don was within minutes of strapping some Odessa on him. Telling Scott to shut up unless he wanted to be grabbed by his ankles and dragged through a trough of shit before he was by-god drowned in Rae's Creek.

Scott's situation was verified for me on the 9th tee. I caught Gwen's eye in our gallery and made a gesture with a nod that said, "What's going on up ahead?"

She responded by mimicking a putting stroke and dragging her index finger across her throat. Easy enough to translate. Scotty was slitting his own throat with his putter.

Claude Steekley, the man who was only out there trying to make a living for his family, played his shot to the 9th green first. He hit too much club, and the ball flew to the back of the green. He was already six over par, and that shot didn't help matters. It was easy for Mitch and me and the fans who were nearest in our gallery to hear him when he shouted at the ball, "That's right, keep going, you Aggie-Baylor-OU bitch! Go on over the clubhouse roof, who gives a shit?"

The tragic thing about my seven-iron shot to the green was that it looked and felt perfect. The ball ate up the flag the second it came off the clubface. I was tempted to hold the follow-through for a photo op.

Mitch hollered, "Be the stick!"

I hollered, "Leave it alone!"

Where it might have wound up—stiff for a gimme three, or no worse than a short putt for a birdie—will remain a mystery, however.

The ball landed a split-second before the swarm of protestors darted out on the green.

There must have been two dozen of them, dancing, hopping around, flapping their arms, screaming death threats to golf and golfers.

Weirdest opera I'd ever been to. Then I heard the noise coming from other areas on the course, and that's when I realized there was a well-timed, inside-job disruption going on. Protestors had skillfully been assigned to all of the leading groups.

Later I'd discover that in other groups on the course there were protestors who picked up the golf balls of contestants, on the greens, in the fairway, and tossed them into the trees and bunkers. Those people thought they were creating havoc with the competition, but they knew nothing about the game. They didn't know that under the rules a contestant can replace a ball without penalty if it's been detoured, deflected, molested, or in any way interfered with by an "outside agency."

Nevertheless, they had their fun.

But now, as I was walking up the steep slope to the green, and as the siren was sounding to halt play, as it would if there was lightning in the area, the protestors began to scatter. All over the course they went sprinting across fairways, dashing into the pines, and plowing through bunkers, being chased by angry fans, Pinkertons, other security personnel, tournament volunteers, and well-meaning golf lovers.

The scene was humorous, is what it was. I stood there and laughed as I watched protestors getting tackled, wrestled, and punched—those who weren't slippery enough to escape through the pines and into the parking lots and out the gates.

It was like watching people trying to herd cats.

But I stopped laughing when I walked up onto the 9th green. My golf ball wasn't there.

# 18

The rules official dispatched to our group was a vice president of the United States Golf Association. I should have known I'd have a big chance with a guy named Jarvis Phillip W. Burchcroft.

This was after things had calmed down, the protest sillies had been abducted or chased off the premises, and General Douglas Anne Marie MacSprinkle had said, "I shall return," and left the Philippines.

The first person interviewed by Jarvis Phillip W. Burchcroft was Mr. Royce Ellis, a red-faced geezer in railroad shoes and a baseball cap with "South Atlantic Waste Management" on it. He'd found my ball in the front bunker left of the green. It was half-buried and nestled beautifully up against a heel print the size of a squirrel.

"Mr. Ellis, did you see the contestant's ball enter this bunker?" he was asked by Jarvis Phillip W. Burchcroft, who was proudly wearing his weak chin and my-parents-are-descended-from-Pilgrims attitude.

"Nope, I didn't see it go in there," Mr. Ellis said.

"Then, if I may ask, why did you think to look for the ball in this bunker, Mr. Ellis?"

Royce Ellis said, "That's where most golf balls is, don't you see? Where my ball always winds up, anyhow—and most of my friends'. Yes, sir, you could say I live in bunkers. You sure could."

Jarvis Phillip W. Burchcroft said, "Mr. Ellis, exactly where were you standing when the contestant struck the ball into this bunker?"

"Hey, whoa!" I said, butting in. "I did *not* hit the ball into the bunker. I hit it perfect. It was on the flag all the way. One of the protestors obviously kicked my ball in the bunker, or threw it in there. That's an outside influence. I'm entitled to replace the ball on the green within a reasonable distance of the cup."

"But we do not know if we have an eighteen–one here, do we?" Jarvis Phillip W. Burchcroft said. "We don't know that's what happened."

Officials love rules-speak. He referred to rule 18-1 in the rules of golf: ball obstructed by an "outside agency."

"I damn well know that's what happened," I said.

"No, you do not, Mr. Grooves. What you *do* know—indeed, what any of us can possibly know at the moment—is that it is something to be determined."

I wanted to ask him if he was a member of one of those country clubs you can't join if you've ever had a job.

But I said, "My ball was all over the stick. Ask any of these people. Ask Claude Steekley." I motioned to Claude. "Tell him, Claude."

"I wasn't watching," Claude said.

"Thanks, Claude," I said. "That's great. Hook 'em Horns."

Mitch stepped in. "Sir, we had a good lie. There ain't no wind. We hit us a perfect shot. You know we ain't gonna hook the ball in that bunker."

"I do not know any such thing," Jarvis Phillip W. Burchcroft said. He turned to me. "Fess up, Mr. Grooves. Are you quite certain you didn't hook the shot a tiny bit? Just a teeny bit? Just a teensy, weensy, tiny bit?"

"Jesus Elroy God Christ," I said, and walked away to calm down. Try to convince myself it wasn't in the best interest of my career to ask Jarvis Phillip W. Burchcroft of the USGA if he'd mind putting on a surgical glove before he stuck his finger up my ass again.

While I smoldered, the official interviewed some spectators to see if they could help him determine whether he was looking at "an eighteen-one situation." He loved reciting the rule number.

A man in a straw hat and green cardigan said, "I didn't see the shot. I was eating my egg salad sandwich."

A skinny woman in a blue sweatsuit said, "There was this man in front of me blocking my view."

An attractive woman in a purple golf shirt and white skirt said, "I saw the ball land on the green, and I'm sure a fat woman tossed it in the bunker."

A burly fellow in a Confederate-flag T-shirt said, "I'd have seen it but this woman kept talking to me about her trip to Vicksburg."

A man in a black suit said, "I was looking when he swung, but that's when the stupid person spilled a Coke on me."

A man in a Hawaiian shirt and Bermuda shorts said, "I think the ball hit the green, but what I was doing, I was looking around to see if anybody knew I was the one who farted."

Having gathered all the information, Jarvis Phillip W. Burchcroft ruled there was inconclusive evidence of an outside agency and concluded in his infinite wisdom that I must play the ball from where it was—out of that hopeless lie in the bunker.

Under normal circumstances I could have asked for a second opinion, even a third, and appealed to the chairman of the competition committee. But there'd been the disruption, no other rules official was available, his decision was final, and I should "move it along, please."

To say I was livid doesn't cover it.

I blurted out, "Why, you insipid, chinless, born-rich—"

But I was stopped before I got to the "fucking shithead" part or took a swipe at his Ivy League head with my seven-iron. Mitch dragged me away and held me in his clutches until I calmed down and realized that spending the rest of my life in prison wasn't worth the pleasure of murdering a USGA rules official. Almost, maybe.

Then came my caddie's pep talk.

Mitch whispered, "We not gonna let this bother us, B.J. We goin' in that bunker, hit us a beauty. Maybe hole it out. Make us a four at the worst, go whip up on the back nine. Now let's keep our cool and do this thing."

I pulled myself together, stepped down into the white sand, and took a firm stance. I closed the face on my sand wedge so it pointed left of the target—the impact would bring it back to square—and I tried to take an upright swing, come straight down on top of the ball. That's how you extricate yourself from a buried lie. I went about it OK, I thought, but evidently not. I left it in the bunker.

As I stared at the ball in the sand, I hoped nobody in the crowd remembered that I'd once lent my name to an instruction article on bunker play in *Golf Digest*. And I couldn't help thinking of what Grady Don once said. That he wasn't a good enough golfer to read golf instruction and still play good golf.

Mitch's second pep talk went like this: "We OK. We only lay three. We sittin' up good now. We just skim it out. Maybe we hole it. Least we do is get down in two, get outta here with a bogey. Bogey don't hurt us. We make it up on the back."

My skim shot was what you'd call haphazard at best. I left it in the bunker again.

Mitch's third pep talk: "We only lay four. Let's put it close, make us a putt. Take our double bogey like a man. We still be one under, and we got birdie holes on the back."

I landed the ball on the green with my third sand shot, but left myself a forty-foot downhill, sidehill, uphill, quad-breaking putt that no human could read or get close to the cup.

Mitch's last pep talk: "Piss on golf. Why don't we just three-putt this thing, go away with a eight? Shoot us a dog-ass seventy-nine, eighty. Don't make a shit to me."

My first putt sped twenty feet past the cup. The second putt swung ten feet to the right. The third putt broke both ways and left me with a five-footer. Big deal, I made it.

But Mitch missed it by one. I four-putted for a fucking 9.

So instead of going to the back side three or four under with a real chance to win the Masters, I was two over, out in 38, out of contention, and sliding off the scoreboard so fast I looked like my chute didn't open.

Which was why, as I walked to the 10th tee, my chat with Gwen took on such an intellectual quality.

"You're off the board," she said. "What in the world happened?"

"Nothing much," I said. "I made a nine, is all."

"You made a *nine*? How is that possible?"

I said, "It was easy. I got zebra'd. Zebras don't always wear striped shirts and stab you in the heart with their phony calls in football games. Some of 'em wear striped ties and fuck people over in golf tournaments."

"I see," she said. "Might I venture the guess you were the victim of an unfavorable ruling?"

"Unfavorable is one way to put it," I said. "Another way is to say a USGA asshole pulled out his dick and pissed on me in front of five thousand people."

Gwen turned to Mitch. He described my tragedy quickly, only touching on the sordid details.

"Bobby Joe, I'm so sorry," Gwen said. "That is so terribly unfair. I'm glad I didn't have to watch it."

"It's not that big a deal," I said. "I'll get over it . . . in about twenty years. Maybe sooner . . . if every incompetent, thieving, scum-licking, criminal zebra cocksucker in the country has his eyes gouged out and his arms and legs amputated, and gets hanged in public . . . and his children are kidnapped, tortured, and murdered by a psycho killer . . . and his wife is sold into white slavery in fucking Uganda."

# 19

After the disruption almost everybody shot straight up, arms and legs. Played like hospital food. Some lost their timing, some lost their concentration, some lost interest. As most sportswriters reported—with an intelligence that was exceedingly rare for them—the only thing Anne Marie Sprinkle's protest did was screw up the contestants. It brought no harm or embarrassment whatever to the Augusta National members.

Here's how the first ten finished in the Masters, although some of the names appeared differently in America's newspapers:

| | |
|---|---|
| Madonna Els . . . . . . | 66-72-69-71–278 |
| Elvis Woods . . . . . . . | 65-72-70-73–280 |
| Cheetah Farmer . . . . . | 67-71-70-72–280 |
| Hard Luck Grooves . . . | 68-72-67-72–281 |
| Desi Garcia . . . . . . . | 70-69-69-75–283 |
| Britney Mickelson . . . . | 66-70-71-76–283 |
| Dunn Matson . . . . . . | 70-69-72-72–283 |
| Grady Don Maples . . . . | 71-71-71-74–287 |
| Froggie Sommers . . . . | 67-74-68-78–287 |
| Chance Minter . . . . . | 71-72-70-76–289 |

Mitch congratulated me on my no-quit act. For not hanging a sign around my neck that said "Donate this round to the homeless."

Mitch said it took a man to dig down and shoot a two-under 34 on the back and fight back to a par 72 and grab fourth in the Masters after he'd been royally screwed by a zebra.

It would be nice if I could say I went to the back nine pumped up to make a valiant comeback and fought my ass off, but that's not what happened. What I did was play loose, casual, nonchalant, swing the club like I didn't much care where the ball went. Christ, I'd already lost the tournament. I honestly didn't even realize I'd shot two under on the back nine until I got to the cabin.

I couldn't blame Mitch for being happy about my finish. It meant $60,000 to him, which was 20 percent of the $300,000 that fourth place paid. But I knew he was happy for me personally. Happy I didn't embarrass myself, do a total puke-faint-die.

I was the leader for twenty minutes. Which found me back in the press room, up at the table behind the microphone in the interview area, flanked by two southern gentlemen in green jackets. My audience was small. A half-dozen writers. Most of them were out on the course or watching TV, rooting for somebody—anybody—to win. Anything but a sudden-death playoff that might drag on into darkness and bring them back the next day.

One of the green jackets said, "Gentmin, we have our Mastuhs toon-a-mint leader here."

Most of the questions were about the murderous ruling that left me buried in the bunker. I said from what I'd heard, I was the only competitor in the field who wasn't permitted to replace his ball on the green without penalty after the protestors did their damage. It was an outside agency, pure and simple, but the zebra blew it.

Still, I said, it was my own fault the way I let the ruling upset me so much. I didn't have to turn the 9th hole into a chopped salad.

I said I would always wonder what I would have done if I'd made a three or a four at 9 and gone to the back with the lead. I might have won or I might have found another way to lose. We'd never know.

After the session I bumped into Irv Klar outside the interview area. He'd interrupted the Pulitzer winner he was clacking on his laptop long enough to come say he was sorry about what happened to me.

He said, "I caught the last of your interview, Bobby Joe. Did you mean you really don't blame the rules official?"

"No, not altogether," I said. "I still hope he'll suffer a long, painful death from a light bulb shoved up his rectum."

Irv stared at me for a second. "I can use that . . . can't I?"

"If it's tastefully presented," I said.

Grady Don was sitting in the players' lounge outside the locker room when I came in. He was alone at a table having a scotch to celebrate his tie for eighth place, the best he'd done in a major. On the TV screen in front of him Madonna Els was winning the Masters again on tape.

The players' lounge connects to the locker room at one end of a ground-level wing of the clubhouse that was added on a few years before my time. The original clubhouse is the two-story white mansion you see in the photographs and paintings, the joint with the wrap-around balcony and the little lookout tower on the roof. The original clubhouse is antebellum, pro-bellum, or uncle-bellum. I only know it's as old as the tournament. At the opposite end of the locker room is a dining room available to anyone with a clubhouse pass. I suppose the best thing you can say about the players' lounge is that it's off-limits to the press.

Grady Don pointed to a Beefeater martini on the rocks with six olives in it. The drink had been placed in front of an empty chair.

"There's your trophy, Slammer," he said. "Sit down and tell me how you blew the Open."

Taking a seat I said, "First of all, Snead made an eight, I made a nine. Second, Snead made his eight on the last hole at Spring Mill. I made my nine with another nine holes to play. Third, Snead didn't have any help from a chinless zebra."

I took too big a swig of the martini and chased it with a whole green olive before my chest exploded.

Grady Don said, "Walk me through your nine. CBS don't have it on tape. They were too busy showing the protestors jumping over flower beds and running through hedges."

First of all, I said, the zebra looked like what you'd expect a sap named Jarvis to look like, and he spoke in one of those upper-crust accents that made you want to tear the leather patches off his elbows. Then I hit the highlights of my artistic 9.

"Man, you really did get fucked," Grady Don said.

"No shit."

"What's the zebra's name again?"

"Jarvis Phillip W. Burchcroft."

"You're lucky."

"I'm *lucky*? Are you crazy?"

"It could have been worse."

"How could it have been worse?"

"He could have liked you."

I hated myself for laughing.

The TV screen was showing the victory ceremony. A cluster of green jackets was watching Ernie Els, the winner, having the green jacket slipped on him by Davis Love the Roman, last year's winner. Tradition.

I looked at Grady Don. "Where'd Ernie win it?"

He said, "Tiger and Cheetah both hit it in the water on fifteen. Ernie didn't."

I wondered what had been said about the protest.

Grady Don said the Masters chairman had gone on TV and said the club had no intention of taking legal action against Anne Marie Sprinkle. The club hoped she and her followers had learned the lesson that their protest was as futile as it was wrong. But the club was going to make every effort to determine whether any of its members had sold credentials to the protestors. If so, they would be kicked out of the club and banned for life.

I nodded at the locker room. "Gwen's kid still around?"

Grady Don said, "He made a hasty departure. That punk. You know how a spaniel dog whines sometimes? For food? Almost sounds like he's singing? That's what Scotty sounded like."

"In here?"

"Out on the course—when he played choo-choo train on the greens. Man, he was a real child star. The kind that makes you walk out of the picture show before he tries to make a fool out of the grownup again. Child-star punk stormed around the locker room a while ago and perfected his act. Throwing things around. Blaming furniture for his three-putt greens. Cussing Jesus, Mary, Joseph, Bobby Jones, Stonewall Jackson, Jeb Stuart, country ham, red-eye gravy . . . and he leaves without tipping the locker-room attendants. He's got some things to learn."

"I'm not sure you can teach anything to a nineteen-year-old who's already worth fifteen million," I said. "You didn't try, did you?"

"Me? Naw. I just laughed at him. Well, I did tell him he was an oblong turd . . . and I said if he couldn't act any cuter than he did today, I wasn't going to any more of his fucking movies."

There was one last room-service dinner at the Magnolia Inn with Gwendolyn Gayle Turner Pritchard.

We dined in her room this time. Her room no longer presented any danger of the kid knocking on the door. Scott had jumped in his Porsche at the club and burned rubber.

Normal people in Toyotas and things can drive from Augusta to Orlando in around eight hours, depending on the number of stops for Cokes and fries. Scott would make it in six and a half, barring speed traps. I estimated he'd be home getting a congenial blowjob by midnight.

So it was that Gwen and I re-created some of our favorite scenes from paperback novels, and did those things before and after dinner.

We finally fell asleep in a tangled heap.

Breakfast the next morning was a leisurely affair on the outside terrace of the hotel dining room. I was driving to Hilton Head, having committed to play in the Heritage. Gwen had arranged for a limo to transport her to the Atlanta airport—just a two-hour drive—where she was booked on a nonstop to LA. Another limo would transport her to La Costa.

"What have we done here?" she said after we'd eaten. She was smoking, toying with her coffee cup. "You played in a golf tournament. I watched a golf tournament. Anything else happen?"

I said, "You mean other than the fact that I met this incredible babe who makes me feel like if I don't see her again pretty damn soon, I'm not going to be worth much on the people market?"

She smiled. "I was hoping to hear something like that."

We came up with an engaging home-and-home series that would begin almost immediately.

You could say we were a couple of crafty old athletic directors working on future schedules for our schools.

Or you could say we were just a couple of crazy kids who weren't going to let golf get in the way of life.

# PART TWO

# DIXIE DREAMS

# 20

The night before the United States Open got under way, Gwen and I were strolling through the charming village of Pinehurst, being suitably charmed but holding our own against the quaint. We'd dined at the Pine Crest Inn, the small hotel Donald Ross used to own, a favorite haunt of mine. Gwen was staying there. The hotel's restaurant didn't fern you out, and its bar was lively—it could turn into a spring-break joint at the drop of two Chi Omegas.

I'd liked to have been rooming with Gwen at the Pine Crest, but we agreed that for the sake of appearances, and perhaps for the sake of my golf game at the year's second major, it was better if I stayed at the Carolina Hotel. This was the big white Victorian joint two par-5s away. The Carolina had been revered in the grand old spa days—when the long, wide, winding porch held more rocking chairs than it did now.

For the week of the Open the USGA had reserved the Carolina for their officials and any contestant who rated convenience ahead of cost. Grady Don and Jerry Grimes were staying there, as were Gwen's kid, and most of the "name" players.

If you were staying at the Carolina, the Pine Crest Inn, or the Holly Inn you were inside the wire. You didn't have to jack with security slugs, gate guards, traffic. Dinks were outside the wire—the press, your penny-pinching pros, a majority of the fans. They were staying somewhere in Southern Pines or out in highway motels.

On our stroll I was telling Gwen how much I liked North Carolina.

"It's the California of the East Coast," I said, meaning that as flattery. "It has good mountains and a nice-size ocean, which is even older than yours. Where we are at the moment, it's only an hour's drive to Raleigh,

Durham, and Chapel Hill, the Research Triangle—where they invented basketball."

"We're back in Dixie, right? This counts?"

"We *are* in Dixie. I don't know if it's still the land of cotton. It's more like the land of golf courses now. The South's not all Confederate battle flags and Cracker Barrel restaurants, you know? I'm talking about the battle flag your liberals raise so much hell about they come down with fevers. The so-called Rebel flag? Libs love it when they see it on redneck pickups—like it was invented in the Sixties. Thousands of American lads fought and died under that flag for the glory of fried chicken and black-eyed peas, but your terminal libs love to compare it to the swastika. I think they teach it at Harvard."

"Didn't the war end? I'm sure I've read that."

"Yeah, we just ran out of time." I grinned. "Bobby Lee wanted Dicky Ewell to take the high ground at Gettysburg when he had the chance, but the lazy sumbitch blew it. We could have stepped on their throats right there."

"*We?*"

"Tell you how the South differs," I said. "In Virginia they spend years trying to figure if they're related to the Queen of England . . . Alabama hasn't come back from Bear Bryant's funeral yet . . . The whole Mississippi coast is turning into another Vegas . . . South Carolina used to be poverty stricken, but Beaufort and Charleston are film capitals now. Three years ago I was driving from Ponte Vedra to Wilmington, North Carolina, for an outing—a payday. I stopped in a rain storm in Beaufort. I went into a 7-Eleven and asked a guy where to stay. He said I could stay at the 'Prince of Tides' house or I could stay at 'The Big Chill' house—they were both good B&Bs. I don't remember which one I stayed in, but I went to this restaurant in town for dinner that night. I expected to find people sitting around arguing about who was the best Confederate general, A. P. Hill or John Bell Hood. But there were these guys at the next table in jeans, beards, sweatshirts, and thick glasses, and I overheard one of them say, 'I think they ought to bring the bitch back and make her re-shoot it.' . . . Some southern states are smarter than others, I admit. A friend of mine on the radio back home says in Arkansas they still point at airplanes."

Gwen said, "North Carolina may be the California of the East Coast, but I've never heard of it having earthquakes like we do."

I said, "No, but it has good hurricanes . . . plus it invented NASCAR."

"That may win," she said.

I remarked that when Pinehurst was built at the turn of the century, it was patterned after a small New England village.

Gwen said, "You recognize New England architecture when you see it, do you?"

I said, "I know a book when I read one. Guy who built it was a pharmacist from Boston. Guy named Tufts. He invented the marble soda fountain. Got rich on that. He wasn't a golfer. There weren't too many golfers in this country in those days, but he turned this into the first golf resort in America."

"Why would you build a golf resort anywhere if you didn't play golf? I have a better question. Why would you build a golf resort anywhere if *nobody* played golf?"

"I'll have to get back to you on that."

"Maybe he wanted to give people something to do after they left his drugstore. You think?"

"Pinehurst is all about golf, nothing else. The people who live here, own a second home here, come here to play, they don't talk about anything but golf."

"I'd never have guessed that, judging by the art galleries," she said wittily. "Why do you like the course so much. Scotty hates it."

"When you're nineteen and fly it out of the county off the tee, you hate every course that won't let you shoot sixty-three. Pinehurst is unique. There's hardly any out of bounds to speak of, and not a single water hazard on it. This is a course with subtleties. It tests your patience."

"Like how?"

"It plays like a links. Like the links courses in Scotland and England. The ninth hole doesn't even come back to the clubhouse. It's way out there. The fairways roll and the greens eat you up. It's tough to get a shot close, and if you miss the green, you have to be the god of chipping to save par. The undulations of the greens can be a nightmare. It's a strong 280 golf course. The pros loved the old North and South Open here in the twenties, thirties, forties. They considered the North and South a major. It was black tie for dinner in those days. Amazing when you think about it. Pros traveling with tuxedos."

"Not to mention their wives traveling with evening dresses."

"This should be a good course for me," I said. "If I'm ever gonna have a shot at the Open, this could be it."

"Really . . . ?"

"I'm not a birdie machine—I don't putt that good. Par's a good score here. These greens won't let anybody run the table. I'm playing good right now, and—on top of everything else—I'm forty-four."

I explained what my age meant historically. In terms of last chances in the major championships of your basic life.

"I like your attitude," she said. "The teenage girl won't be a distraction?"

"She shouldn't be."

The teenage girl was Tricia Hurt. She was the fifteen-year-old phenom who had been capturing the hearts and minds of golf fans for over a year. The USGA had gone sick in the head and lobbed her a last-minute invitation to play in the Open.

A teenage girl in a men's major? For publicity reasons? For financial reasons? For *any* reason?

Like everybody else on the PGA Tour, I couldn't decide whether to laugh at the USGA or be hot at the USGA for doing it.

For the time being, however, it wasn't worth thinking about.

I said to Gwen, "Pinehurst No. 2 is Donald Ross's masterpiece, but it was famous even before he put in grass greens."

She said, "What kind of greens did it have to begin with, grits?"

Gwendolyn Pritchard, standup.

I said, "Sand. Sand and oil. Small, flat sand greens. Most courses in a hot climate had sand greens in the old days. The golfer was obliged to drag an iron rake across the green to smooth out a line from his ball to the cup before he putted. Or after each group left the green, a worker would smooth out the sand by dragging a big heavy wet rug over it. Ross didn't find a strain of Bermuda that could take the hot climate until 1934. That's when No. 2's sand greens were switched over to the grass greens you see today with all the humps and swales. Bent came along even later."

She made a "hmm" sound.

I said, "Donald Ross built four courses to start with, and numbered them. Each course was for a certain kind of player. Long, short, pro, beginner. This was between 1901 and 1920. But he didn't intend for No. 2 to be the gem until later. Until Bobby Jones hired Alister Mackenzie to help design Augusta National. Ross was upset when Jones hired Mackenzie instead of him. He felt snubbed."

"And it was so unlike Jones to snub someone."

"I'm giving you history and you give me smart-ass."

"I'm sorry, Bobby Joe, but you talk about these people like I'm supposed to know them."

I said, "I'm sorry. Donald Ross and Alister Mackenzie were both Scots. Ross was a golf pro and architect all his life. Mackenzie was a doctor the first half of his life. He was in the Boer War and World War One. Then he discovered golf. Just think of them as two chunky guys with mustaches who wore tweed coats. Augusta was what inspired Ross to devote the last years of his life to turning Pinehurst No. 2 into a great layout. He was trying to out-monument the Augusta National."

"You don't think he did, do you?"

"Pinehurst is tougher. But Augusta has more variety, more drama. And it wins 'Best Postcard.' Mackenzie and Ross were both great designers, but Mackenzie had done Cypress Point, and that may have been the reason Jones picked him to collaborate on Augusta."

"That would swing it for me—especially if I owned one of those homes on Seventeen-Mile Drive."

"I couldn't live on Seventeen-Mile Drive."

"You *couldn't*? Why not? It's obscenely beautiful."

"Too far to drive for baloney and light bread."

We stopped at the window of a gift shop and studied a carved-glass table lamp. A bug-eyed golfer in knickers was crouched over a putt, the light bulb and lamp shade growing up out of his shoulder blades.

Electricity meets golf and does humor.

I said, "Here we have proof that they really don't talk about anything but golf in Pinehurst."

She said, "Only a person with impeccable taste would buy that."

In what must have been a world-weary tone, I said, "Well, people do this and that . . . but everything's pretty much what it is."

Laughing, she said, " '*Everything's pretty much what it is*'? I'm taking that. It's mine now. It goes in there with 'Fate don't have a head.' "

"I've always been deep," I said.

# 21

Tricia Hurt could outdrive most guys on the pro tour by ten to twenty-five yards. Make a man look like stepped-on shit.

"That's her," I said quietly to Gwen with a nudge.

We were sitting on an outdoor bench. We'd walked over to the sprawling Mediterranean-style villa that Pinehurst calls a clubhouse, and walked back to the village. Gwen was having a Merit Ultra Light when the teenager appeared.

Meaning the fresh-faced six-foot-tall teenage girl, rather pretty, who'd come strolling along. She was with a slender, arrogant-looking man who could only have been Dabney Hurt, her rich daddy.

Dabney Hurt was one of those facelifted, hair-too-long-in-the-back, Wall Street–looking guys. He wore sneakers, creased jeans, and a golf shirt with the collar turned up, and a cashmere sweater was carefully draped around his shoulders. Rumor had it that Tricia's mother, Millicent, spent most of her time on the computer at home, collecting the stories written about Tricia. Daughter was the family future, the franchise. Sad, really.

Tricia Hurt's broad shoulders and sturdy bronze arms were hard to ignore in her waist-tight white sleeveless blouse. Her snug-fitting khaki slacks suggested the strong, sculpted legs of a figure skater.

She was from Connecticut, but she'd spent every moment since she was eight in a combination golf instruction camp and boarding school near Palm Beach, Florida. She'd been winning girls and women's amateur titles since she was ten.

I said, "The kid's got a set of legs on her. It looks like she could play any sport she wants to."

"Katarina Witt does golf," Gwen said.

Tricia was the heiress. The latest in a line of chick golfers put on earth to embarrass guys—like Annika Sorenstam and Michelle Wie, who blazed the trail ahead of her. Tricia had been invited to enter four PGA Tour events last year when she was fourteen, her against the guys. The corporate-sponsor dummies turned flips with excitement. She not only made the cut in all four, she finished in the top 20 at Doral and Reno.

Grady Don Maples and Jerry Grimes were among the guys who'd been outdriven and outscored by Tricia on separate occasions.

Jerry said there was no doubt she was from another world, and furthermore she had not come here on a friendly mission. Grady Don sometimes referred to Tricia and her daddy as "Anastasia and the Czar," but mostly he referred to Tricia as the space-alien teen bitch.

After being paired with Tricia in the third round at Doral last year—and having her 71 beat his 73—Jerry Grimes reported that she wasn't only long with the driver, but she was long all through the bag, like Scott Pritchard.

Jerry observed that her grip was a classic Vardon. Her swing was big, slow, picturesque, a thing of beauty. It was said by noted swing gurus that she "possessed a genius."

Jerry admitted he was stunned on the first hole at Doral, a par-5, when she John-Daly'd him off the tee by twenty yards.

He said, "I thought she hit a rock in the fairway, but no such luck. She hits this little foomp out there with her Bertha, but it goes, man. She only went with the driver five more times, or I'd be in traction. She Americaned me at the second . . . Continentaled me at the sixth . . . Air Force One'd me at the tenth . . . space-shuttled me at the twelfth."

There were four or five of us listening in the locker room at Doral that day. I was as fascinated as the others.

Jerry said, "I couldn't believe she was outknocking me. I decided I'd get her at eighteen. I came off the ground at it. I solid clubfaced it. I laid titanium on Titleist's ass—and *bam*!" He smacked his palms together.

"Did you get her?" somebody asked eagerly.

Jerry shrugged. "She Goodyear-blimped me."

How Tricia made it into the Open at Pinehurst was no big mystery if you knew how much the U.S. Golf Association liked money.

The USGA didn't used to like money so much. It just wanted enough to run its annual tournaments smoothly and pay the hired help. But one day the organization looked around and saw a group of fools getting rich for no good reason, and somebody said we have to get in on this cake.

That's when the USGA jumped on the greed train. Waved goodbye to most of the organization's honorable traditions. Started partying with their two best new friends, network TV and corporate sponsors.

This led to Dabney Hurt. He owned UniCorp and LifeData. UniCorp sold something by the millions that nobody needed. LifeData did something to help hospitals kill old people faster.

It so happened that UniCorp and LifeData bought the two largest corporate hospitality tents for the Open at Pinehurst. Some of Dabney's other companies bought space. In all, Dabney's "participation" was worth $20 million to the USGA.

But the USGA was aghast when Dabney Hurt asked that in return for his generosity his teenage daughter receive a special exemption to compete in the men's Open championship of the United States of America.

To anyone's knowledge, dating back to the first National Open in 1895, there'd never been a female in the championship, although the unknowing could be excused for wondering about such names in the record book as Laurie Auchterlonie, Val Fitzjohn, and Fay Ingalls.

The current USGA president, Jameson Swindley, said under no circumstances would such a request be granted to Dabney. Jameson Swindley said he was appalled by the request.

First, Dabney Hurt said he'd changed his mind about the hospitality tents and was keeping his $20 million. When the USGA said he couldn't do that, Dabney said, "Did I mark my lip?"

Jameson Swindley then made the mistake of telling someone he should have known Dabney Hurt hadn't gone to Yale.

Big mistake. The remark drifted back to Dabney, and Dabney said he was going to buy Jameson Swindley's Manhattan law firm and fire Jameson Swindley and see that Jameson Swindley spent the rest of his life living in the doorways of abandoned buildings in Queens.

Other high-ranking USGA officials likewise suffered financial threats from Dabney Hurt. They dwelled on that, and they dwelled on losing the $20 million. But they didn't dwell long. They were busy voting unanimously to grant a special exemption to Tricia Hurt.

None of that made the papers. The news release from the USGA only quoted President Jameson Swindley saying, "The USGA has a long history of granting special exemptions. We believe a young lady competing against the men in the U.S. Open Championship is an idea whose time has come. We are therefore delighted to grant a special exemption to Miss Tricia Hurt of Greenwich, Connecticut."

When I was done relating all this to Gwen as we sat there on the bench, she said, "I think it's great, don't you? It'll be interesting to see how she does against you guys."

"It could be more fun," I said.

"How so?"

"It could be Anne Marie Sprinkle."

Got smoke blown in my face.

# 22

Nine events on the Tour had been played between the Masters and the U.S. Open, which had long since been scheduled for the sandhills of North Carolina in June.

I'd entered only five of the nine, what with my busy home-and-home schedule requiring me to visit Gwen twice in California and entertain Gwen once in Fort Worth.

La Costa's hotel bar and golf course were familiar territory, as was the whole area. I'd played in the Tournament of Champions six times at La Costa before it moved to Kapalua, and a number of San Diego Opens at Torrey Pines, but when I visited Gwen she treated me like a guy in a Hawaiian shirt and flip-flops with a throw-away camera from Wal-Mart in my hand.

I saw the Pacific Ocean from numerous vantage points. Sunshine was often called to my attention. Surfers and surf babes were pointed out to me, as were sailboats and aircraft carriers.

I was shown the flocks of thin ladies doing their daily shopping and lunching in downtown La Jolla. We had cocktails at the La Valencia Hotel, "the Pink Lady." Mandatory. I'd done it before. It's like missing a step and falling into the 1930s. Bump your head on Jean Harlow.

Die Shopping, Gwen's store in Del Mar, was in a made-to-look-rustic strip mall with other stores. Places that sold yogurt, bagels, ladies' shoes, paintings, Rolls-Royces.

Gwen's shop sold prints of fish, birds, and rock formations, mugs, vases, cushions, datebooks, leather goods, ladies' sports togs, and coffee makers that grind the beans and do everything else but pour it for you.

I was introduced to the two Gwyneth Paltrows who worked in the shop, and I met Gwen's partner, Sandy Knox. Sandy was a pert little blonde with a rack. That day she wore baggy slacks and a slipover dark blue knit shirt with a message stitched on it in gold sequins: GET TO THE POINT.

"He's a doll," Sandy Knox said to Gwen, referring to me. "Can I have him when you're through?"

"Lay one hand on him and you're a dead bitch," Gwen said.

I was grateful to discover that Gwen's house at La Costa didn't have a fake waterfall amid the landscaping, like the houses on either side of it. Hers was a Spanish-style split-level deal, white with a red-tile roof, large rooms, fireplaces, patios, view of the golf course.

Some of Scott's trophies and medals were easy enough to spot in the living room and den, especially the tall silver replica of the U.S. Amateur trophy. The hardware sat on tables and book shelves, and the medals were displayed in a glass case that Gwen called a vitrine. I think that's right.

Gwen said half of Scotty's cups, goblets, pitchers, pie plates, and medals, dating back to when he won the world junior something-or-other at the age of ten, were with Rick, his dad, now the president and CEO of International Sports Talent.

I asked why her kid didn't keep some of the treasures in his own home in Florida. She said, "He's into different kinds of trophies now. Of the female and automotive variety."

I was curious to know if Gwen had heard of any new clients Rick the Agent might have signed. I hadn't read of any in the golf magazines. She said she'd heard from her kid that Rick was trying to sign two teenage girls who might achieve fame and fortune in tennis and ski racing, and he was working on a top-secret prospect.

The best thing I could say about Gwen's home was that the master bedroom was cozy and comfortable.

When Gwen visited Fort Worth I did what you do with other friends who come to the city for the first time. You mix the cowboys in with the culture, and add barbecue, Tex-Mex, and chicken-fried deals.

Gwen admired our downtown, the modern towers rising above turn-of-the-century buildings. I explained that it was once a rowdy stop on the Chisholm Trail. That Butch and Sundance used to frolic in Fort Worth. That Etta Place had died in Fort Worth of a broken heart in

Mary Porter's Sporting House after she found out she didn't look like Katharine Ross.

Gwen gave high marks to the "historic stockyards district," to the real cowboys, play-like cowboys, saloons, and boutiques, and she enjoyed learning that the Stockyards Hotel, having been overwhelmed by nostalgia, offered a luxury accommodation called the Bonnie and Clyde Suite.

She sampled Tex-Mex cuisine at Joe T.'s, at the Original, at El Fenix, and at Mi Cocinita, the little café in the converted garage in a neighborhood over by the grain elevators on the south side. As for barbecue, she swooned at Railhead's ribs, the sliced at Angelo's, and the chopped at Cousins.

She ate the three good corners of a chicken-fried steak with cream gravy at the Paris Coffee Shop and again at Herb's Café, a haunt for almost everybody who'd ever gone to TCU, or played golf locally, but I mainly took her there to meet the legendary waitress, Lois "Get It Yourself" Deaton.

Lois didn't disappoint me. She gave Gwen the once-over and said, "Where's the Christmas tree you found this one under, Bobby Joe?"

I ran Gwen through our world-famous art museums, the Kimbell, the Carter, and the Modern. She pronounced the Kimbell sublime, inside and out, the Carter fabulous, and said everything in the Modern was badly in need of an explanation.

I drove her around Colonial, River Crest, Shady Oaks, and Ridglea, the country clubs where in my college days I made Phi Beta Kappa in smoking, drinking, and automatic one-down presses.

Mira Vista had come along later, after I was on the Tour. It was a lush country club and residential community inside security gates on the southwestern edge of the city.

A surprisingly sporty golf course was woven up, down, and around Mira Vista's mansions and townhouses that were built on the hills and in the bottomland. Some of the mansions were so staggeringly large they were sometimes mistaken for the clubhouse itself.

Gwen saw Mira Vista and all that went with it the night we went to dinner with my folks.

# 23

In preparing Gwen for Louise and George Grooves, I said my mom was a sweet-natured, still-attractive lady in her early seventies who'd be wearing slacks and a turtleneck, and I added that she still liked to drink coffee, play bridge, and smoke cigarettes. As for my dad, I said he'd be the silver-haired grump in the blue golf shirt and gray cardigan who wasn't nearly as unhappy as his expression might lead her to believe—not when there was still a lot of chili and rice to eat in this world.

Soon as we arrived—Gwen in pants and a lightweight sweater—my mom whispered to me, "My word, Bobby Joe, she's lovely as a spring day."

My dad said hidy and immediately asked Gwen if she knew what was good for arthritis—right now he couldn't tell whether his left leg hurt more than his right shoulder or the back of his neck.

When Gwen shrugged and said, "I don't really know—Advil?" my dad said, "Naw, that don't get it done, but make yourself at home, anyhow, seeing as how you're prettier than a homemade waffle. You're the best one he's ever run through here."

Gwen acknowledged the compliment with a hunched-shoulders smile.

My mom served a cottage cheese and pear salad, a ham steak with navy beans, rice and brown gravy, and cornbread. Nothing green anywhere near the plate. Anything green on a plate, other than green beans cooked with bacon, or canned asparagus, would put George in such a foul mood it wasn't worth the trouble to Louise.

Gwen commented on how good everything was, the cornbread in particular. She'd never had better cornbread, she swore.

"Louise don't put sugar in it," my dad said. "Life's too short to eat cornbread with sugar in it."

Our dinner conversation covered a range of topics.

According to my dad, Mira Vista's security gates were the envy of the other country club neighborhoods in town, which didn't have any. Mira Vista was built and developed in the eighties, but the security gates were envied more than ever nowadays, he said, since burglary, car theft, kidnapping, armed robbery, child molesting, and murder had become more popular in the United States.

"What would help more than security gates," George Grooves said, "would be if we could find us some courtroom judges who weren't so eager to put criminals back on the street every day of their lives . . . or I should say every day they don't have an early tee time or haven't gone off to shoot birds or ducks."

Gwen made the mistake of asking my dad what people should do if they didn't live in a neighborhood with security gates.

Looking at her like Lyndon Johnson used to look at the American people, he said, "Arm yourself and wait."

Which caused Gwen to make one of those "*ulk*" sounds you make when you're trying to catch an out-loud laugh before it gets away from you and flies through the room.

Gwen learned that my mom loved movies and went to every movie that came out, except for the ones where people live on other planets.

"Your interest in movies must come from your mom," Gwen said to me. "You're always saying lines from old films."

I said, "No, I've just always liked the ones where everybody smokes."

My dad wouldn't go near a movie if the theater was in a mall next door to a discount golf store.

He said, "Don't even try to trap me into going to a movie. Ever since we've owned a washing machine with a window in it, I've been able to see things that make more sense than anything Hollywood has to offer."

Gwen said, "You must watch a lot of sea epics, huh?"

That made my dad chuckle.

"You got you a comedian lady here," he said to me. "I'd hang on to her, if I was you, for them days when your putter stabs you in the back."

"I'm doing my best," I said.

My folks were happily retired from their dry-cleaning and florist businesses, which had been successful because they worked hard at it. My dad spent most of his time these days playing golf from the whites by his own rules—mulligans are free, roll it over everywhere. Another hobby of his was letting local sports teams and anti-American politicians piss him off.

The "overpaid sissies" who played for the Cowboys, Rangers, and Mavericks annoyed him almost as much as the "jock-sniffing egomaniacs" who owned the Cowboys, Rangers, and Mavericks.

He didn't recognize ice hockey as a Texas sport, therefore he didn't much care what went on with the Dallas Stars.

Of all the things that annoyed him, however, he was certain that if our TCU Horned Frogs didn't develop a reliable pass defense it was going to give him a heart attack quicker than CBS, ABC, NBC, and CNN.

"I don't wander too far away from Fox News," my dad said.

I said to Gwen, "I ought to explain that he hasn't learned how to say things to the TV screen without having it bother his heart."

"Say what things?"

I said, "Oh, like, you know, 'Get off my TV set, you rug-hugging, bug-eating, raghead pissant cowards.' "

"Oh, that," Gwen said.

Louise said, "I do believe Omar Sharif is the only Arab I have ever liked . . . Gwen, I want a cigarette. Will you join me?"

"Don't mind if I do," Gwen said, reaching in her pocket.

They lit up their own brands, each with a Walgreens lighter, the kind people leave on table tops and in car seats.

Gwen innocently offered my dad one of her long slender lights, unaware that evil doctors had taken my dad's heart off cigarettes years ago.

He said, "I'd love one, honey, but there's undercover cigarette police all over the house. I'll have one of my skinny cigars on the patio later."

My dad moved on to one of his favorite subjects. "We're in an all-out war with terrorist filth. We didn't start it, but we damn sure better win it if the world wants to survive. What I don't understand is why there's folks in our own country who think we can win it with hugs and kisses. Only thing the hydrophobia, shit-in-the-street, fanatical shitasses understand is an ass whippin' . . . You a Democrat? You're too pretty to be a Democrat."

"George, I'll swan," my mother said.

"I have a mind of my own," Gwen replied.

"You a liberal?"

"I like to think I'm an independent."

He said, "How do you feel about people burning the American flag?"

"I think most of them do it to be on TV."

"I don't think it ought to be against the law."

Gwen looked shocked. "You don't?"

"No, I don't. But I also don't think it ought to be against the law to beat the livin' shit out somebody who *burns* the American flag."

I said, "My dad was too young for World War Two by a year, I guess it was, but he served in Korea."

George Grooves said, "I was in the seventh grade at E. M. Daggett Junior High when the Japs bombed Pearl Harbor. Miz McGuire brought her RCA Victor radio to our home room so we could listen to President Franklin D. Roosevelt declare war on the yellow-belly sons of bitches."

Louise said, "He talks like that and we both drive a Toyota."

"That's 'cause we scrubbed 'em up," my dad said.

"But you were in Korea later on?" Gwen said to him.

"I was."

"Kill any gooks?" she asked playfully.

"I shot at some. I hope I hit somebody. What I mainly did was freeze my ass off and wish I was back here having a piece of chocolate ice box pie at the Toddle House. You take politics seriously, young lady?"

"I vote."

"That's not what I asked."

"Politics don't consume me. It would take a politician I have yet to see or hear about to make me work on a campaign for him—or her."

"Good. You know what kind of people take politics serious enough to work on campaigns?"

"I'll bet you're going to tell me."

"People who don't have a football team to root for."

Now Gwen did laugh, and said, "I do believe you've hit on a fine direction for our country. Watch football, be happy."

George Grooves said, "That's my domestic agenda. I'd have a damn good foreign policy, too, if I was the boss."

"Oh?" she said. "What would that be?"

He squinted like Lyndon again. "If they give you any back talk, nuke their sorry ass."

In general, I thought the evening was a success.

# 24

All of my ex-wives had been keeping busy at work, or we would have run into at least one of them during Gwen's visit—over a rib, an enchilada, or a stray Picasso.

Terri Adams still worked for the criminal lawyer, Red Taggert, so she was obviously helping him keep human waste out of prison. She enjoyed it. "Crime pays us pretty well," she liked to say.

One of Red's big cases recently involved the famous rapper, Snot Fishy Poot Stain.

While he was changing planes at the Dallas–Fort Worth airport one afternoon, Snot Fishy Poot Stain's next flight was delayed by weather. This prompted him to pass the time by entertaining the other travelers at his gate. One of the other travelers was a Viola Dipwick, an elderly lady with a cane. When the famous rapper put his baseball cap on her head and turned it sideways, she turned it forward. He turned it sideways again, but she turned it forward. He turned it sideways one more time, but she turned it forward—and poked him in the thigh with her cane. That's when the famous rapper shot Viola Dipwick between the eyes with the .38 he carried.

Red's plea in the famous rapper's behalf was self-defense. Where Terri came in, she was Red's bag lady. She paid two dopeheads to claim they were eyewitnesses to the shooting. They testified that the elderly lady had violently tried to poke Snot Fishy Poot Stain in the nuts, and he'd only been defending himself. The jury deliberated a little under an hour before reaching a "not guilty" verdict.

"I was only doing my patriotic duty," Red said to the press. "Americans don't want no harm to come to their celebrities."

Terri also helped Red in a real estate transaction that centered around many of the felons he had put back on the street to rob and kill again.

It happened when the city was asked to relocate more than two hundred criminals from the downtown public housing project where they'd been living. The housing project had been sold to a company and was going to be demolished to make way for a "corporate campus."

On the advice of Red, its attorney, the city housing board urged the city to buy the luxurious Shadow Haven apartments in an affluent west side neighborhood and use it for the relocation of the criminals. All of the apartments had two bedrooms, were air-conditioned, and came with TVs, computers, fireplaces, gardens, and use of the swimming pool.

There were raucous public hearings on the issue. Hundreds of homeowners in the affluent neighborhood expressed fear for their safety, and argued that their property values were bound to nosedive.

Terri posed as a resident of Shadow Haven. She pleaded for the relocation. Speaking to the homeowners at a hearing, she said if they would only "look into their hearts," they would know the city housing board was doing the right thing "for those less fortunate than ourselves"—her description of the felons.

The homeowners might have known they were fighting a lost cause since the city housing board consisted of two Al Sharptons, two Barbra Streisands, one Alphonso Bedoya, and the chairman, Emiliano Zapata.

Shortly after the deal was completed, it came out that Red Taggert was a part owner of the Shadow Haven apartments that the city had purchased for the sum of $58 million.

For a while the *Fort Worth Light & Shopper* received letters, faxes, and e-mail whose gist was "I sleep better at night knowing Red Taggert and everybody on the City Housing Board will die someday."

I knew the real story on all this because Terri bragged to me about her part in the scam.

"Life is about who's got the fix and who don't," she said. "If you haven't learned that, Bobby Joe, you haven't learned nothin'."

Cheryl Haney was undoubtedly busier these days with her volunteer work and social-climbing duties than she was with selling mansions, new and used. She was a certified *Vogue* lady now. I imagined her days filled with meetings involving the Jewel Charity Ball, the Van Cliburn piano competition, fund-raising for the symphony, and all things to do with finger sandwiches and white wine.

She was no longer the saucy lady I'd first known. The chick in a low-cut blouse who'd loved tooling around town in her top-down Chrysler convertible, zipping in and out of traffic, proud of her bumper sticker that said, "I Date Your Husband."

Cheryl did leave me a phone message that Gwen found amusing.

"Hello, dirt-fuck," she said. "Hard Reach here. How dare you call me Hard Reach. I was having lunch Wednesday at the Fort Worth Club with Jolene Frederick and she said she'd seen you at Colonial, and you said, 'How's Hard Reach doing? Has she washed all the Trinity River off yet?' Hard Reach, my ass. And when did you get to be a fucking Bass brother? How about in the future you stay on your fucking side of town and I'll stay on my side, you short-wad shit-pile."

Gwen asked, "How long has Cheryl been in the Junior League?"

Alleene was still the leader of the ex-wife tribe, and my good pal and business partner, and I'd wanted Gwen to meet her. I was sure they'd get along.

But the day we dropped by the office of Alleene's Delights on Berry Street over near the TCU campus, we found out she'd left only moments earlier. One of the Gwyneth Paltrows who worked for Alleene said she had gone off to cater a dinner for "rich socialites."

"Rich socialites," I said. "The best kind. Rare, though."

Overall, Gwen got a nice flavor of my city.

# 25

Those weeks when I went back on the Tour—for the Heritage, Colonial, Memphis, Memorial, Houston—I didn't play well enough to skirt into the win column, but I did manage to grab my share of clip.

"Clip." Grady Don's word for prize money. As in what you stick in your money clip.

"Gonna scoop me some clip this week," he'd say, "if my flat stick don't catch diabetes-meningitis."

"Flat stick." The putter.

Putters can catch other things, as Grady Don saw it. Heart trouble, flu, ulcers, constipation. He claimed he once owned a mallet-head putter that actually spoke to him one day after it rimmed out a one-foot putt.

I was aware that the putter is the most independent club in the bag. At times you can hardly talk to it in a civil tone. The best thing you can do with a putter that betrays you is kill the sumbitch.

But you have to make sure it's dead. Drowning may not do it. Grady Don insists that putters can swim, and some can grow into sharks and work their way into oceans where they cruise close to beaches and wait to bite the leg off a vacationing golfer when he goes in for a dip.

He's on record as saying the best way to kill a putter is break it in half and drop the head down a sewage drain. You can keep the other half, the handle with the jagged edge of the shaft. It can help you open boxes of crackers and cereal.

Most putters don't have a long life.

Ben Hogan's center-shaft brass putter, made out of a doorknob, the putter Ky Laffoon gave him, enjoyed a good run. It won him ten majors.

But it finally betrayed him. Cost him two more Opens and another Masters.

You could say Bobby Jones's blade putter, "Calamity Jane," has been the most fortunate. After all of its success, fame, and transatlantic travels, it lives on. Mounted in a glass case on the wall in one of the Augusta National's dining rooms, it can gaze down on the occasional plate of country ham or dish of peach cobbler.

Grady Don firmly believed that nobody could manufacture a putter that wouldn't catch syphilis eventually.

I played mediocre again in front of the home crowd at Colonial—too many distractions. I did finish tied for ninth and couldn't complain about the hundred and thirty grand I pocketed.

I started off worrying about whether Gwen's kid would enjoy his first visit to the tournament and my city. His first night I took him to dinner at the Railhead, and I discovered he'd never had barbecue before. "Why would you ruin good beef?" he asked.

I said, "Just try a rib, if you don't mind."

He did, and with a surprised look, he said, "This is good!"

And went about eating two dozen more.

I shouldn't have bothered to worry about a big good-looking celebrity like Scott Pritchard having a good time in my city.

He was snapped up the next night by "Do It All Delia" Williams, the paralegal, and then for the rest of the week he was entertained in succession by "Audible Amy" Walters, the dental assistant, "Slam Dunk Shirley" Cotton, the receptionist, "Motel Marilyn" Boyd, the happily married mother of two, and "Dirty Talk Dottie" Martin, the bank officer, who was known for serving all your needs, even banking.

"I love Texas," Scott gasped to me between adventures.

This was before he finished shooting the 261 that tied the seventy-two-hole Colonial record. He won by six strokes in the tournament Ben Hogan and halter tops had made famous.

Gwen thanked me over long distance for helping Scott play well and have a good time in Fort Worth.

"I had very little to do with it," I said, leaving out the part about introducing him to some of our local all-stars.

"I'm surprised he shot so low. He looked tired on TV."

"He may have been," I said. "Colonial's a different kind of Tour event. Lot of social functions connected to the golf."

Someday, if Gwen ever attended the Colonial, the fully loaded halter tops, miniskirts, and spike heels would speak for themselves.

I nabbed a nineteenth at Memphis and a twelfth at Memorial, and Grady Don did some top twenties himself, but the big moment for both of us was a visit in Memphis from Smokey Barwood, our agent. Smokey showed up at the Peabody Hotel downtown where we were staying. Us and the ducks.

The three of us walked over to the Rendezvouz for a plate of ribs and pull. At dinner, after Grady Don said, "It ain't Texas, but it ain't bad," Smokey presented us with a business proposal.

There was this new company called Miracle Golf, Inc., headquartered in Fat Chance, Louisiana, and the product it was most proud of was the Flip Me container featuring a pull-the-trigger top to prevent insects from flying into your drink as it sat in the cup holder in your golf cart. We would own one third of Miracle Golf if we agreed to be the "spokespeople" for its golf products. Many more exciting products were in the works.

Smokey produced a Flip Me container from his briefcase.

"What do you think?" Smokey asked at the table, demonstrating the trigger-top. Flip up, flip down. Two times. Three.

Grady Don looked at me. "Some people get millions from Nike."

"When you win your first major, we'll have more bargaining power," Smokey said.

"Thanks for the reminder," I said.

Speaking for both of us, Grady Don said, "Smokey, when I get through with this pulled pork and these beans, I'll show you what else you can do with that container."

Grady Don and I drove to the Houston tournament in his Lincoln gunboat. We'd taken to doing it since 9/11 had caused all the inconvenient bullshit at airports. Me and Grady Don and the little gray-haired ladies are always the only ones who ever get strip-searched while the diaper-heads, turbans, and bedsheets go straight on board. We actually liked driving to tournaments if it wasn't so far it gave you a limp.

We'd take the scenic routes, the back roads. Like going down to Houston—only four hours—you could stop for lunch at the Burton Café near Brenham. Enjoy the lush, rolling countryside that isn't beautiful by Lake Tahoe standards but looks plenty beautiful to most Texans.

The Burton Café is a place that makes you want to eat the whole menu, even things that aren't fried, then lick the grease off the wrists of everybody in the joint.

Taking the back roads from Fort Worth to Houston also means you can avoid I-45. Leave it to the speeding, cell-talking wizards who lose control of their Chevrolet pickups, leap over the median, and become Texas State Highway Department statistics. Not to mention the overturned eighteen-wheeler that spills shit everywhere, blows up in flames, and causes a six-hour delay, by which time the driver may be awake from his nap.

The reason I played in the Houston Open this time was because they played it in Houston for a change. Houston proper. Instead of some far-flung residential development that seems closer to Saturn.

It was played at graceful old River Oaks Country Club. The clubhouse looms like the White House at one end of River Oaks Boulevard in one of the prettiest neighborhoods in America. The original Donald Ross design has been toughened up by others through the years, but it still weaves through willows, Spanish moss, stately oaks, and money.

Jimmy Demaret won the Western Open at River Oaks in 1940. The first Houston Open was played at River Oaks in 1946. Which was the last time Byron Nelson, Ben Hogan, and Sam Snead finished one-two-three in a golf tournament.

I'd once captured a college trophy at River Oaks, and liking a place often helps your game. My 275 landed me in seventh place and was worth $150,000. If it hadn't been for the 17th hole, where I made a double in the last round, I'd have been fourth.

The 17th at River Oaks requires a big drive over a lake, and offers a shot to an upraised green with a blind pin. You can cut across as much of the water as you wish on the tee ball, then you have to take it up top and spin it. Try to land a wedge on top of Yul Brynner's head and keep it there. Your poor old average River Oaks member has to fire a long iron at the green. Makes you wonder why rich people want to live like that.

Grady Don didn't fare so good in the tournament. He wasn't too enthralled with the River Oaks history I laid on him. He said, "Lord, Bantam, and Slammer finished one-two-three here, did they?"

"You can look it up."

"Well, you can add to your lore that Grady Don Maples finished thirty-fucking-fifth here."

The subject of Gwen didn't come up until we were on the way back home and stopped for lunch again at the Burton Café. This time, we ordered the cheeseburger for an appetizer and the chicken-fried steak for the main course—with cream gravy, mashed potatoes, pintos, corn on the cob, and black-eyed peas.

"Where you going with the shapely mom?" Grady Don said. "Y'all thinking about marrying yourselves to one another? Or maybe that thought ain't got here yet—excuse me for asking."

I said honestly, "We haven't talked about where we're headed. She seems to be happy with where we're at. I know I am. It's the most fun I've had in a long time with a female woman-type lady."

"She's a female woman-type lady, all right. My money says you're gonna make her number four, the way you're acting."

"I don't have any idea if she's interested in being married again. We've only been jacking around together two months."

Grady Don leaned back and said, "Gwen's a dandy, I'll say that. If I've ever seen one that don't need her teeth cleaned and coat brushed, it's Gwendolyn Pritchard. She'd make a bulldog break his chain."

"I won't pass that along to her as one of your compliments, if you don't mind."

"I hope you don't get your heart broke one day, that's all—when she goes chasing after a Frisbee."

"I won't pass that along either."

"It's not like you haven't been down this road before, B.J. You're a big-time scholarship donor. You've recruited some serious debutantes in your time, son. But this one . . . man, she could go to Egypt and give the mummies a hard-on."

"She has a lot of pluses."

"I'm just saying you better think about it careful before you make her number four."

"If we do marry, she wouldn't be number four."

"How you figure?"

"Alleene counts. So does Cheryl, although her cussing and bitching took up most of our time. But Terri Adams was a walk-on. I'm not counting Terri Adams."

"You married the walk-on."

"OK, she gave good audibles. But we weren't together long enough for me to unpack. Let the guys who screwed her while I was out of town count the walk-on."

"Babes as good-looking as Gwendolyn aren't trustworthy, B.J. It's not only a city ordinance, it's an international law. You know that. Shapelies bring you to your knees, make you give up sweets. But one day you go out to run an errand, and they're off doing the quarterback, the drummer, and the dope dealer."

"You left out the deckhand and the tennis pro."

"Them too."

"I'm sorry to disappoint you, Grade. Gwen's not that kind of chick. She's mature, she's a mom, a businesswoman, and she has a great sense of humor. We laugh a lot. We talk about things."

"Talk about things. Now *I'm* gettin' a hard-on."

"We don't agree on everything, but we agree on most things. Like music. We both grew up on James Taylor, Carole King, Carly. I say Kris and Willie and Billy Joe Shaver never wrote anything but anthems. She agrees with me."

"She like Patsy? She better."

"She has Patsy Cline in her car, in her home, and in her store, is all. She does confess she once liked the Stones. I was never a good judge of that, I've told her. I still had a hard time calling it music when an unwashed, stringy-haired asshole scooted around the stage fucking his guitar."

"Have you straightened her out on politics?"

"Not totally. But you'll like this. The other night on the phone we were talking about the suicide terrorists. How dumb you had to be to let one of the slime buckets talk you into killing yourself. 'Here, kid, strap this bomb on your waist and blow yourself up in that building over there. Maybe you can kill some women and babies.' Like what happened to, 'Do it yourself, Mohammed, I got your bomb right here.' Gwen says the death penalty is too good for terrorists. They ought to be locked up in solitary and forced to listen to rap the rest of their lives."

"I like it."

"See?" I said. "There's more to Gwen than you think. You've just been judging her on her looks."

"Yeah, I have. I guess that makes me a fucking retard."

# 26

Just another lucky break, is all it was. On the first day of the U.S. Open, when there should have been nothing on my mind but how to handle Pinehurst No. 2, it was my honor and privilege to meet Rick Pritchard.

Yep, that Rick Pritchard. Gwendolyn's ex, Scott's dad, and—if first impressions count for anything—a recent inductee into the California Hall of Copper-Riveted Gold-Plated Four-Star Major-League Assholes.

He wasn't hard to spot on the practice range. Standing behind Scott, watching the kid launch eight-irons into the realm of Eastern Europe, was a big, tan, muscled-up guy, around six-three, with thick layers of wavy blond hair doing what Maurice of Beverly Hills instructed it to do.

Rick was a hulk in tight-fitting white slacks and a bright red long-sleeve cotton shirt, the sleeves pushed fashion-consciously up to his elbows. A brown leather bag hung from his shoulder on a long strap.

Precious shoulder bags for guys? They were back?

Even though my mind should have been solely on Pinehurst, I wanted to meet him for two key reasons. One was to look at his jewelry up close. I'd seen the lights sparkling from a distance. He was wearing more gold shit than three Palm Springs divorcées combined. The other was to see if those really were black velvet slippers on his feet.

When I sauntered over, I first spoke to the kid.

"Can I borrow your forearms today, Scott?"

Humor.

He was hitting 200-yard eight-irons.

Dad was on his cell, his back turned to us.

"Do you like this course, Bobby Joe?" Scott said.

"I do. But it's tough. It takes patience."

"It's a junkyard. Put a tee ball down the middle, what are you looking at? A stupid unmade bed or something. Geeeaah."

Delightful reference to Pinehurst No. 2's classic crowned greens. What Donald Ross had in mind—a bunch of unmade beds.

I looked at Rick. He was clicking his cell off, putting it back in his shoulder bag.

"Hi," I said pleasantly.

Blank stare from Rick.

Scott said, "Dad, this is Bobby Joe Grooves. Bobby Joe, my dad."

Rick broke into a smile. "Hey, hey, hey." He extended his hand.

I went with a firm, defensive grip, expecting Rick to be a guy who tries to crush your hand, let you know how manly he is. Off and on, my right hand was still a little sore from five years ago in Dallas when I shook hands with a car dealer named Shorty who was on my Pro-Am team.

Rick gave me a civilized handshake. I noted his jewelry—the hefty gold Rolex, the gold necklace, the two gold bracelets, the treasured gold ring from the Rose Bowl. I wanted to tell him I was relieved his gold ring came from the Rose Bowl and not from Maurice of Beverly Hills.

"I owe you a debt of gratitude," he said.

"You do? What for?"

"For keeping my wife occupied these past two months. Gwenny says you guys have had a ball."

Gwenny.

Now I knew the real reason she divorced him.

I said, "She's your ex-wife, I believe."

"A big mistake on my part, you can lift that out of the fine print," he said. "But if we get back together someday, it'll only be a bump in the road. Right, Scotto?"

Scotto. Filed it.

"Yeah, whatever," Scott said, taking a divot the size of Godzilla's foot and sending an eight-iron into eternity.

"I'm a little slow," I said to Rick. "Are you saying you're planning on getting back with Gwendolyn someday?"

"Who can predict world events?" he said. "Women are like porn flicks—you have to look at fifty to find a good one."

I tried to force a smile at that. Failed.

He continued to laugh.

I said, "What happened to Ashley, if I may ask?"

"Oh, wowser. Another bump in the road. Women. Like the man said, 'You can't live with 'em . . . pass the beer nuts.' Eh, Scotto?"

"Fatage," Scott said, ignoring dad, speaking to his eight-iron. He flipped the eight-iron aside, picked up his sixty-degree wedge.

I said to Rick, "I take it the lovely Ashley's been traded to the Redskins? Is that it?"

"Good way to put it, Bobby Joe. She had a pretty good arm but couldn't hit the deep post. Heh, heh. Costly but necessary. I have the sense Gwenny hasn't filled you in on what's been going on."

"I'm getting that sense, yes."

"Short of the long, I'm working on Gwenny to come on board. She's playing hard to get, but if I know Gwenny, she's interested."

"On board what?"

"International Sports Talent. My company. IST. Damn thing's running away with me. That's mostly thanks to Scotto here, the big wage earner, but I'm on the verge of signing a new client that's going to contribute heavily in the *ka-jing* department. It's hush-hush, but I see no reason why I shouldn't let you in on it—you being a friend of the family, *n'est-ce pas?* I'm going to sign Tricia Hurt. Is that any good? Huh? Tell me that's not any good?"

"You're going to sign a fifteen-year-old girl to a pro contract?"

"*Pardon, monsieur,*" he said. "If I may rephrase . . . I am going to sign a fifteen-year-old *locomotive* . . . to a professional contract."

"Tricia Hurt doesn't need to turn pro yet. She's too young. Besides that, her daddy's rich."

"Her daddy happens to be in financial doo-doo."

"He is?"

"Two years ago the Dabster went public, tried to become pope. Now all of his stocks are in the shitter. He's leveraged up to his facelift. The banks own him and the banks are restless. It's not generally known, but everything he has is for sale—the ranch in Idaho, the house on Nantucket, the penthouse in Manhattan, the Palm Beach mansion, his yacht, his Citation, and, sad to say, his entire barn of eighty-five mint-condition vintage cars, including the incredible '36 Cord, the '39 Continental, the '47 Cadillac Woodie, the '33 Dodge Brothers sedan, and the incomparable '53 Cunningham C-3 Cabriolet, one of only nine ever built. *C'est magnifique.*"

Car guy. California deal.

Rick said he normally charged 30 percent of a client's earnings, but he was nailing Dabney Hurt for 50 percent of Tricia, the Dabster being in financial difficulty. Dabney would settle on half of the annual gross in exchange for a $10 million signing bonus. The ten mill was a bagatelle, Rick said, considering he could guarantee Tricia $20 million a year for the first three years. "With elevators," he said.

"Deep as he's in the ditch, how much good can ten million do?"

"It'll keep him afloat till he can think of something else," Rick said. "The important thing is, I shall have the two hottest young players in the world—Scotto and Le Tricia. *Le roi est mort, vive le moi*."

"What?"

"The king is dead, long live me."

"Did you major in French at Southern Cal?"

"Took a year. Polishing up. Good for the Euro biz."

I looked off, took a breath, looked back.

"Does Gwen know you're going to sign Tricia Hurt?" I said.

"I told her at breakfast."

"You and Gwen had breakfast this morning?"

"At the Pine Crest."

"I had breakfast with Gwen at the Carolina."

"Must have been later."

"No wonder she only wanted coffee."

I would have appreciated a moment to myself to control my anger, pull the dagger out of my heart, but Rick was still talking.

"The best way for me to drive this bus is move the main office to New York City, New York. That's Manhattan Island, Big Town, Gotham, the Big Apple. I'm there most of the time now anyway. What I'm trying to talk Gwenny into doing is running my Beverly Hills office. She should sell the La Costa house, sell her half of the boutique in Del Mar to Sandy, and find herself a place in the Beverly flats."

"Gwen would be your employee?"

"Surely you know Gwenny better than that. She would have an ownership position. And that ain't just *ka-jing*, Groovo. We're talking blimpo coinage. Centavos meet drachmas, krona meet guilders, liras meet rupees, and whammo. Multo shekelroids."

"So it's strictly business? You and Gwen?"

"Well, not to tread on your turf-o-rama, Bobbo, but Gwenny and I do have a history. Who can say what the future holds?"

His cell beeped.

Rick answered, listened, handed it to me. "It's the ex-o-rama."

I took the phone, stepped away, turned my back.

"Gwenny," I said. "Is it really you?"

"I know you're pissed," she said.

"Boy, you got that one right off."

"You have every reason to be."

"Something else we agree on in life."

"We'll talk about it later."

"What will we have to talk about? The round of golf I'm getting ready to play in a major championship when I'm totally mind-fucked?"

"I know. The timing is not good."

"Where are you?"

"I'm on the clubhouse terrace. I'm looking at you through binoculars. I was on my way to the range when I saw you with Rick. I came back here. I'm sorry I didn't tell you he was here this morning, but I didn't want to upset you. I never dreamed the two of you would meet up, damn it to hell."

"What will your title be at International Sports Talent?"

"Bobby Joe, I'm not sure I want to do that, but a great deal of money could be involved. We need to talk about it."

"Why did you lie to me?"

"I didn't lie to you, Bobby Joe. I just didn't mention something."

"I've got to tell you, *Gwenny*. I am really hot."

"And I am really, really sorry. Play good."

"Hey, no problem. As good a mood as I'm in."

I punched off the cell.

"Yo, Rick," I said. He looked. I pitched him the cell. He caught it. Good hands for an old SC fullback.

"Nice meeting you," I said. "I have to go feather my irons and nestle my wedges now."

# 27

Sometimes you play better when you're mad. That was the theory of Baldy Toler, my old high school basketball coach. When you went into a fray, he wanted you to be "hot as a pot of collards." I recall making every effort to be exactly that, even though at the time I didn't know what a collard was.

A knee in a rival's stones was Coach Toler's idea of setting a good screen. Same as breaking a guy's rib with your elbow representing the correct way to snare a rebound. Accomplish two things at once.

As per Coach Toler's instructions, I thought our anger was put to even better use on defense. "Make the scogies pay for ever golldang bucket they make," he'd say.

I never knew what a scogie was either, mind you, or whether it had anything to do with a collard, but Baldy said the best way to make somebody pay for a bucket was to knuckle up a fist and stab the shooter in his armpit when he went up for a long jumper, a midrange jumper, or a put-back in the paint. "Give the sumbitch something to remember."

We played full-court man defense at all times, and this involved talking to your opponent throughout your time on the floor. Mention such things to him as you knew for a fact that your uncle was fucking his mom. Or if you noticed a cross around his neck on a chain, call him a Catholic dick, tell him St. Ignatius was a queer, and say you stopped by Our Lady of Victory yesterday and got a good blowjob from Sister Mary Agnes.

Many life lessons were learned from Coach Toler, who consistently led his youngsters to city, regional, and state championships. Torture and discipline were his allies. He made practice such insufferable agony, the games were cake.

You also learned from his long wooden paddle, which he laid on your butt instantly if you made any semester grade below a B. You learned from his fondness for ordering fifty fingertip pushups every time you missed a layup in practice. And you learned from his penchant for making you run so many 400-meter laps after practice that half the squad annually developed emphysema.

But I suppose most of Coach Toler's warriors would remember him best for what he'd say to us before we left the dressing room and took the court for a game.

"Awwight, men," he'd say. "What are we gonna do tonight? I'll tell you what we're gonna do. We're gonna eat lightning and shit thunder!"

How to resurrect such competitive anger and transfer it to golf?

That was my question for Mitch as we stood on the number 1 tee waiting to begin the first round of the Open.

"You mad at Gwendolyn," Mitch said, "and you want to take it out on the golf course?"

"I would, yeah."

"How that old coach tell you to get over a girlfriend did you wrong in high school?"

"It's too vulgar to repeat."

"But you remember it."

"I've never forgotten it."

"I know vulgar. We friends. What the coach say?"

"What he'd say was, 'Think of the tomato-mouth bitch sitting on the toilet taking a big shit.' That's what he'd say."

Mitch shook his head. "Wouldn't work on today's generation."

"It wouldn't? Why not?"

"Be a turn-on."

I pinched my arm to keep from laughing. I wanted to stay hot at Gwen and International Sports Talent and Rick Pritchard and meaningful relationships everywhere.

I said to Mitch, "Gwen didn't tell me her ex was in town for my own good. You know what bothers me as much as anything about it? People who do things for you for your own good. It makes me want to say, you know what you can do for me for my own good? Don't by-god do anything for me for my own damn good."

Mitch said, "Let's punish Pinehurst and all them other things with the driver today."

"Go with the Show Dog?"

Made some sense. The course was set up unlike any Open course I'd ever played. A man was encouraged to take out the driver. Pinehurst's greens were so brutal when it came to putting and chipping, the USGA, in an uncharacteristic mood of fairness, opened up the fairways and kept the rough at a sane level. The landing areas were fifty to sixty yards wide, the rough was only three inches high.

The U.S. Open was normally known for having fairways only thirty yards wide in places, so narrow, as Dave Marr once said, you couldn't walk down the middle of them without snagging your shirt. And the rough was so high, like halfway up your leg, you could lose your shoes in it while you looked for your golf ball.

It was the tricked-up difficulty of the courses along with the pressure of trying to win a title as big as the U.S. Open that inspired Dr. Cary Middlecoff to make a remark back in the fifties that's found its way into the hearts of most contenders. What he said was "Nobody wins the Open—it wins you."

# 28

The first two rounds I was in a threesome with Claude Steekley, he of the furrowed burnt-orange brow, and my old pal Knut Thorssun, he of the wooden dick.

This put two unique ladies in our gallery Thursday. One was Pookie Steekley. I wasn't keen on overbites, except for Gene Tierney's, but Pookie's made her seem sexy in the same sort of aristocratic way. Too bad she liked Bible study. Claude had shared that tidbit with me.

Pookie was wearing a sleeveless orange polo shirt, white golf skirt, saddle oxfords, and a wide-brimmed straw hat with orange feathers in it. Her hat, I felt, had escaped from a *Masterpiece Theatre* series on PBS. Crawled right out of their TV screen in Austin.

The other lady was Vashtine Ulberg, or I should say Snapper, Sweden's own rap diva—and Knut Thorssun's bride-to-be unless Bobo shrunk up on him.

Vashtine was dressed like she was there to make a music video with a plot revolving around the roller derby.

She wore crack-tight cutoff jeans, a yellow V-neck tank top barely holding in her magnificent lungs, and black patent-leather whore boots, and her wild blond hair was almost as long as Knut's.

Vashtine drew a larger crowd off to the side than our threesome on the tee. She was surrounded by droves of her music-loving fans, an indication that none of them had finished the sixth grade.

It might not have been Vashtine's outfit alone that caused the incident. Her fame among imbeciles may have contributed.

We heard the shouting and saw the shoving and scuffling before the golf carts arrived. I followed Knut into the crowd to see if we could help calm things down.

A half-dozen USGA officers unpiled from the carts, some of them in their white button-down shirts and striped ties of yesteryear, all of them armbanded and walkie-talkie'd up.

I recognized Jameson Swindley, the tall pinhead who was the current USGA president, and Dace Fackle, the executive director. Swindley led the group into the middle of things, saying, "Young lady, you are causing a disturbance at our Open championship."

I suppose he shouldn't have grabbed her arm . . . or maybe it wouldn't have mattered. Vashtine still might have let loose.

She snarled, "I am here to vatching the focking golfik! Vut you donk to me, you focking ateshatten slakfort! You dat knownin who the focking shitek you focking wit?"

Knut said to one and all, "This lady is my fiancée, it is so. She is to be my wife as soon as I can work it into my commitments, to be sure."

Jameson Swindley said, "If that's the case, Mr. Thorssun, I suggest you tell her not to dress so indecently at our championship."

Knut said, "Her way is not to be considered indecent in Stockholm, or anywhere in our homeland, the point you are making. But to make an effort for peace in this matter, I must say to Vashty, my love, it is perhaps best for you to rethink your costume for today, is it not?"

"Oh, jah?" she screeched at Knut. "Vut taken dot side of the pussy lickink dirgen shiteks? Vell, vut you tank of these, you clocksocking modderfockings?"

With that, she lifted up her top and flashed her tits. It was more like a full display than a flash. She turned this way and that as thunderous applause and joyous shouts accompanied her act.

That clinched it. Vashtine was forced into a golf cart and told she would be transported to the clubhouse and given the option of changing her attire and behaving herself or spending the rest of the day under house arrest.

"Voo tellin the modderfockers, Noots!" she yelled as the cart rolled away. "Callin jag lawyers, Noots! . . . I vant sue ever focking rotter assenholin golfik dinkin!"

Dace Fackle, the executive director, smiled apologetically at Knut. "I'm terribly sorry about this. We'll see that she's comfortable in our private hospitality suite in the clubhouse. She'll be with some of our officers and their wives. There'll be food and some rather nice wines."

" 'Noots'?" I said to Knut.

---

It so happened I Lucilled it off the first tee with the Show Dog and gestured a thanks to the appreciative souls who applauded.

I hoped it would be a trend, parking my tee ball in the fairway.

Thus, after settling down to a medium boil over Gwendolyn Pritchard's treachery, and after having accidentally been in the right place at the right time to observe Vashtine Ulberg's healthy set of lungs, I was able to devote the rest of Thursday—for whatever financial or sentimental value it might have—to my golf game.

An unexpected incident occurred at the second hole, which was one of the holes where you could hit it out of bounds on Pinehurst No. 2. Elsewhere you can hook it into the houses at the 3rd, slice it into the houses at the 5th, and hook it into the practice range at the 18th, but to do any of that you have to try very hard.

A village road runs along the left side of the 447-yard second hole, and Claude Steekley's looping hook off the tee found it. He reloaded and cautiously steered the next one into the fairway, leaving himself about 180 yards to the green, from where he was shooting four.

But he snap-hooked this one to the left with his six-iron, and he knew it could wind up OB as well. He played another provisional.

"Brown shit Aggie boot!" he shouted.

His words rang through the pines.

We started looking for his ball in the pines near the road, his wife, Pookie, included in the search party, milling around, nudging leaves and pine needles with the toe of her saddle oxford. She didn't look happy about the situation. Wives seldom do.

Claude found his own ball. It was one foot out of bounds.

"Baylor, Aggie, Sooner squat!" he shouted.

Claude stomped around in a circle, grumbling, kicking at the dirt, leaves, pine needles. He knew he'd have to march out to the fairway and would now be shooting six, and was on his way to no better than an eight.

It was while Claude stormed around in the pines that everybody's attention was drawn to the automobile.

This blue Lexus pulled up and stopped. How the lady at the wheel, a complete stranger, managed to slip through all of the Pinehurst security check points was a mystery that Lucas Davenport would have to solve someday, but there she was nonetheless.

A window slid down and the lady hollered, "Do any of you know where I can find a hotel room?"

Most of us only stared at the lady in the car, but Pookie Steekley dryly called back to her: "In a few minutes you can have ours."

# 29

A lesser man would have shuddered at the sight of his name at the top of the dreaded scoreboard.

I say dreaded because if you're not Ben Hogan, Jack Nicklaus, or Bobby Jones, you're not comfortable on top of the scoreboard after the first round of the United States Open. It's an engraved invitation for destiny to put his foot on your throat.

Or her foot. It depends on what the meaning of "foot" is.

There's a long line of first-round leaders of the Open who not only didn't win the Open they led, they double disappeared. Some vanished without a trace while others spent the rest of their days in club jobs, handing out prizes for low-gross, low-net, and fewest putts in the ladies weekly nine-hole play day.

A partial list of guys who led the Open and dropped off the world would include Lee Mackey Jr., Henry Ciuci, Al Krueger, Les Kennedy, Al Brosch, Bobby Brue, Dick Knight, Bob Gadja, Tim Simpson, and T. C. Chen. I'll take a breath and add Nolan Henke, Mike Donald, Charles Hoffner, Stewart Gardner, Wilfred Reid, Harry Hampton, Charles Lacey, Frank Ball, Tommy Shaw, Clarence Clark, and Terry Diehl.

And I haven't mentioned Sam Snead.

Sam was hardly a nobody. He was a huge somebody. But he never won a U.S. Open, as even Kurds know by now. Never won it despite the fact that he led the Open after the first round five times. In '37 at Oakland Hills, '39 at Spring Mill, '40 at Canterbury, '46 at Canterbury, and '51 at Oakland Hills. He finished second four times. By two strokes to Ralph Guldahl in '37, by one stroke in '47 to Lew Worsham at St. Louis, where he missed a thirty-inch putt on the last hole of their playoff, by one stroke in '49 to Cary Middlecoff at Medinah, where he three-putted the 71st green, and by six strokes to Ben Hogan at Oakmont in '53, where he was only one back with seven to go but Hogan put a 3-3-3 finish on the case.

Snead's four silver medals say nothing about the time he truly, seriously, honestly should have won the damn thing. This was on the Spring Mill course at the Philadelphia Country Club in '39 when he made that eight on the last hole.

Eight. Compulsory figures. Two Olympic rings.

A routine par-5 on what was actually an easy hole would have won it for him. A bogey 6 would have tied it for him. But the eight slung him down to fifth place behind Byron Nelson, Craig Wood, Denny Shute, and Marvin "Bud" Ward, the finest amateur of the era.

Sam found a creative way to make the eight. He unwisely chose a driver off the tee and hooked it into the rough. He impulsively tried to hit a brassie out of the rough—a two-wood for those too young to remember persimmon—but he pull-topped it into a bunker. He slashed into another bunker. Slashed out. Pitched on in five. And three-putted from thirty-five feet.

Delve into the literature of the game and you'll find Sam's explanation for the catastrophe. Find him saying, "I thought I needed a birdie on eighteen to win. There wasn't no scoreboards on the course in those days. Nobody in the gallery told me anything. Hell, if I'd known what I needed, I could have played the dern hole with a seven-iron and made a five."

When I first started going to the Masters I made it a point to meet Sam, spend time around him, listen to his stories in the clubhouse. I asked him about making the 8, if it caused him to lose his hair and nearly have a nervous breakdown. Things I'd read.

"Aw, I made that up," he said. "It was only my third National Open. I was a young feller in my twenties. I thought I'd win the thing five or six times before I got done. I believe I would have, too, if I'd won that one back there in Philadelphia."

I don't know how many people I put to sleep with my history lecture at the press conference. I didn't keep up with it. But some of the media looked less like they were characters in *The Day of the Living Dead* when I said the fifth hole was the key to my 67 and three-stroke lead.

For those who never left the TV sets, food, and beverages of the press lounge, I felt an obligation to let them in on the fact that the

482-yard 5th hole on Pinehurst No. 2 was undoubtedly the greatest par-4 in America that doesn't have an ocean, bay, lake, pond, river, creek, or irrigation ditch on it. Or a bulkhead, waste area, or quarry.

Just golf shots. That's all it required.

Start with a long, rumpled fairway tilting left through a corridor of pines, leaving more room for your tee ball on the right side. Best drive is a slight fade. Then you need a precise long iron to a well-bunkered green with humps and slopes and ripples all over it, and a dangerous drop-off to the left. Try not to overpure it to the back of the green. Try not to thin it or fat it short and hang it up on the front of the green. Dead in both places.

After opening up with four straight pars, I was fortunate to make good swings on the drive and the approach at the 5th. My three-iron bounced neatly into the green and caught the right curve on a hump and left me with an eighteen-foot birdie putt. When that putt hit nothing but net, the three there felt like a double eagle. Made a man say, "Oh, shit, oh, dear."

I described my other two birdies for the press. The seven-foot birdie putt at the 15th, a 200-yard par-3, where I almost holed out a four-iron. And my no-brain forty-foot birdie putt at the 490-yard par-4 16th, which is longer than the 5th hole but flatter, wider, and more forgiving. The putt wandered over hill and dale and hung on the left side of the cup, then dropped.

Which sent Mitch prancing around the green, doing a baton thing with the flagstick in his hand. I thought he looked like he was leading the Grambling band, and said as much to him.

"Ohio State," he said. "Doin' the Buckeye Battle Cry."

I remembered he was from Columbus originally.

I took the opportunity in the press center to publicly congratulate Knut Thorssun and Claude Steekley, my playing partners, on their rounds. They'd each fought their way to a respectable 74.

It's easy to shoot a low score when everything goes your way, I said to the press. The toughest thing to do in golf is turn it around, hold it together, when you're off to a bad start.

Claude had been four over after his quadruple bogey on the 2nd hole when he'd worn out the boundary stakes. Knut had bogeyed the first three holes after the embarrassing incident with Vashtine before we even started.

Knut expected to find Vashtine waiting for him when we completed the round, but she wasn't anywhere near the 18th green. He asked Dace Fackle, the USGA's executive director, where she was.

That took a moment. The executive director was in the midst of explaining to three angry golf writers why they could no longer have clubhouse parking passes, and why he didn't think this should make him a prime candidate to have the shit beat out of him—he was trying to please as many people as he could at the same time.

The writers walked away after telling the executive director not to leave his wife and children unguarded.

Dace Fackle then turned to Knut. "Vashtine was taking a nap in the clubhouse, the last I heard. I'm told she said it was no problem for her to mix rum, gin, Crown, beer, and red wine, but apparently it was."

The first thing I was asked after I went to the interview room in the press center was about the "Vashtine problem" on the first tee.

"It was a misunderstanding," I said. "There are autograph hounds everywhere she goes. Sometimes they get out of control. Today it just happened to be on a golf course."

OK, I lied. It was for the good of the game.

They wanted to know if I knew Vashtine personally.

"Not well enough," I said and smiled.

Some laughed.

They wanted to know if I liked her music.

"I didn't know rap was music," I said.

Some laughed again.

I said the only funny thing that happened today was on the 2nd hole, and told them about the woman in the car stopping and asking about a hotel room, and related Pookie Steekley's response to her.

What I didn't share with the press was the shock I received after I walked off the 18th green, courtesy of Pookie, she of the sexy overbite.

While Claude was examining his scorecard, Pookie rushed over and gave me a tight hug and a tongue-exploring kiss, and left me with a look that said, "Next time you're in Austin, Bobby Joe, call me up—we'll slip away and slide your Jimmy Dean sausage roll into the warm, juicy oven of my Krispy Kreme donut ring."

Well, that's how I interpreted it, anyhow.

---

The press heard that I went with the Show Dog off every driving hole and still kept it in play. I missed only three greens but was lucky to pull off good chip shots when I did.

I made a stab at humor, saying, "It's fun to play that way. I find golf less stressful when you hit fairways and greens."

I envisioned a humorous headline—"Golfer Says Low Rounds Less Stressful"—and figured my interview would make their day.

But that was before the space-alien teen bitch came in with a 70 that put her in second place.

# 30

The current lady in my life had been in my gallery since the 5th hole—I'd heard Gwen's whoops and caught her glimpses—but I pretended I didn't. I played Ben to her Valerie.

Legend has it that at times Hogan concentrated so deeply in a major, he frequently didn't recognize his own wife. It was as if he'd stare at Valerie when she'd offer him a sip of iced tea out of the thermos she always carried, and he'd say, "Have we met?"

The first time Gwen and I spoke was after the round, a moment after Pookie Steekley retrieved her tongue from my mouth and moved on.

Gwen walked up and faced me with her arms folded and a look.

"Saddle oxfords?" she said.

Some people might have called that an accusation. Others might have called it wise-ass.

I said, "Saddle oxfords have always turned me on. Some guys like a woman in a sailor hat and a garter belt. What are you doing here? Shouldn't you be on a computer or a cell phone or at a board meeting?"

"Who was that woman?"

"The woman congratulating me?"

"No, the one hanging from the tree."

"That was Claude Steekley's wife."

"They must be quite happily married."

"I don't really know her well."

"I could tell."

"Where's your husband today, Gwenny?"

"If you mean Rick, my *ex-husband*, he's back in New York by now. He was here overnight. He ate dinner with our son and breakfast with me this morning."

"What will your title be at International Sports Talent?"

"Are we going to fight this out right here?"

"No. I have to do something. I need to go to the merchandise tent and buy caps and stuff for the pals back home. I want to get it out of the way before I forget about it."

"I'll go with you. Maybe they have saddle oxfords."

The merchandise tent was a huge temporary plastic bubble, but it might not have covered all of Luxembourg.

You entered at one end and checked out at the other. It was a department store of golf. Shirts were here, other shirts were there. Sweaters in that corner, windbreakers beyond. Caps hard right, visors hard left. Mugs and plates in between. Bag tags, watches, money clips, divot tools, towels, and headcovers were here, there, everywhere. Everything with a logo. A person could even purchase a golf ball or a golf club.

The combination book store and art gallery located over in a corner was where we stumbled on Irv Klar. He sat at a table behind a stack of his books and in front of a wall of bad paintings of golf holes. He was signing his name in copies of his new book—for nobody in sight.

"Put your name in it, good as a sale," he said as we stood looking down at him. "Long line an hour ago."

The title of his new bestseller was *Three and a Half!*

At the bottom of the jacket in smaller print you could read what it was about: "The Story of Howie Berger, America's Greatest Jewish Golfer."

I explained to Gwen that Howie Berger was a pro back in the thirties and forties. A guy who won the Canadian Open and not much else. But he was a mainstay on the Tour, a friend of the big names, and was said to have a sense of humor.

Old story. When Howie would hit a wild shot, a ball that might fly into the gallery, he was known to holler, "Three and a half!"

Get it? Three and a half instead of fore? A nice saving? Him being Jewish? And having this keen sense of humor?

"Hence, the book title," Gwen said.

"Funny, huh?" Irv spoke up, still writing his name in the books. "That popped right out at me in the research. I knew it was the title."

Leafing through the book, Gwen said to Irv, "Is there much about anti-Semitism in here?"

"What for?" said Irv.

" '*What for*'?" Gwen said.

Irv said, "Oh, you mean the Jewish thing? No. I didn't come across much in the research. Howie's dead or I could have asked him."

I seized the moment to introduce Gwen to Irv.

I said, "Irving Klar, *Washington Post* columnist and famous author, say hello to Gwendolyn Pritchard. Gwen is Scott Pritchard's mother."

"Hi, hi," Irv said hurriedly, signing a book.

A good-looking chick meant nothing to Irv Klar—unless she was a book reviewer or hosted her own radio or TV show somewhere in America.

Gwen said to him, "I was assuming your book deals with prejudice. I remember hearing from the golf teachers who worked with my son that the club pro in the old days—Jewish or not—wasn't allowed to dine in the clubhouse. The members would insist he take his meals in the kitchen. That was apparently true at country clubs everywhere."

"Really?" Irv said, glancing up for a second. "I can use that in the paperback edition. I know a good spot."

"That'll help me sleep better tonight," I said.

Irv looked up. "What'd you shoot today, Bobby Joe?"

"I carved out a little sixty-seven, is all."

"Hey, did you hear me on *Imus* this morning? Three book mentions. Maybe you weren't up that early."

"I don't believe I was, Irv."

"I got four minutes."

We left him writing his name in his books.

A truce was declared and Gwen and I even vowed not to touch each other until after I won or lost the U.S. Open. To make sure the truce got off to a good start we invited other people to join us for dinner that Thursday evening.

I invited Grady Don and Jerry. She invited her son. We were a table for five in the Carolina Hotel dining room. The conversation was almost exclusively about golf. Grady Don ordered an expensive bottle of red wine and proposed a toast to me and my 67.

Looking around the table, he said, "Here's to the man who went out there today and bit off Pinehurst's head and sucked out its lungs."

Gwen lifted her glass and said, "I couldn't have put it better myself—although I would have tried."

The same group assembled for dinner Friday night, minus one.

Scott Pritchard shot a hard-luck 79. "Geeeaaahh" was his personal critique of the round. When Scott added it to his opening 72, he missed the cut by three strokes. Which put him in a carefree mood to wander over to the lively Pine Crest bar instead of dining with boring grownups.

"I'm gonna go hang," he announced to his mother at our table. "Catch some pour, scope out a bim."

Gwen said, "Be choosey, please. Don't connect with a bim you might bring something home from."

There were more things to celebrate Friday night.

One was my even-par 70. It gave me a thirty-six-hole total of 137 and kept me in the lead by two. The score was good even if the way I went about it wasn't. I saved par six times. I got up and down from Charlotte, Winston-Salem, Asheville, and once from Richmond, Virginia.

Mitch had said, "You a lucky thief today. We ought rob us a bank when we done here. Won't nobody catch us."

I thought my best quote in the press center was "I hit a lot of greens today—my ball just didn't stay on very many of them."

It was the wind coming up and the firmer greens that made the day tough for everybody. There were only two sub-par rounds, J. J. Henry's 68 and Fred Couples's 69. They played early when it was calmer, and were back in the pack, barely made the cut.

Knut Thorssun and Claude Steekley both shot 72s and made the cut with a little room to spare. I credited their solid play to the fact that their ladies weren't around.

Vashtine stayed in the hotel to work on a new rap "song," Knut said, using the word loosely. She'd been inspired to create by her experience yesterday with rum, gin, Crown Royal, Budweiser, and a nice Merlot.

Knut said, "It is to have words to recommend bloody murders on golf officials and uniform police. Also to make green and yellow vomit and dainty piles of shit on the wives of golf officials. This is the song I am hearing as I left the hotel room, to be sure."

I said, "It'll run a year, Mr. Kern."

"I am to do what?"

"Nothing. Talking to myself."

Claude didn't say what Pookie was up to, but I guessed she'd found a devout young gentleman to study passages in the Bible with her at a motel in Southern Pines.

Grady Don and Jerry were among the cut survivors. They were particularly happy about it because three of the big favorites, Woods, Els, and Mickelson, all missed the cut. They shot 78, 79, and 81 in that order.

It was a cruel blow to the championship, losing three marquee names such as those, but it gave the press a chance to refer to the second round as "gloomy Friday." In the days before political correctness, of course, the press would have referred to it as "black Friday."

Jerry Grimes said at dinner, "Bobby Joe, it don't hurt your chances to know Elvis and them have gone to Downtown Cut City."

I said, "There's still plenty of heat on the board. Cheetah Farmer's right there. So's Stump Bowen . . . Rainey Walters . . . Julius . . . Knut."

Grady Don amused himself by saying, "I like your pairing tomorrow, is what I like."

I was paired with the space-alien teen bitch.

# 31

The day of the third round started for me with the thrill of breakfast and the agony of a business proposal. Looking back on it, I'd say there was an omen in there somewhere.

Smokey Barwood, live-wire agent, arrived in Pinehurst during the night by plane from New York and by limo from Charlotte. Grady Don and I met him for breakfast in the Carolina dining room.

Smokey was wearing a black suit and a dull tie in a white pin-collar shirt. He looked more like a man at a funeral than a golf tournament.

As he shook my hand, he said, "I came here to be with you."

"In his hour of need," Grady Don said.

We talked about the Open for a while before Smokey brought up the business proposal. He removed a folder from his briefcase.

"What have either one of you heard about cerelixopone?" he said.

"Spell it," I said.

He did. No help.

"What is it?" Grady Don asked.

Smokey confidently said, "Only the greatest leap forward in club performance since titanium. It's the result of a secret process that mixes a ceramic material with nylix and suropone. Metal will never be the same again. Take my word for it. The cerelixopone driver is a killer. Tests prove it gives the average player twenty percent more distance, thirty percent more accuracy. Launch Golf is the company that developed and owns the process. Headquarters in Carmel, California. The owner is a delightful gentleman named Gavin Saunders. I've met Gav. Hell of a guy. We have a chance to get in on the ground floor as stockholders with you two as the spokespeople for the product on TV, in print ads, billboards, everywhere—and the company has a great marketing idea for the launch."

"Gav?" Grady Don said.

"Right," Smokey said.

"He likes to be called Gav?" Grady Don said.

"Yes," Smokey said. "Their surveys show that the greatest growth in golf over the past four years is among homosexuals. Therefore, they plan to hit this group hard, right from the get-go. They're going to market three cerelixopone models at once—the Big Gavin, the Bigger Gavin, and the Biggest Gavin."

Grady Don and I were laughing before Smokey finished.

Looking serious, Grady Don said, "Hi, I'm Grady Don Maples. I'm here to talk to you about the Big Gavin. That's Gav's new driver, not his cock. Bobby Joe will talk to you in a minute about his cock, which is bigger than a rechargeable flashlight and available at any Ace Hardware."

Smokey observed Grady Don with deep sadness. "I take it you're not interested in pursuing this opportunity?"

"Damn, you're shrewd, Smokey," Grady Don said.

The agent turned to me.

"I'm with him," I said.

"You don't even want to hear the financial details?" the agent said.

I said, "Let me put it this way, Smokey. If I was sprawled out in a gutter with my head on a curb and a bottle of vanilla extract in my hand, I might listen."

Smokey closed the folder, put it away, and ran a couple of other opportunities past us.

Grady Don could do an outing and clinic for a group of plumbing executives who were going to a retreat in Mexico.

"Can't handle it," Grady Don said. "I don't speak Spanish."

"It doesn't matter," Smokey said.

"Sure it does," said Grady Don. "I wouldn't know how to say, 'No, I don't want to fuck your sister.' "

The deal Smokey proposed to me was a $5,000 appearance fee if I'd go to Germany and play in the Stuttgart Open. The son of Field Marshal Erwin Rommel was the tournament chairman.

"That's a lure?" I said, laughing again. "Where's von Rundstedt? Maximilian Schell? Hardy Kruger? If you have Nazis, you gotta use 'em."

"I'll take that as a no," the agent said.

Stuttgart and the Big Gav kept me smiling on the practice range and putting green while I prepared for the third round.

Gwen gave me a thumbs-up sign and a good-luck grin as I walked past her on the way to my two-thirty tee time, where a gallery of four hundred million people was waiting for the last group of the day.

All those fans who would no longer have Elvis, Madonna, or Britney to follow. I wondered how disappointed the crowd would be with my pairing, those who weren't out there strictly for a swing tip. Half of them would be thinking, "I paid good money for this ticket, but now I don't get to see Tiger, Phil, or Ernie? Maybe the little babe will be interesting to watch, but who's this geek?"

My fifteen-year-old playing partner came over and introduced herself on the first tee, saying, "Hi, Mr. Grooves, I'm Tricia Hurt."

I shook her hand.

"Tricia, my treasure," I said. "Make it Bobby Joe."

"OK, sure," she said. "Bobby Joe."

She was as tall as I was, but had better legs. Sweet face, I thought. A tap-in from beautiful.

"Play good today," I said.

"You, too," she said, and walked back to the other side of the tee.

I noticed her daddy, the Dabster, had worked his way up to the ropes by her caddie and was giving the caddie a last-minute lecture. The expression on the Dabster's face was stern, threatening.

The caddie chewed his gum and looked straight ahead as he listened to his orders from the man who was apparently telling him that if his daughter didn't play well today, he would rip the caddie's heart out of his chest with his bare hands and jump up and down on it in his Guccis.

I stood with Mitch on the tee while we waited for the group in front of us—Cheetah Farmer and Stump Bowen—to make their way to the green.

Mitch said, "We got enough candy in our pocket, you reckon?"

I smiled. "I have Caramel Nips, what have you got?"

"Lifesavers."

"That's it? You forgot the Butterfingers?"

"I have hundreds. They like those, don't they? Don't hundred-dollar bills make young girls horny?"

"They used to. I believe it takes a Jaguar now."

The first hole at Pinehurst No. 2 is a straight-away par-4 of 404 yards, relatively easy. I didn't care for the idea of a teenage girl outhitting me off No. 1 in front of a sizable crowd, which was why I went with the Show Dog.

I made a smooth pass at it. Felt like I stung it pretty good. My tee ball split the fairway down the middle about 295 yards. Walking back over to Mitch, I was thinking, "Chase that one, muffin . . . puddin . . . princess."

But I stopped thinking it the minute she took that big, graceful swing and launched her own tee shot.

I knew she'd FedEx'd me.

# 32

The muffin, puddin, punkin princess lost her genius at the 8th hole. It must be a terrible thing to lose your genius.

The 8th is a rigorous par-4, 485 yards, curving to the right, but it's not as tough as Tricia made it. Her problem began when her approach slid off the green and wound up in a swale, leaving her with a long chip up a severe slope.

She chose to chip with her three-wood. It's a shot Tiger introduced to the world in the nineties, and I might add, a shot only Tiger had been able to make work with any consistency. The times I tried it, I thought I was playing croquet.

Tricia's first chip rolled halfway up the severe but smooth slope and came back down to her feet. She looked up and said something to the heavens. She chipped her next one a little harder. But not hard enough. It came back down the slope to her feet again.

Furious with herself, she took two steps forward and met the ball as it was rolling back toward her and almost rapped it again before it stopped rolling. Her third try made it onto the green, and she two-putted from forty feet for a triple-bogey 7.

She had started the round trailing me by two strokes. We had both parred the first seven holes, so when I managed a par to her triple on number 8, she was quickly five back—and steaming.

As we walked to the next tee, I tried to console her. "You're only three over for the championship," I said. "There's still a long way to go. Now's the time to call on your patience."

She didn't say anything. Head down. Trying not to make eye contact with her dad.

I said, "Incidentally, you *do* know if you'd hit that second chip back there before it came to rest, it would have been two more. That's a two-stroke penalty."

"I don't need you to tell me the rules," she said.

I was startled by her response.

"I know the rules," she said.

I said, "I'm sure you do. You've been in a lot of competition for someone your age."

"I know the rules as well as you do."

"That may well be true."

"It *is* true."

"Hey, I surrender."

"I scored one hundred on the rules quiz at the golf academy."

"I'm impressed. Everyone there must have been."

"They *were*," she said. "Nobody had ever scored a perfect hundred before I did."

"What do you say we drop it and play golf, huh?"

Our conversation ended with her muttering something under her breath.

I'm sure it couldn't have been "Fuck you," even though it sounded faintly like it. They wouldn't have taught her that at the golf academy, would they?

Suddenly, Tricia wasn't as beautiful and gracious as she'd been back on the first tee. Before my very eyes, she'd turned into what may have been her true self—the space-alien teen bitch.

I found myself dwelling on teenagers again for a moment. Grady Don and I often talked about how we'd been raised to say yes ma'am and no sir and dress properly and sit still and keep your mouth shut in restaurants and respect authority and compete hard but fair at sports. But today's teenagers, guys in particular, liked tattoos, body-piercing, noise for music, bloomers for clothes, didn't respect anything but money, and their idea of humor was a stupid remark they'd heard somebody say on a sitcom. Grady Don was fond of saying he'd like to take every affluent white kid who wore his baseball cap backwards and make him live in a poor black ghetto for six months, then let him out and ask him how he'd like to wear his cap now?

Tricia and I didn't speak for the next two hours. We were busy grinding, struggling to make pars, which we did.

Up ahead, I tried not to let something else annoy me.

It was Cheetah Farmer holing every putt he stood over. The scoreboards told me he was four under on the round. That moved him to within a stroke of me.

He was working on a 66, low round of the tournament, and when I stood on the 18th tee and listened to the roar coming from the green, I could tell he got to the house with it.

Chandler "Cheetah" Farmer had no friends on the Tour, and didn't care. He liked being a jerk. He seemed to take pride in it. He came out five years ago with a gunnysack of arrogance, having been a big winner in amateur golf, and unfortunately for the rest of us he proved himself as a pro right away. He became a consistent money winner, a tournament winner—Greensboros and things—and he pulled in two majors, the British Open at St. Andrews and the PGA at Southern Hills. Having become a marquee name, he took to firing people. First person he fired was his dad, the bull-neck crewcut dullard who caddied for him. He accused his dad of stealing his money. He replaced him with a guy who'd been caddying for Wu Sing Fu on the LPGA tour. Cheetah had fired all of his gurus twice—Butch Harmon, Rick Smith, Dugan Cockrell. But he was now back with Butch. He'd fired three agents and lately was representing himself. He'd even fired three girlfriends—Kitty, Jackie, and Angela—all of whom were known for the hot pants they wore and the tattoos on their thighs and shoulders.

Cheetah didn't occupy my thoughts long. Soon enough came the incident that was either a tragedy or a comedy, depending on whether you were a fan of mine or a Nazi Commie Islamic rodent.

# 33

A tragicomedy is what Miz Dinker would have called it. But my old continental lit professor would have been talking about Europeans who wrote books thicker than their beards. Not golf.

It started when I couldn't decide what to hit on 18, the Show Dog or a steer job. The last hole at Pinehurst No. 2 is a dogleg-right par-4, 450 yards, slightly uphill, trees on the right, practice range on the left.

If you don't hammer a big drive out there, you're left with a long difficult second shot to a well-bunkered green where a lucky bounce counts for as much as skill.

But you need a tee ball in the fairway at all cost or you can wind up in worse trouble. Like deep in the rough. Dead. Deader than a stock tip from a rich guy.

Confused is the worst thing any athlete can be in competition. I'd only known that since high school, but I momentarily forgot it.

Which was why I made an indecisive swing with the driver—let out or let up?—and hit the looping, out-of-nowhere, Baker-Finch hook that looked for all the world like it would sail over the pines and into the practice range, out of bounds.

"It could be OK," Mitch said.

"Or not," I said disgustedly.

I looked over at Tricia and said, "I'm gonna reload, just in case."

Meaning I was going to hit a second ball to play in the event that my first drive was, in fact, out of bounds.

I steer-jobbed a three-wood this time, making sure I threaded it into the fairway. Damage control.

Stroke and distance is the penalty for out of bounds. Thus, if I was forced to play the second ball, I'd be laying three, shooting four—and still 200 yards from the green. I'd be looking at a double bogey or worse.

As you might imagine, I was overjoyed to find my ball inside the boundary stakes. It was in bounds by a few heartwarming feet. Not only that, I had a clear shot to the green.

My stupid hook had hit a tree or something that kept it in bounds. Whatever the case, it was a pure Lucille.

Standing there, I took a silent moment to thank the Skipper for looking after me. Told the Big Guy if he'd come down here and play a round with me sometime he could have a mulligan on every hole, he could use titanium, I'd use hickory, he could hit a Pro V1, I'd hit a gutty, he could have Ben Hogan for a partner, I'd take Glenn Ford or Anne Baxter. All that was the least I could do to return the favor.

Tricia Hurt's voice interrupted my thoughts.

"I'm calling a ruling on you, Bobby Joe."

"Excuse me—?"

Had I heard the child correctly?

She said, "I'm afraid I'm going to insist you play the second ball. You lie three, playing four."

"What are you talking about?"

"I'm talking about a violation of the rules."

"I violated a rule?"

"Yes."

"What rule did I violate?"

"It comes under rule twenty-seven. You committed a verbal."

"I did what?"

"Back on the tee, before you hit your second tee shot, you did not announce to me that you were playing a provisional ball."

"Yeah, I did."

"No, you did not."

"I damn sure did."

"Do you remember what you said?"

"Sure. I said, uh—I said what I always say—I said what we say on the Tour—I said, 'I'm gonna reload, just in case.' My exact words."

"Precisely."

"Precisely *what*?"

"You did not use the word 'provisional.' A player must say, 'I am going to play a provisional ball.' It's in the rulebook. You admit you did not specifically use the word 'provisional.' That is a clear violation. I invoke the penalty. You must play the second ball."

"Like shit I will," I said. "I want a rules official."

"You have one."

Another voice falling out of the sky.

I wheeled around to find a middle-aged woman in a navy blue blazer, white blouse, khaki pants, and a USGA armband. She might have been attractive if she hadn't been with the USGA.

In as pleasant a voice as she could muster, she said, "I'm Brenda Claire Hopkins. I'm a vice-president of the United States Golf Association, and the rules official on this hole. Tricia is correct about the rule. You must play the second ball."

I said, "Do you know what's riding on this? I believe I'll find me a higher opinion than . . . Brenda Claire . . . whatever your name is . . . whoever you are."

"You are entitled to another opinion," Brenda Claire Hopkins said calmly. She spoke into her walkie-talkie.

"Bunny, are you there? Come in, Bunny. Need you on eighteen."

"*Who*?" I said.

"Bunny Pemberton is the rover on this nine."

"Man or woman?"

"You've never heard of *Bunny Pemberton*?" she said. "My goodness, he won the Senior Amateur two years ago at Ridgewood!"

I said, "Ah, *that* Bunny Pemberton. Of course. Gosh, I've followed his career for years."

Brenda Claire Hopkins turned away and made a social call on her cell as she strolled among the pines.

I stood around. Wished I smoked. Stood some more. Tricia Hurt, meanwhile, walked up to her own ball in the fairway.

Bunny Pemberton arrived in a golf cart and didn't take long to make up his mind after he listened to Brenda Claire Hopkins explain the situation. He upheld her decision.

"You people are dead wrong," I said. "I want to appeal to the chairman of the competition committee. Call him up, please."

Bunny Pemberton said, "He may be out of touch at the moment. He was in a hospitality tent a moment ago. I'm sure he won't overrule us—he's more of a stickler for the rules than anyone I know."

"Who's the chairman?"

"Jarvis Phillip W. Burchcroft."

"Jesus Christ."

"Do you know him? He's known as Mr. Rules."

" '*Mr. Rules*'?" I said, looking like I smelled sour milk. "I know the lightweight, chinless fuck-face. He gave me a horseshit ruling at the Masters."

"Mr. Grooves! Your language!"

"Get him down here."

Bunny Pemberton summoned the chairman on his walkie-talkie. They had a long discussion. Then Brenda Claire Hopkins had a discussion with him on her walkie-talkie.

Five minutes later Jarvis Phillip W. Burchcroft showed up in a cart.

He said, "Mr. Grooves, you and your rules problems are becoming a habit, if you don't mind my saying so."

I thought he may have hiccupped.

He said, "My ruling is the same one I gave Bunny and Brenda when they interrupted me as I was putting a delicious dab of Beluga on a wedge of toast in the Bank of America tent."

Bunny said, "I hope you tried the quail eggs in the mushroom cap."

"The foie gras was exquisite, too," Brenda said.

"It most assuredly was," the rules chairman said. "But I must say the caviar went very well with the Cristal Bellini and fresh peach."

I said, "Does anybody mind if I find out what my ruling is?"

"Indeed not," Jarvis Phillip W. Burchcroft said. "You of course must play the second ball. It's covered under twenty-seven–two."

He produced a little spiral notebook and pen from his blazer pocket, wrote "27-2a/1" on a piece of paper and handed it to me.

He said, "It's a rule that's usually excused or ignored by competitors, but when it's invoked, I am obligated to investigate and enforce it if necessary, as in this case. You'll find it under the decisions section in the rules of golf. Twenty-seven dash two . . . small letter 'a' . . . slash . . . numeral one. Are we clear? Everyone?"

With that, Jarvis Phillip W. Burchcroft hopped back into the golf cart and sped away.

I glanced at Mitch. "We just lost the Open."

"It ain't over," he said.

"Yeah, it is," I said.

Bunny Pemberton said, "Mr. Grooves, I strenuously suggest you move ahead and finish the hole. I'm putting you on the clock."

"I'm on the clock? You're putting me on the clock? We're the last group on the golf course! Who the fuck are we holding up?"

"Your language, sir! Honestly!"

"Aw, crawl up my ass and die, Bunny!"

I lobbed several more f-bombs into the atmosphere before I reached my ball. Having done that, I proceeded to make sure I lost the Open. I made a lovely 10 on the hole.

# 34

Gwen was saying she'd never heard of John L. Black or Roland Hancock, much less Mike Brady, and she wasn't sure she'd heard of Miller Barber and Frank Beard, but those names sounded vaguely familiar—maybe she'd seen them in print somewhere—and what did it matter anyhow?

I said, "Those names matter in history. My name will be right there with the other losers. You look through the record books, you come across guys who blew the Open. Years from now, people will see my name, see my seventy-six in the third round. They'll say, 'That's where he lost it, right there.' They'll wonder what kind of truck hit me—if it was a new pair of shoes I threw up on."

We were at a table in a back corner of the Pine Crest dining room, the place empty except for three weary British journalists and their third bottle of wine. It was Sunday night, the Open was over, most people had cleared out of the village, gone.

I was on my third martini rocks and my ninth olive. Gwen was nursing a vodka soda, poking around at the fried-shrimp appetizer.

I'd finished second to Cheetah Farmer. I made an admirable comeback in the last round with a 70, which gave me a 283 total, but it was two shy of what I needed. I'd blown it in Saturday's third round. With a considerable amount of help from the space-alien teen bitch and the USGA's rules clowns.

As Gwen dipped a shrimp in the red sauce, she wondered why the $700,000 second-place money and the silver medal for runner-up hadn't eased the pain. Not everybody could say they were a runner-up in a major, she said.

If it was all the same to her, I said, I'd rather have the trophy with the names of Jones and Hogan and Nicklaus all over it—and they could keep the prize money.

I said, "People look in the record book, they see my scores . . . sixty-seven in the first round, great . . . seventy the second day, good . . . I close with seventy, fine . . . but what's this shit in the middle? This seventy-six here? There's still blood and pus running out of that thing."

"Could you be more graphic?" Gwen said.

"Just call me John L. Black."

"If you wish."

"John L. Black, white man, forty-three . . . Came to the last two holes of the '22 Open at Skokie needing four-four to beat Sarazen, four-five to tie. Easy holes, but what does John L. Black do? He snap-hooks his tee shot out of bounds on seventeen, makes a double, loses by one—never heard from again."

"Hardly the same as you."

"Just call me Roland Hancock."

"Hi, Roland."

"Roland Hancock, white man, twenty-two . . . Comes to the last two holes of the '28 Open at Olympia Fields, needs five-five to win. Bogey-par, is all. Jones and Farrell are tied, sitting in the clubhouse. The crowd starts patting Roland on the back, yelling, 'Stand back, make way for the new champion.' So what does Roland do? He goes choke-dog sideways, finishes six-six, loses by one, never heard from again."

"Misery loves company. Is that the subject tonight?"

"Miller Barber and Frank Beard," I said.

"Yes," said Gwen. "I was afraid you'd forgotten them."

"Good players, proven winners. You'd think they'd be locks. Shows you what a major can do to a man. Miller Barber leads by three through fifty-four holes at Champions in '69, but he shoots seventy-eight in the last round. If he shoots seventy-four, just a sloppy, ordinary, everyday, four-over seventy-four, you'd have never heard of Orville Moody."

"I still haven't."

"Frank Beard at Medinah in '75. He's leading by three after fifty-four but he shoots a pitiful seventy-eight in the last round, and yet he only misses the playoff by one. Turns out if he'd shot himself a poor old seventy-six—it's not asking too much, a poor old seventy-six—he'd have won easy."

"Fate don't have a head, is all I can say about it. Want a shrimp?"

"Mike Brady. There's one for you."

"Who's he? Does he want a shrimp?"

"Mike Brady made losing the Open his hobby. He was the early-day Sam Snead. He lost two playoffs, in 1911, to Johnny McDermott . . . in 1919 to Walter Hagen. He always finished in the top ten. In 1915 at Baltusrol he shot an eighty in the last round when a seventy-five would have beaten Jerry Travers. He shot an eighty in the last round to let Hagen make up five shots on him at Brae Burn, then he lost the playoff by a shot. Mike Brady butchered more last rounds in the Open than anybody ever."

"Why don't you look at it differently?"

"Like how? Play like I won?"

"Put yourself in another category. There must be a lot of great golfers who were second in the Open, but never won it. You're one of those."

"Let's see. That puts me in there with Sam Snead . . . Jimmy Demaret, Harry Cooper . . . Denny Shute, Macdonald Smith, Dick Metz . . . Vic Ghezzi."

"Good. Think of it that way."

"I will. They're all dead."

"That's not what I meant."

"You know what?" I said. "I'm ass-deep in condolences."

Cheetah Farmer was first, at the trophy ceremony in front of the clubhouse. He congratulated me for "bringing out his talent." He said my comeback from yesterday's "bad break" had forced him to play his best.

My bad break. Like a bank got a bad break one time when John Dillinger robbed it.

I performed OK at the ceremony. I was a gracious loser, a smiling runner-up—when all I wanted to say to Cheetah Farmer was, "I know it was you, Fredo. You broke my heart."

Numerous fellow competitors in the locker room offered me warm handshakes and looks of heartfelt concern.

There were the sympathetic phone messages taken by the locker-room attendant and passed on to me.

George and Louise Grooves had called to say I was still their son, and my clothes fit better than Cheetah Farmer's did—anybody watching TV would know that.

Buddy Stark and Cynthia called to say they were in the top-floor suite at the Victoria-Jungfrau Grand Hotel in Interlaken, Switzerland, but would soon be going to the Hotel du Cap–Eden Roc in Antibes, and wanted to know if people still took golf seriously?

Witty pals, Buddy and Cynthia.

Grady Don Maples and Jerry Grimes left notes in my locker before they bailed for Westchester, the next stop on the Tour.

Grady Don's note said, "Hell of an Open, son. You came as close as a man could, considering there's no God."

Jerry's note said, "Great try, B.J. You had everybody in the locker room rooting for you."

Smokey Barwood, the live-wire agent, left a note. "Tough loss," it said, "but I have an idea that could turn this into a positive."

Knut Thorssun even left a note. It said, "Vashtine and I are to feel great sorrow in your behalf. It is a plight that should not happen to nobody. She says your plight is definite to inspire her talents and she must write a song about a person who is cheated in life by butt wipers."

Alleene Simmons, my first ex-wife, business partner, and still my pal, sent me a message that actually made me smile. The locker-room attendant wrote it down word for word because he didn't understand it.

Her message was: "So your fifth-grade teacher gave you a D. Let it go, dude."

# 35

A little later, after my steak had barely been touched and my fourth or fifth martini had rudely shoved the cup of coffee aside, Gwen lit a cigarette, and said, "Not to be insensitive, but there's another way to look at it, Bobby Joe. You didn't have to make a ten."

Piss me off was what that remark did. So in a tone of pissed-off-ness, I said, "Boy, you've got that right. I should have given it more thought. I should have realized I could win the Open by three if I could make a five on eighteen Saturday . . . Or I could win by two if I could just make a double-bogey six . . . Hell, I still could have won if I'd only made a seven. I can't imagine why none of that occurred to me."

"Is that what I meant?"

"I know what you meant. I didn't have to let the ruling bother me that much. Well, I wish I hadn't. I wish I hadn't red-assed my fourth shot into the rough . . . red-assed my fifth shot into the bunker . . . red-assed my bunker shot so bad it stayed in the bunker . . . red-assed the next one on the green but left it in a place that Jesus Christ himself with Ben Crenshaw's stroke would have three-jacked the fucker."

"It was a learning experience. I gather that's what your buddy Alleene was trying to tell you in her message. I'm looking forward to meeting your favorite ex someday."

"Yeah, another life lesson for me," I sighed. "Another character builder. I'll tell you what. I'm about ready for the Skipper to start building character on somebody else's ass."

"I'm sure you are."

"How'd the space alien finish? I haven't bothered to look."

"Her inexperience must have caught up with her. She shot a seventy-seven. She tied for ninth."

"Gee, what a shame . . . but I have to admit it's not too bad for a teenage girl in a guys' major. She's some kind of talent, the little bitch."

"She says she's sorry about what happened to you Saturday. She feels badly about it now."

"Who'd she say that to?"

"She said it at her press conference yesterday. It's in the paper today."

"I didn't read the paper this morning. It's bad luck to read the paper before the last round if you're a contender. I guess I'll rethink that shit."

Gwen said, "Tricia told the press she was just trying to play with your head when she used the rules violation on you. She didn't think it would be upheld. She said she was surprised when it was."

"She was 'playing with my head'? She said that?"

"That was the quote. She was five back at the time and trying to gain ground in whatever way she could. She was trying to upset you mentally. She hoped you'd lose your concentration and bogey the hole. She said they teach it at the academy in Florida. She said high school and college coaches teach it. You do whatever you can to unsettle your opponent. Rattle the clubs in your bag when the opponent is addressing a shot. Raise your umbrella up and down when your opponent is getting ready to hit. Play slow if they play fast. Play fast if they play slow. All kinds of things. Gamesmanship."

"She said they teach that at the golf academy? To teenagers? To *girls*? Jesus. You might do shit like that when you're a kid, when you're learning how to gamble, but no golf coach I ever knew taught it, and if you tried anything like that on *our* Tour, you'd have two chances to get away with it—slim and fucking none."

"I'm only telling you what was in the paper. It seems to me the real culprits in your case were the officials."

"Taking up for your new client, are you?"

"That's not called for."

"Why not? She's going to be your client. Yours and Rick's. He told me that. Your ex in the funny hair. He said he has a verbal agreement with Tricia's father."

"I am *not* a part of IST. Not yet. Maybe never. It's something we're going to discuss, right?"

"Not now."

"I should say not."

"What's that tone supposed to mean? I'm not allowed to be pissed because I lost the Open?"

"Bobby Joe—"

"You know what's occurred to me, Gwen?"

"I'd be delighted to know what's occurred to you."

"You and I have been together—what?—three months? I've been practically the same thing as in love with you for three whole months . . . and it's been great. It's something I never thought would happen to me . . . not after I married three women who hated golf—until we were divorced. But I get lucky. One day I meet you and we connect, and it turns out you not only love golf, you care about *me*, even though I'm zero-for-heart-stopper. I mean, I don't edge out too many guys in the romance department. And you're so gorgeous, I feel like I may go blind every time you walk out of the room. But while I'm wallowing around in this love, something else happens. I lose two majors. Two I deserve to win. I'm out here almost twenty years and I finally get two real shots at a major—hell, I'll settle for *one*—but I get screwed out of the Masters when I'm playing really good, and then I come here and I get screwed out of the Open when I'm playing really good. So guess what, babe? You may be the all-time dynamite lady, but I have to tell you. Since I'm a golfer, I'm about to believe you're a fucking voodoo curse."

She may have set a new PGA Tour speed record for a lady slamming a napkin down and leaving a dinner table.

# PART THREE

# SHOOT THE HAGGIS

# 36

The main thing I had to do in the two weeks between the U.S. Open and the British Open was fetch my love life out of the sewer.

As any sober person might have guessed, Gwen bolted out of Pinehurst early the next morning, hot as a pot of collards that my martinis had accused her of bringing me bad luck in the majors. I didn't realize I'd made her that angry until I discovered she hadn't even left a note.

I took a flight home later that Monday, cured my hangover, and started trying to find Gwen a day later. There weren't many places where she could be. At her home in La Costa was one place. At her shop in Del Mar was another. On the outside, I figured, she might have gone to meet her ex-husband, Rick the Agent, in Beverly Hills or New York City, to accept his offer of a highly lucrative position with International Sports Talent, although I didn't think my martinis had been the decider on that all-important question.

Interestingly enough, when I called both IST offices in Beverly Hills and Manhattan, the secretaries I spoke with had never seen or heard of anyone named Gwendolyn Pritchard. In fact, they were surprised to learn that Rick had ever been married.

Sandy Knox, Gwen's partner in the Die Shopping boutique, came clean in the second phone conversation with me. Yes, Gwen was home but no, she wasn't talking to anyone. She was "disappointed . . . hurt . . . bruised . . . depressed."

"Infuriated?" I said. "Would that be part of it?"

"It's in there," Sandy said.

"I gather she's leaning hard on the asshole word when my name comes up, would that be fair to say?"

"You have assumed correctly. This isn't something you can fix with a phone call, Bobby Joe."

"Please tell her I need to speak to her."

"It won't do any good. She's too upset."

"OK, try telling her to stop acting like I broke a date for the dance."

"You should come out here if you really care about her."

"She knows damn well I care."

"A woman can't hear it too often."

"Boy, I knew I shouldn't have canceled my subscription to *Cosmopolitan*. I'd have known that."

"Sarcasm. That'll fix it."

"Maybe I can shout how much I care for her. Hold the phone up so she can hear me."

"She's not as amused by the situation as you seem to be."

"I'm not amused either, Sandy, but it's frustrating to try to fix something with somebody when the somebody won't even *talk* to you."

"Do the romantic bit, Bobby Joe. Come out here, take an ocean-view suite at the La Valencia, lay in champagne and flowers, invite her over for a visit, see if one thing leads to another."

"That's a very romantic suggestion, Sandy, but considering the mood she's in, it could be a big waste of time and money."

"No it won't. If Gwen doesn't show up, *I* will."

I laughed at her joke—if that's what it was.

While I was home I dropped by the office of Alleene's Delights to check out my mail and see if my bills were being paid on time, or if my part-time secretary's social life was keeping her too busy to worry about it.

Ever since I'd been on the Tour, traveling thirty-five weeks or more a year, I'd hired someone to do secretarial work for me. The big stuff like investments and taxes and retirement funds, that was handled by Smokey Barwood's money managers and accountants in New York.

Smokey's people had done well by me. I'd been with the agency fifteen years and nobody had run off to Buenos Aires with my money yet.

The same wasn't true on the local scene. Over the years I'd been through a half-dozen bookkeepers who thought my money was their money, and by the time I discovered it and fired them, they were driving away in new Celicas and Corollas.

My latest had been working out OK for the past two years. She was one of the Gwyneth Paltrows who worked for Alleene. She managed the catering office. She'd agreed to take on my chores in her spare time and I paid her well for doing it. Her name was Tina or Frieda, I could never remember, always being on the road. Maybe if she had a bigger rack . . .

There was a signature stamp for the fan mail she answered in my behalf. Not that I received much. Four or five desperate requests a month to cure somebody's slice. Four or five letters a month from people wanting to know if I could help them get on Augusta National, Cypress Point, or Pine Valley to play eighteen holes.

"Get born rich and start your life over," is what I would advise them, but I left it to Tina or Frieda to say it more delicately in letter form.

My sec didn't open letters that were personal from names she recognized, and while I was there she called my attention to one. It was from Terri Adams, my second ex-wife, the one who enjoyed helping Red Taggert keep criminals loose on society.

Terri had a talent for conning me out of money. If it wasn't a problem with her car or a kitchen appliance, it was a medical emergency regarding herself or a close relative. Sometimes this was true. But most of the time, I knew she wanted cash to lavish on herself at Neiman's or give to her latest live-in, some out-of-work slug with a talent for rolling joints—a guy she would have become infatuated with because he reminded her of some handsome dimwit in a TV series.

I frowned as I read the letter from Terri—she wanted to "borrow" $30,000. "Alleene has to see this," I said.

"She's in the kitchen," Tina or Frieda said. "We're catering a gala tonight at the Fort Worth Zoo for the deep-pockets. She's probably in there reminding the staff not to beurre-blanc the poached salmon until they serve it."

"Jesus, that would haunt me forever," I said.

I summoned Alleene out of the kitchen. She was wearing a white food-stained chef's coat and a pair of old jeans and her hair was pulled back in a bun, but she still looked terrific. She poured us a mug of coffee from the fresh pot she kept ready in her office at all times.

She sat back in her leather desk chair and started reading the letter from Terri out loud.

"Dear Bobby Joe: I know I am always asking you for something, but this time it is urgent. I have nowhere else to turn because, as you know, my whole family is dead from various sick causes.

"Now I have received another severe blow. I find I cannot get health insurance because of a pre-existing condition—I have fibroids in my uterus."

Alleene laughed. I was shocked by her reaction.

"She has fibroids in her uterus?" Alleene said, a smile lingering. "*Everybody* has fibroids in their uterus."

"They do?"

What did I know about fibroids?

Alleene said, "Well, not everybody. I don't have them. But it's a common thing. Almost every woman I know either has them and her doctor watches them, or she goes ahead and has the hysterectomy."

"Terri's had a hysterectomy," I said.

"She has?"

"I gave her money three years ago for a hysterectomy."

Alleene laughed again. "B.J., if Terri's had a hysterectomy, she doesn't have fibroids in her uterus because she no longer *has* a uterus. She really does take you for a sap, you know that?"

I shrugged. "It's easier to give her the money."

"You don't have to listen to the yelling, right?"

"That's it. I want to talk about something else, babe. I have a bigger problem than Terri Adams."

Alleene knew I'd been taken with someone named Gwendolyn Pritchard. I'd told Alleene about Gwen a month earlier when I was in town and we were having one of our business lunches. Now she listened while I told her I'd decided that Gwen was the greatest lady I'd known since Alleene herself, and how I was certain I'd fallen into serious love with her, but how I'd messed up in Pinehurst and had run her off with a hurtful remark I didn't mean, and what would she suggest I do to go about repairing the damage?

Alleene and I had gotten married twenty-one years ago because we liked screwing each other. Then we got divorced a year later because we didn't have any money. We were living in a tiny garage apartment where the couch made into the bed and the kitchen was a hot plate.

I was still trying to become a pro and didn't know much about anything other than golf, gambling, movies, hanging out, and sitting around. She'd suggested we split and I agreed it was for the best. I assumed we'd still screw now and then, and we had, for old times' sake—until I started marrying other people.

We'd remained close friends through the years. She'd found excuses for my marriages to Terri Adams and Cheryl Haney, and she hadn't heaped too much ridicule on the swell dancers and fun ladies I dated in between.

Alleene was still a great-looking woman and it baffled me that she'd never married again, that a smart guy hadn't scooped her up. She went out with guys, and she'd enjoyed one or two meaningful relationships in the past, whatever a meaningful relationship is. But lately she wasn't involved with anyone. Which was fine with her, she insisted. She'd reached the point in her life where nothing was more important to her than her successful business, her golf game, and her two dogs—Victor, the Maltese, and Ilsa, the poodle. Alleene was a good golfer, ladies' division, despite the fact that she hadn't taken up the game till her thirties. She was still winning country-club trophies around town.

When I was finished describing my Gwen problem, Alleene couldn't deny herself the fun of saying, "If you were a star in the NBA, you could buy her a four-million-dollar ring. That tends to square things."

"Very helpful," I said.

"I have another piece of advice."

"Strap it on me."

"Have you thought of going out with ugly women for a change?"

"That wouldn't work. They'd take it out on me because they're ugly."

"A cripple, maybe?"

"Would *you* go out with a cripple?"

"It would depend on what's crippled."

"His dick, let's say."

She giggled, stood up. "I have to go back to work, B.J. Go to your shapely adorable in California. It's obvious the lady's in love with you or she wouldn't have been hurt so badly. Throw yourself on the mercy of the court. Begging helps. It'll work out."

We parted with our usual wet kiss and feel-up—for old times' sake.

# 37

The best place to sit in the Whaling Bar & Grill at the La Valencia Hotel, in my judgment, was a table by a window where you could gaze out at the blue Pacific and still see Gwen Pritchard if she entered the room in a slinky white dress.

That's where I was when Gwen came in and moved across the room toward me. The joint was crowded at cocktail hour and she couldn't have turned more sun-tanned faces if she'd been Rita Hayworth at the top of her game. Which would have been the year she made *Gilda*.

As I pulled out a chair for her, she said, "I'm only here because Sandy Knox would have come if I hadn't."

"Sandy wouldn't really have come here, would she?"

"Like a shot out of a cannon. You're single, aren't you?"

Gwen ordered a potato vodka on the rocks from the waiter who pounced on us. I motioned for another tall scotch and water.

"No martini?" she said cunningly.

"Martini is a speed horse. Junior lets me go a distance."

"Junior?"

"J and B. His close friends call him Junior."

"So here I am. Start talking your way out of it."

I opened up with the confession that I was in deep-type love with her, back-seat high school love, the kind I'd never been in before despite my unfortunate marital history, and I wanted us to get married and live happily ever after in whatever place she preferred, as long as it wasn't San Francisco—at this stage of my development I couldn't live around that many Commie dupes.

"You have to drop in a joke, don't you?" she said.

"It wasn't a joke."

She battled a smile.

I said, "Gwen, I'm sorry about the other night. I should have caught you when you ran out of the restaurant and apologized right then. Instead I went and sat with the Brits and kept drinking. I was bitter about the tournament. I let it get the best of me. You haven't brought me bad luck. That's the best I've played in the Masters *and* the Open. You must know I think you're the greatest thing that ever happened to me. I hope you're somewhere close to thinking you might want to forgive me."

"Do you really have a suite here?"

"I do."

"Let's check it out."

I was hoping Gwen wanted to check out my suite so she could slip out of her duds and plunder my body, but the main reason was because she wanted to smoke.

Smoking had turned into a sneak deal in California. Thanks to the powerful lobby of busybodies and carrot cakes, it was now against the law to smoke a cigarette anywhere in the state, even in the middle of your own forest fire burning out of control on your own hillside. As Grady Don had commented on the situation so eloquently, "It's OK for fags to go down on strange dicks in San Francisco, but you can't light a cigarette."

Gwen was aware that she could smoke in my hotel suite. Or she could until one of the illegal immigrants on the housekeeping staff reported it to the management.

While I made us a fresh drink at the well-stocked living-room bar, she recruited a decorative plate for an ashtray, put it down on a table, sat in a chair at the table, crossed her legs, and lit up her Merit Ultra Light.

"You only came up here to smoke," I said observantly.

"That's part of it."

"I thought you might be going to lose the dress."

"Why would you think that?"

"I'm a silly old romantic. I came all this way—"

"We have things to discuss."

"Yeah, we do. I want you to go to Carnoustie with me."

She looked stunned. "We haven't even made up! You're asking me to go to Scotland?"

"We're making up."

"We are?"

"I told you how I feel."

"You make one speech and that's it?"

"Like my dad says, life's too short to put sugar in cornbread."

"We have things that need to be settled, Bobby Joe."

"The big thing's already settled. I love you. You love me. The only thing left is my town or yours?"

"It's not that simple."

"Why not?"

"It just isn't."

"Why do you want to complicate it?"

"We have differences to work out."

"What differences?"

"Politics, for one."

"*Politics*?" I almost yelled it. "What did I ever say to make you think I give a shit about politics? Have you ever heard me say politics is more important than golf . . . football . . . barbecue?"

Slight grin. Recovery.

I went on. "You say you care about human rights, and if that makes you a liberal, you don't apologize for it. Fine with me. Hell, Gwen, if liberal means open-minded, I'm a semi-liberal and everybody I know is . . . well, everybody but my dad."

Another grin. Another recovery.

I said, "But that doesn't mean I have to vote for Fidel Castro's cousin. You talk about human rights. Hey, I'm all for it—if the sumbitch'll step out of the unemployment line long enough to mow my lawn. Abortion? It's OK if my own daughter needs one, not for anybody else . . . Same-sex marriage? Here's my deal on that: if I'm a chick and Sharon Stone wants to tie the knot, count me in. What else?"

"That about covers it."

"You want to know who most of your quivering liberals are?"

"I have a feeling I'm going to hear it."

"In high school they always had to sit in the middle."

"Middle of what?"

"When they rode in the back of somebody's car."

"I'm so glad you shared that with me."

While she sat and smoked, I paced, stood around, leaned against walls, paced again. Frustration deal.

I said, "Look, we have the rest of our lives to cancel out each other's vote. I'm going to Carnoustie early to practice, but you don't have to come till the tournament starts if you don't want to."

"Where am I?" Gwen said, throwing up her hands. "What am I doing? Have we just walked out of a movie holding hands and we're on our way to the ice cream parlor?"

Now I grinned.

She said, "There's a whole future out there, Bobby Joe. I want to know if we're going to fit in it. You and me . . . us . . . together. What do you plan to do when you grow up? What do you *want* to do?"

"What do you mean? With my basic life?"

"Yes. When you're no longer competitive on the golf course. Do you have a long-range goal? Do you want to design courses . . . take a club job . . . run a golf school . . . Has TV made any overtures? What?"

"I've got a lot more golf to play, Gwen."

"I understand, but you're forty-four, Bobby Joe."

"Damn, I forgot about that. We do have a problem."

She looked at me impatiently through the smoke.

"I've got it," I said. "When the day comes that I'm no longer qualified for the Tour, I'll move to Palm Springs. Marry one of those rich-widow dolls. That'll take care of food and shelter—and I'll get to wear a pink blazer."

Her look changed to pathetic.

Then she said, "I talked to Rick yesterday. He drove down from LA. It was very interesting."

"How's his hair?"

"Do you want to talk about his hair or the offer he made me?"

"I choose hair."

"I don't. Bobby Joe, I am absolutely convinced of something. Rick is going to become the biggest sports agent in the business. I don't say this because he's starting out with Scott Pritchard and Tricia Hurt. I say it because he's shrewd at finance, a great talker, a masterful liar. He's a little bit smart and a whole lot devious—and all that is a powerful combination."

"Sounds like he ought to enter politics."

"I'm only saying Rick has every quality it takes to become an enormous success as a sports agent. I did leave out his other trait. He's a Lolita collector. Very bad where marriage is concerned."

"Take me to the offer."

"I would be a thirty percent owner of the company and the starting salary is half a million a year."

"Christ, he must not be getting laid at all."

"Ordinarily that would be funny . . . Rick knows he can trust me. He knows I can do a good job . . . and it's another way to protect Scotty's earnings. He brought an agreement for me to sign, a deal memo. A contract will be drawn up later. I would run the West Coast office. He wants to operate out of New York. Travel, do his PR and selling thing. I would look after the details he doesn't want to fool with. And I would have input on everything. I told him I wouldn't even begin to consider his offer if I had to live in Beverly Hills. I said I don't own enough pairs of shoes to live in Beverly Hills."

"I hope he laughed at that."

"He didn't laugh as hard as he does at Three Stooges reruns."

"What did he say about you moving the office?"

"He asked me where I would move it."

"And you said . . . ?"

"I said, well, since I was in love with this guy in Texas—don't get overwrought—I might move it to the Dallas–Fort Worth area. He thought about it a minute, and said OK, he was good with that, the air travel works, and half the Tour lives there anyhow, the half that doesn't live in Florida."

"What did he say about the guy in Texas you're in love with?"

"He wished me luck."

"Did he call me Groovo?"

"Not that I remember."

"So you took the job, right?"

"I haven't yet. That's why we're talking. Think about this for a moment, and try not to interrupt. Consider the day comes when you no longer play golf as good as you'd like. For whatever unforeseen reason. Injury. Loss of desire. Or maybe age starts to take an early toll. Wouldn't it be a good thing if you already had something else to do? And it was something to keep you around golf, and it was interesting and financially rewarding? What if you were already in an executive position with International Sports Talent?"

"You want me to be a fucking *agent*?"

"God," she said with a give-up look that said she must be speaking to me in an unknown tongue.

I said, "This is pretty good. The woman I'm in love with is offering me a job making plane reservations for her kid!"

She said, "Can we chill here?"

"Probably not."

"Did you hear what I said? I said *executive* position. I'm not talking about today . . . now . . . next year. I know you're exempt on the Tour for two more years, and I know what that means. I'm a golf mom, remember? I know for two more years at least, you'll be one of the select hundred and twenty-five pros who've earned the right to enter as many as forty-eight tournaments a year and play for a five million purse in each one. It beats air-traffic control, right? I'm talking *someday*, Bobby Joe. Eventually, OK? But sooner than later . . . and you wouldn't be working *for* me, you'd be working *with* me. You would be a big asset to the company. You're an athlete. You know golfers, you know athletes in other sports. You know how they think, what they want, what they need. You'd be invaluable to the company."

I walked over to her. She stood up. I put my hands on her hips.

I said, "So . . . what you're saying is, I'd better give this serious consideration or there's no more us?"

"No, not at all. But I guess I *am* saying I'm probably going to take the job, and you and I will just have to work our romantic thing around it."

I said, "I have another in-depth question. What happens if I say your long-range plan for me is not that bad an idea—I might go along with it?"

She put her arms around my neck.

"I lose the dress."

# 38

Small hotels in towns where British Opens are played tend to fall into the category of your typical rundown British seaside resort dump. They inspire thoughts of old black-and-white English mystery-movie titles—*The Condemned Stove*, *Separate Faucets*, *The Toilet at the Top of the Stairs*, *The Spiral Closet*, *The Hot Water Vanishes*.

My small hotel in Carnoustie, on the North Sea coast north of Edinburgh, bore the simple name of Smith House. The name had nothing to do with the Smith brothers of Carnoustie—Alex, Willie, and Macdonald—who came to America and won tournaments and taught golf.

In the center of town, Smith House was two doors from the Maiden Arms, a bed-and-breakfast that had nothing to do with another of Carnoustie's favorite sons, Stewart Maiden, the only teaching pro Bobby Jones ever had.

The Maiden Arms did have something to do with my caddie. Mitch was staying there with my golf clubs. He'd come over ahead of me, spent a week in London, shopping, dining, getting laid. He'd taken the train from London to Edinburgh—first class on the *Royal Scotsman*—and hired a taxi to drive him from Edinburgh to Carnoustie, for three hundred dollars.

Some of the caddies said Roy Mitchell had a more enriching life than they did.

Smith House was easy to find. The directions of the owner, the widow Smith, were good. It was on the road that closely bordered Carnoustie's 18th fairway, halfway between Huggan's Cranes and Stone-Cutting Machinery at one end of town, and the little gray stone Catholic church at the other end. The church had been vacated, I'd heard from the widow Smith, and was now a pub and bowling alley.

There'd been an opportunity to stay in the Carnoustie Hotel Golf Resort & Spa, the big white four-story edifice—relatively new—that sits directly behind the course's number 1 tee and 18th green. But Tiger, Ernie, Phil, Cheetah, Knut, and the rest of the stars had seized ten rooms apiece for their friends, families, and entourages, and after all of the Royal & Ancient gentlemen and their volunteer rules officials from the U.S. Golf Association and PGA of America had been taken care of, I was offered the last available broom closet.

Gwen was coming later on the weekend, and I knew she would be happier and more comfortable in the suite at Smith House, which consisted of a bedroom, sitting room with fireplace, kitchen, and full private bath. Next to a castle and the title that goes with it, a full private bath in Scotland is the greatest treasure you can stumble upon.

I'd learned another valuable lesson in my first trip to Great Britain. You can rent a car and drive yourself on the wrong side of the road and encounter a near-death experience at every roundabout, or you can spring for a limo and enjoy the scenery.

The choice was simple, as I saw it. Live or die?

My usual driver, Charles, met my flight at Edinburgh Airport and gave me a comfortable, no-thrills ride to Carnoustie. Around St. Andrews, around Dundee, around the Firth of Tay—a body of turbulent water in the distance, brownish-grayish, that looked to be headed for a vicious firth-off with the Firth of Forth, the firth that rubs up against St. Andrews, which is not to be confused with the Firth of Clyde, the firth on the west coast of Scotland that rubs up against Troon and Turnberry—and along the coast road to Carnoustie.

Your Scot has no trouble keeping his firths straight, but Americans generally do.

When we reached downtown Carnoustie, I couldn't resist. I asked Charles to show me the church pub first. I went in and found it to be an agreeable place to have a lager if you liked low ceilings and plywood walls, and cared to watch somebody try to pick up a spare back there behind the area where the altar had been.

I went to Carnoustie a week early to practice, and not because that's how Ben Hogan did it in '53. Our Open convinced me I was playing good golf on a consistent basis. I was on a streak—in a zone, as they say. I figured I had another chance to do well in a major, so why not give it my best shot? Go early, do the homework.

Although I'd played all of the other British Open courses—Sandwich, Lytham, and Birkdale in England; St. Andrews, Troon, Muirfield, and Turnberry in Scotland—I'd never seen Carnoustie.

I'd missed the one there in '99. I wasn't exempt for it and didn't feel like traveling all that way to try to qualify. That was the Open the French guy messed up and lobbed into the lap of Paul Lawrie, an obscure pro whose name was so unfamiliar he might as well have wandered in from a sheep-shearing.

I'd heard all about Carnoustie. I was aware that it was the longest, mistiest, coldest, windiest, dreariest, and toughest of all the British Open courses. Somber. That's the word most often used by the golf historians to describe Carnoustie.

The course and town were all mine for four days, before the other players started arriving. In practice I played three balls off every tee, trying to figure out where I wanted to be on each hole.

In the early evenings I did the Hogan thing, which I'd read about. I walked the course backwards, starting at the 18th green, to give myself some other ideas about what to expect from the troubles that were out there. The moguls, the winds, and the meandering Barry Burn where it comes into play on the 10th, 17th, and 18th holes. Barry Burn is the poetic name of a wide treacherous creek that likes to drown good scores.

At night I strolled the town. Up and down the streets of old gray buildings mixed with residences, pubs, butcher shops, fishmongers, news agents, laundries, golf shops, knickknack stores.

I dined in places that offered the "all-day breakfast," my favorite thing at British Opens: fried eggs up, English bacon—hold the trichinosis—bangers, hash browns, baked beans. But I ventured into two pubs and sampled slices of name-this-meat, which came with sauces of uncertain origin and unrecognizable vegetables. I found a takeout joint where I could order fish and chips or a mad-cow burger. One night I did try the Indian restaurant on top of the shoe store—and set my body on fire.

Otherwise, those first few days were given over to stocking the suite with necessities and becoming familiar with my quarters.

Stocking the suite meant more than laying in snacks and drinks. It meant buying light bulbs that burned brighter than those supplied by the widow Smith, Lavinia. Those in the suite when I arrived were the kind that when you turned them on, you turned them off. It meant finding bars of soap that were larger and more plentiful than the two used slivers on hand. It meant searching for a brand of toilet tissue that was softer than sandpaper. It meant acquiring more clothes hangers, enough to accommodate two adults. Just two would have doubled the one lonely, misshapen wire hanger dangling on the rod in the closet. Last, it meant going out and buying towels and washcloths after being informed by Lavinia that the one washcloth I found in the suite was actually my towel.

It was another matter to become familiar with my quarters.

I slowly learned the secrets of the hot-water switch after I found it behind the dresser. After that came finding the drinking glasses that were where the cutlery should have been, finding the dishes that were where the pots and pans should have been, finding the silverware that was where the cups and saucers should have been, finding no trash baskets anywhere, learning how to turn on the stove, learning how to turn off the stove, and figuring out how to open and close the windows in the bedroom without the help of a crowbar or two Bulgarian weightlifters.

I was definitely ready for female companionship. Someone besides the widow Smith, who could give Cody Jarrett's mother two-up a side.

# 39

I'd lived many years thinking there couldn't be anything longer than a tune on a bagpipe, but that was before I played a round of golf in the wind and rain at Carnoustie.

How hard did the wind blow in the first round?

It blew so hard it ripped the swoosh off Tiger's shirt. It blew so hard it took Jesper Parnevik's cap to Denmark. It blew so hard it knocked another letter out of Vijay Singh's name. It blew so hard it made cereal out of the heather. Take my wind, please.

Jerry Grimes said, "Boy, it was a bad-hair day out there. When my cap blew off, I looked like Albert Einstein."

Grady Don said, "I looked like Don King."

"Who?" said Jerry.

"That boxing guy. Has his hair done by Lufthansa."

"This deal saved me," I said, touching the bill of my brown checkered cashmere Hogan cap, or what some might call a James Cagney cap. "You can buy one in the exhibition tent for only two thousand dollars."

It was routine to joke about the prices in the exhibition tent at the British Open. Once upon a time you could go to the Pringle booth or the Lyle & Scott booth or any of the other booths in the tent and find bargains, but that was before the people who run Tibet figured out how much the rest of the world likes cashmere.

The exhibition tent itself had lost its charm. Some wizard talked the R&A into throwing out all the fun stuff and turned it into nothing but a great big golf shop with booths for tourist info. It used to be like going to a state fair under a big tent. Along with the golf apparel and golf equipment, you could find tractors, speed boats, sports cars, golf carts, driving nets, bizarre putting devices, antique jewelry, gems and silver ornaments created by Garrard, the Crown jeweler, excellent paintings and prints, rare books . . . Only at the British Open could you find a copy of *The Brigadier Breaks 90* by Sir Arthur Dragoon Fusilier.

We were having a lager after the round in the bar on the ground floor of the Carnoustie Hotel Golf Resort & Spa. We'd discarded our rain gear and were enjoying the warmth of cardigan over slipover over golf shirt, and the indoors. We had finished our rounds within thirty minutes of each other.

The bartender was a middle-aged Scot who'd been listening to our comments on the weather.

"Aye, it's just a wee summer breeze, lads," he said.

Grady Don laughed. " 'Wee summer breeze.' Fucking sky's purple, the rain's horizontal, I'm pissing ice water, but this guy's going to the beach today. What time you going, Jock? I'll meet you there."

The bartender said, "Part of our defense, you see. The elements. You have titanium and sports psychologists. All we have is nature."

Jerry said, "All I know about the weather is what Scotty Pritchard said about it."

"Tell B.J.," Grady Don said.

Jerry laughed. "Scott said, 'Geeeaaah, the wind.' "

They kept chuckling.

I said, "You guys might be making fun of my future son-in-law."

Grady Don said, "It must be tough on your future son-in-law, having to go through life looking like Ride the Wild Surf."

I said, "Charlie don't surf."

Grady Don said, "I don't accept that."

I said, "I'll grant you he can pass for a surf unit, but he's never done anything but play golf. Gwen says he's never even gone to the beach to pick up a chick."

Grady Don said, "I guess if you look like Scott Pritchard, you don't have to go to the beach to pick up a chick. All you have to do is stand around and see who scores highest on the quiz."

"Old Scotty got himself beat up today," Jerry commented.

"Clobbered good," I said. "I'll bet he hasn't shot an eighty-nine since he was eight years old. He was in tears when I talked to him. He was humiliated. He said he made a seven on the first hole, and that was as good as it got all day. He's out of here today. Sayonara."

Grady Don said, "Those eighty-nines will WD you every time."

I said, "His mom's upstairs with him . . . helping him pack . . . being a good mom."

I volunteered the services of my limo and driver, Charles, to transport Scott to the Edinburgh airport, where he could catch a shuttle to London or Manchester, and from there he could find a flight home.

"Geeeaaah, Carnoustie," Scott said as he climbed into the limo. "Somebody needs to buy this place some lawn mowers."

The three of us—Grady Don, Jerry, and I—called on all of our experience and wisdom to shoot first-round numbers that were satisfying under the circumstances of wind, rain, and bad bounces.

We dug out middle-of-the-pack scores. I shot a 74, three over, which was only three behind the leader, but there was a gang of brand names between us. Guys with 72s, 73s. Grady Don had a 75, Jerry a 76.

The leader with an even-par 71 was the usual puzzling stranger, a tall, gangling, mystified young Brit named Alfie Crangburn. He'd chipped in three times and holed out a five-iron for a deuce.

His name fit nicely in there with other first-round leaders of past British Opens. Such curious chaps as Flory van Donck, Fred Bullock, Peter Tupling, Bill Longmuir, Paul Broadhurst, Nick Job, Lionel Platts, Neil Coles. Like most of those before him, Alfie Crangburn was expected to disappear at the first opportunity.

Gwen cooked dinner for the two of us that night. She'd been in town three days. Long enough to conquer our stove, find a grocery market, rearrange everything in our suite, and make friends with the widow Smith.

I discovered Gwen knew how to make a shepherd's pie, which, next to golf, is the best thing the shepherds ever gave us.

Gwen's was superb. She mixed ground beef with the ground lamb before adding the chopped celery, carrots, onion, and beef broth, and she sprinkled grated cheese on the layer of mashed potatoes that covered the whole top of the casserole.

While I came close to eating myself into a coma, I said, "Gwen, this is so good it makes me want to throw rocks at France. Of course there's more than one reason to do that."

Gwen said, "It's easy to make."

"It's great, I mean it," I said, and leaned over to give her a kiss.

She smiled. “And me not wearing my sex bracelets.”

We toppled over after dinner and settled in for an evening of watching television—four channels were available. That particular night our choices consisted of a panel of educators and literary critics discussing *The Utter Failure of Yorkshire Poets*, a documentary on Hebridean sheep, a special on Dundee’s dental hospital, and a news show on which we learned that the first-round leader, Alfie Crangburn, was not, repeat *not*—as inadvertently reported earlier—the great-grandson of Lieutenant Alfred Crangburn of the Royal Engineers, V.C., D.S.C., D.S.O., the man who had killed more than eighty Zulu warriors in a single day at the Battle of Rorke’s Drift.

# 40

The wind and rain came back for an encore in the second round. The Skipper ordered it in case Carnoustie's narrow fairways, high rough, and unlucky bounces weren't enough to expand a golfer's vocabulary.

My threesome went off early on Friday, shortly before noon, having played late on Thursday. But it didn't help us beat the weather. The round still took close to six hours, windy and wet all the way. The slow play did give me time to learn the names of my companions. The Korean was Kang ju, the Bolivian was Santiago.

The pairing reminded me that the British Open has the most international field of the four majors. A third of the contestants come from countries where it seemed to me that trying to stay alive would rank well ahead of golf as a pastime.

I became aware of this the first time I played in the championship, which was at St. Andrews fifteen years ago. I was excited about watching the opening ceremony. I intended to be out at the number 1 tee at 7 A.M. before the first group went off in the opening round. But that was before my chance meeting in the clubhouse bar the day before with Peter Dobers, a highly respected British golf writer having a large glass of red wine at what I recall was midmorning.

When Dobers overheard me saying I wanted to rise early and go out on the first tee the next morning, he said, "What on earth for?"

"I want to watch the opening ceremony," I said. "Don't they raise flags . . . Doesn't a band play and a guy say, 'Gentlemen, start your engines,' and somebody sings 'My Old Kentucky Home' . . . that kind of thing?"

"Good God, no," he said.

"What do they do?" I asked.

"Well," he said thoughtfully, "I suspect the starter simply looks at his watch and tells the Nigerian to hit it."

There was a long delay at the 6th hole, the par-5 with the out-of-bounds fence on the left. Up ahead, guys were tromping around in the heather, looking for balls. I took the moment to share the news with Mitch that with this tournament, this week, I would complete my Hogan's Alley slam.

I explained how there are almost as many Hogan's Alleys in golf as there are Hogan stories, and now I'd played all of them.

Pinehurst No. 2 was the first. It was called Hogan's Alley because he won the old North and South Open three times on Pinehurst No. 2. The second Hogan's Alley was Riviera, where he won the Los Angeles Open in '47 and '48, and returned later in the summer of '48 to win the U.S. Open and set a new seventy-two-hole record doing it. The third Hogan's Alley was Colonial Country Club, in our hometown of Fort Worth—his and mine—where he won the Colonial National Invitational five times.

"Colonial your alley, too," Mitch said.

"It is," I said. "I think I won a back-nine press there one day."

Now we were standing under umbrellas on the fourth Hogan's Alley, the 578-yard 6th hole at Carnoustie. It's the only Hogan's Alley that consists of one hole. It acquired the name after Hogan birdied it three times in '53 when he won the only British Open he ever entered, completing the Triple Crown—he'd won the Masters and U.S. Open earlier that year.

The 6th at Carnoustie was first known for something else. The land on the other side of the out-of-bounds fence is a firing range belonging to the Ministry of Defence, and has been for years. I'd seen a photo of the old sign that once adorned the fence. The sign said:

DO NOT TOUCH ANYTHING.
IT MAY EXPLODE AND KILL YOU.

You could say the left side of the fairway on Carnoustie's number 6 had once ranked among golf's most daunting hazards.

The 6th that day was where I started keeping myself in the championship. I was three over on the round after five holes, courtesy of evil bounces, but I birdied the 6th into the wind. Drove it good. Threaded a three-wood into the criminally narrow layup area, which was only eleven yards wide. My best shot of the day. I pitched on and made an eight-foot putt.

It was a fistfight trying to save shots all day. The only other par-5 on the course, the 515-yard 14th, dogleg left, was where I made my other birdie. Since it was playing downwind I was able to bite off a hunk of the dogleg. My tee ball was big enough to take the Spectacles out of play. The Spectacles are the two side-by-side bunkers in the middle of the fairway. They stare at you from about seventy-five yards short of the green. I cleared them easily with my second shot. That set up my bump-and-run pitch from in front of the green, which left me with a birdie putt of three feet. No short putt is easy when the wind is trying to blow you off balance, but after backing off twice I side-doored it.

My one-over 72 gave me a thirty-six-hole total of 146. Normally that number wouldn't mean shit, but in bad weather on a tough course it was a Lucille. At the end of the day I was only two back of the five players who were tied for the lead.

Defying the odds, one of the leaders was still Alfie Crangburn. He scrounged out a 73 to go with his opening 71. Keeping company with him were four names that would give anyone a restless night—Sergio Garcia, Nick Price, Darren Clarke, and Cheetah Farmer.

A swarm of people could be found three and four shots back. Grady Don and Jerry were included in the swarm, as were the usual marquee suspects, Phil, Ernie, Tiger, Knut.

Mitch studied the situation and said, "Everything too bunched up. Time somebody thin the herd."

Gwen and I dined that evening at a pub called The Goose and Garter, one of the places offering the all-day breakfast, which I ordered and savored. Gwen tried the fried fish that badly wanted to be Dover sole but may have been plaice and was most likely cod.

We took a small table where we could see and hear the TV, and watched highlights of the day's golf. There was a brief glimpse of me. I was bent into the wind, clutching my Hogan cap. The voice on TV described me as "a veteran American campaigner."

Gwen said, "The veteran American campaigner. I guess it was pretty rough, huh, going up that cliff on Omaha Beach?"

The most interesting moment on TV was Alfie Crangburn's interview with a reporter. The unexpected co-leader said, "Oh, I haven't a prayer of winning. My knees are already wobbly. I dare say none of you chaps will want to speak to me tomorrow night. Not after I've returned an eighty-five or ninety, what? It will all be gone, then. But I shall be proud to say I once led the Open Championship."

Reading the daily papers in England and Scotland was always a treat when I was there. They ranged from intriguing to outrageous. One of the things I asked the widow Smith to do was supply the suite every morning with the papers I'd come to prefer over the years, and add them to the bill, please, which was something I shouldn't have even bothered to mention.

Each day I received the best of what you'd call your real newspapers, the *International Herald Tribune*, the *Daily Telegraph*, the *Times*, the *Independent*, and *The Scotsman*, and I'd also receive the fun-filled tabloids: the *Daily Mail, Sun, Mirror, Express, Star, News of the World.*

After dinner that night we relaxed in the suite. I built a fire and Gwen made a pot of coffee. I rummaged through the papers while she smoked, sipped coffee, and read a chapter or two in *The Vicar's Rector's Bimbo*, a paperback novel she'd picked up. I could have the title wrong.

One of the things I explained to Gwen about the London newspapers was that certain stories could be a good riddle. You could come across big headlines that jolted you with such news as "Gooch Says No," or "Hadley Tops It Off," but you'd have to read ten paragraphs before you could tell whether the story was about cricket, soccer, or rugby.

I confessed something to Gwen. The fact that I'd accumulated a list of words that, if those words appeared in the headline, I wouldn't read the story. It was particularly so in the papers back home.

"No matter what?" she said.

"Never."

"Why not?"

"The story couldn't possibly interest me."

"What words?"

I wrote the words down on a piece of paper for her, not necessarily in order of my intense noninterest.

Deficit
Merger
Steroids
Teenage
Congress
Hollywood
U.N.
Gay
Hip-hop
Hunger

She read them aloud. Maybe it was my imagination, but I thought I saw her fight off a smile at the end.

Gwen had vacationed in Europe more than once, but she hadn't been abroad in five years, so she was shocked by some of the things she found in the London tabloids today.

Like skin.

Nude slatterns of every make and model, usually hung, shouting in the headlines that they'd like to shag a royal or any celebrity from the world of show biz or sports.

Gwen said, "Shag was a dance when I was a girl. We did the shag."

"It means something else over here now," I said.

Our favorite of the day was the full-page layout in the *Star* of Vashtine Ulberg, the future Mrs. Knut Thorssun. Nothing on but a thong. Sitting on a stool. Legs spread. Cupping her stunning breasts. Bedroom look. The headline blazed:

*Vashtine to the Open Golf Field:*
I WOULD SHAG THE LOT!

"Knut must be very proud," Gwen said.

# 41

The weather in Saturday's third round was an authentic wee summer breeze, the kind any American could identify, and there were welcome patches of sunshine with it. Otherwise I don't think I would have bit off Carnoustie's head and sucked out the lungs.

My three-under 68 was the low round of the day and the championship, but it wasn't the only one. There were two others Saturday. Fortunately those players were well back in the field. A 68 was carved out by somebody named Kahiko Katsuyo, and the other was fired by somebody named Tosayo Suyoshi. I'd never heard of them, but I'd seen *Back to Bataan* on TV a couple of times.

What my own 68 did was slide me into what you call your thick of things. My fifty-four-hole total of 214 was only one stroke back of Alfie Crangburn's 213. He was still refusing to go away.

Alfie shot a 69 by holing out another five-iron for an eagle, sinking five putts longer than sixty feet for pars and birdies, and benefiting from a favorable ruling a drunk official gave him which saved him a par. The rules official was so loaded he gave Alfie a free drop out of thick heather and into the fairway at the 15th hole.

The official ruled that a TV camera tower had been in Alfie's line of sight, but the tower clearly hadn't been in his line of sight, and Crangburn admitted later he had frivolously asked for relief, never dreaming he'd get it. Nobody blamed him for taking advantage of the ruling.

That evening on the BBC 2 sports lineup you could see and hear the rules official up close on the 15th hole.

"Absolucally," the official said to Alfie. "Temporanny Immovable Obstruption. Rule Twenty-four tube. Place on, please."

I could only laugh when I saw that the gasolined official was Jarvis Phillip W. Burchcroft.

The key to my round, I told the press, was staying out of the purple flowers. That's a kind way to describe heather. A thick clump of heather can make your hand ring when you try to hit out of it.

My round included five birdies and two bogeys. Bunkers caught me at the 5th and 13th. Deep as they were, I was happy to escape with bogeys. I birdied the two par-5s again, 6 and 14. Unlike Alfie Crangburn, the longest putt I sank was a twenty-footer for birdie at the 17th. The best club in my bag was the four-iron, I said. I hit it to three feet at the 12th, and it took me home over the Barry Burn at the 18th for a par.

Gwen had walked the full eighteen. She was hard to miss in my gallery. Good-looking babe in a bulky white turtleneck, snug gray slacks, her long raven-black hair swirling in the wee summer breeze around her jazzy sunglasses.

It should have been obvious to any thinking person that Gwen was following me. She couldn't have been interested in Cheetah Farmer.

I was somewhat disappointed no writer asked me about Gwen. I could have been a wit. Said she was a notorious golf groupie from the States who followed me everywhere, and I didn't know what to do about it.

I did get a laugh when a British writer brought up Sunday's final pairing, which would consist of Alfie and me. He mentioned that we wouldn't be going off until very late, like 3:20 in the afternoon, and asked what I'd do to kill the time?

I said, "Oh, I'll probably do some shopping, have a long lunch, take in a movie."

In all of the excitement of my round and the media attention, Gwen and I had forgotten a dinner date and were only reminded of it when we returned to our hotel and found the note.

The widow Smith, Lavinia, had insisted on cooking something special for us on Saturday night. A gourmet surprise.

Gwen took her hot bath first. I napped. I took my hot bath. She smoked. We dressed comfortably. I made cocktails. A potato vodka and club soda for her, an off-brand scotch and water for me. Junior didn't do this part of Scotland. And we were off. We carried our drinks and the bottles of vodka and scotch down to the owner's flat on the ground floor.

"Oh, I see you've brought spirits," the widow Smith said. "I don't allow alcohol in the home, but I will make an exception in this case. Now start on this while you have your drinks."

She put down a plate of smoked salmon and Melba toast on a coffee table in the living room.

"Please make yourselves comfortable," she said. "I shall be going back and forth to the kitchen to prick the boil. I made a decision. I hope you don't mind. Some people like minced tripe in the haggis, some do not. I've included it. I do hope this will be all right."

Panic. I knew what tripe was. I might not have known much about haggis, but it had been my staunch belief throughout my entire life that tripe was something to be dodged at any cost.

Gwen caught my look and called out to the widow Smith, "Uh, I'm sorry you've gone to so much trouble, Lavinia, but we really can't stay for dinner. When we accepted your kind invitation the other day, we had no idea Bobby Joe would be in contention for the Open. Surely you can understand. He never allows himself to eat much before the last round of a tournament . . . and I do want to make sure he gets his rest tonight."

The widow Smith called back from the kitchen that she understood completely. She should have thought of it herself. She would share the haggis with her neighbors. But she would prepare two platters for us to take to our suite. She did want us to try it. We hadn't been to Scotland, she said, if we hadn't eaten the haggis.

Gwen looked at me. "Didn't I do good?"

"Tripe," I whispered. *"Tripe."*

She shushed me.

"First you obtain the large stomach bag of a sheep," the widow Smith was suddenly saying as she trotted into the living room, picked up a slice of salmon on toast, and trotted back to the kitchen. Next thing I knew I was hearing about washing and scraping the sheep's stomach, and she was saying, ". . . and nurture the pluck, which is the lungs, the liver and the heart, of course." I was reaching for the bottle of scotch by then. Next came something about leaving the windpipe hanging over the side of the pot to allow "the impurities to pass out freely." I poured more scotch as she went on about "the lights," which were the lungs. I gulped and refilled as she continued discussing "the pluck" and "the King's hood," whatever that was. It was when she mentioned chopping up the beef suet—"fat" in my lingo—that I was forced to hold in a monster groan. But I hung in there, as did Gwen, who was pouring herself a straight vodka. Then we heard about adding the beef fat to the mixture, and this was followed by throwing in the handfuls of toasted oatmeal with the minced tripe and the grated lungs and the ground liver and the finely sliced heart, and adding salt and pepper, and giving it a "good shaking," and dumping all of it in the stomach bag, and sewing it up with thread before putting it in the large pot of water to boil for three hours, making sure to prick the bag occasionally to let the air out.

"Delicious," Lavinia said. "Don't spoil it with garnish or sauce."

"Top of the world, Lavinia," I said as we left to go to our suite, me carrying a platter of haggis and the bottle of scotch, Gwen carrying a platter of haggis and the bottle of vodka.

There was a lively race to the commode. I wasn't about to lose. My haggis was flushed first, but Gwen was raking hers off the platter and into the john an instant later.

I said, "Forget a stab in the eye with a hot poker. Before I'd even *taste* this deal, I'd go to the Congo, take off my clothes, and let a family of pygmies shoot poison darts at my naked body."

# 42

Three tall scotches and a Tylenol PM made me sleep like a run-over possum. But I still woke up mad. The haggis did it. First thing I thought Sunday morning when I opened my eyes was: What if I'd eaten any of that and stuff and *then* found out what was in it? I'd have been long gone to Downtown Vomit City, and due to lingering illness I might have had to withdraw from a major championship I had a better than slim and none chance to win.

Gwen prepared a mammoth brunch. Eggs, hash browns, beans, sausages, English bacon—she trimmed the trichinosis—scones, toast, honey, and good coffee, as opposed to British coffee, which tastes like a combination of stewed dirt and melted wrought iron.

The sun was out, I noticed through the windows, but the wind was whipping around. Good, I said to Gwen. The course would still play tough. It wasn't likely to give up any low scores to Els, Mickelson, Tiger, Cheetah, Knut, or any of the other heroes who were five to ten shots back. A 72 or 73 would be a good score in the last round.

I wasn't meeting Mitch on the practice range until one o'clock, a full two hours before I would tee off. There was plenty of time to watch the early action on television, see how the course was playing, and browse through the Sunday papers.

Not much in the papers about the veteran campaigner from America. A man who'd been fourth at the magnolia joint and second in the U.S. Open. A man who was considered the actual British Open leader instead of one shot back by those who took experience into account.

The papers were all about the youthful Alfie Crangburn. Except for Monty in Ryder Cups, the Brits had been short of golf heroes since Nick

Faldo hit the skids. Even their adopted Spaniards had become unreliable. But here was Alfie popping up, a heartwarming story.

Best of all, Alfie was a socialite. At least he was in the minds of the British press slugs. He was upper middle class, which was hardly royalty, but it meant that his dad didn't drive a lorry for a living.

Alfie, now twenty-four, had been raised in a large house with hedges and gardens in a plush suburb of London. His father, Oliver Jeremy Crangburn, commuted to work in a Jaguar. The father was a vice-president of a firm in London that passed pieces of paper up and down halls.

His mother, Constance, confessed that her hobby was shopping. She preferred shopping at "Forty's" and "Harvey Nick's." Alfie had a younger brother, Bowles, who liked to take things apart but not put them back together, and a teenage sister, Julia, who loved "going to clubs."

The family liked to eat bubble and squeak and neeps and nips and baugers and mash and drink stickies and fizzies, but Alfie was partial to the Wimpies and whipsies, which Americans would recognize more easily as hamburgers and milkshakes.

Alfie had been playing golf only eight years, having taken up the game at sixteen. He had fiercely wanted to be an athlete of some sort. But he was too slow for tennis, track, or soccer. Too weak for rowing. Afraid of water anyhow—couldn't swim. Not nimble or crafty enough for cricket. Horses frightened him terribly—equestrian events were out of the question. All outdoor winter sports were insane, especially bobsledding. And he was too intelligent to race motor cars. Subsequently he looked to golf.

Alfie turned pro because he'd never won anything as a junior amateur or even as an adult amateur, therefore it seemed pointless to remain an amateur. He had been playing the European Tour for the past three years, but without any success whatever. His biggest paycheck was sixty pounds from a tournament in Algeria. He wasn't even listed among the first 1,200 players rated in the world rankings. He had gone unnoticed through the qualifying process to enter the British Open, and had barely made it.

Asked to explain his performance in the championship, Alfie was quoted saying, "Well, it has something to do with the course, doesn't it? I rather like the fact that as one goes round somber old Carnoustie, a bloody good shot can wind up in the hay while a perfectly horrid shot might very likely find its way to the green."

Of all the players who were out on the course ahead of Alfie and me, nobody had made a move by the time we started.

One reason was because Carnoustie was playing differently. It had dried out and the winds were coming across on one hole, and from another direction on another hole. Helping here, hurting there. And the ball was running farther on the firmed-up fairways and hardened greens. Running too far in some cases, like across a fairway or over a green and into the rough.

We began the round amid the pomp and circumstance that goes along with the final pairing in a major. There must have been a dozen black-blazered Royal & Ancient officers and invited observers inside the ropes with us as well as the "foot soldiers," the ex-players turned announcers who were working for British, American, Euro, and Japanese TV.

The group included Jarvis Phillip W. Burchcroft, "Mr. Rules," who was a guest official. He had the gall to give me a broad, well-wishing smile and go-get-'em gesture with his fist before I teed off.

Like we were two old buddies from the USA over here on foreign soil. Like I couldn't possibly harbor a grudge against him for the two crippling rules interpretations he'd given me at the Masters and our Open—he'd only been looking after the integrity of the game, after all. Surely I understood that.

I gave him a straight-faced nod. Didn't want to. Did.

I was dressed in a white golf shirt under a tan slipover cashmere sweater, gray slacks, black shoes, and my checkered Hogan cap. The bareheaded, shaggy-blond Alfie wore a too-tight red sweater over a blue knit shirt, brown slacks, and white shoes.

Keeping the ball in the fairway off the tee was helpful at Carnoustie. I knew this, but it didn't seem to matter to Alfie. He consistently found other ways to play the course.

The 1st hole was a good example. The 400-yard hole was a straightaway par-4. My drive found the center of the fairway and I put a pitch shot on the green twenty feet from the pin. Swinging good.

In contrast, Alfie duck-hooked his drive into the rough, and was forced to chip out sideways. But no problem for Alfie. He hit some kind of long iron about 220 yards to the back edge of the green, and sank a monster putt for a par. After I two-putted for my own par, I walked to the second tee saying to Mitch, "Well, I tied him."

Tee to green, over the next eight holes, I hit nothing but good shots. Cruise-controlled it off the tee. Clubfaced it into the greens. No drama with the flat stick. I birdied Hogan's Alley again, number 6, and made routine pars everywhere else.

I was out in thirty-five, one under for the day, even for the championship, and under normal circumstances, on any other day, in any other British Open, against any other opponent, I'd have been working on the victory speech I'd be making while I fondled the claret jug.

But despite my excellent display, I gained only two shots on Alfie, and I was only one ahead of him with the tough back nine to go.

After his miracle save on number 1, some of the things Alfie did on the front nine would have brought permanent disfigurement to his face and limbs if he'd done any of them in certain gambling games back in certain parts of Texas.

Examples:

He got up and down out of a greenside bunker for par on number 2.

He scooped his approach shot on number 3 but holed out a pitch from twenty-five yards for a par.

He clumsily played three shots out of the rough on number 4 and then chipped in from eighty feet for a par.

He sank a thirty-foot putt for par at number 5.

He drove out of bounds on number 6—into the firing range, where I should have gained at least four strokes with my birdie—but he sank a sixty-foot putt for a bogey, holding it to a two-shot swing.

His second shot to number 7 hit a spectator's chair on a hill and bounced down onto the green to save him a par.

He hit a goofy slice at the 183-yard 8th—he must have been fifty yards from the green—but he got up and down for his three.

He butchered number 9 with a top, a chunk, and a balloon ball, then bladed his fourth shot from forty yards away, but the ball hit the flagstick, popped up in the air, and dropped down in the cup for a par-4.

The roars of the British grew louder with each one of Alfie's exploits.

In the instances when I caught Gwen's eye in the gallery, I could only shrug and turn my palms up in bewilderment.

Tee to green on my chart, Alfie Crangburn had *played* a nine-over forty-five but he'd *scored* a one-over 37.

On our way to the back nine, Mitch shook his head, and said, "What we got goin' on here is somethin' else. I'd volunteer to turn into one of them gay dudes if I could kiss this motherfucker goodbye."

# 43

The last thing on my mind was that I'd contribute to the lore of the 10th hole at Carnoustie. Lore isn't good for anything but a page in a history book. Near as I can tell, your basic lore doesn't do anything but sit around like a gravestone in the weeds of an old cemetery and wait for lore people to care about it.

Carnoustie's 10th is a 470-yard par-4, up a slight rise, with the burn crossing in front of the green and angling around to the right of it. The hole was another place where Hogan planted lore in the '53.

Or his caddie did.

Hogan's caddie was a Brit named Cecil Timms, and Cecil dined out for years on both sides of the Atlantic with the story about the one and only time over the seventy-two holes when he helped the Wee Bantam Ice Hawk.

They played thirty-six the last day back then, same as the U.S. Open—this was in the days when stamina was thought to be a more vital part of the game than TV money—and in the morning round Hogan had parred the 10th with a good drive and a crisp four-iron to the green.

Cecil Timms said Hogan's drive in the afternoon was close to the same spot, but the second shot had more riding on it now. Hogan at the moment was holding a slender one-stroke lead over his challengers, who were formidable. They included Robert de Vicenzo, Dai Rees, Bobby Locke, Peter Thomson, Tony Cerda, and Frank Stranahan.

There in the 10th fairway, Hogan reached for the four-iron again. But Cecil bravely—Cecil's word, "bravely"—put his hand on top of Hogan's hand, preventing Ben from taking the club out of the bag.

Hogan glared at him, as only Hogan could.

Cecil said, "The wind's changed, sir. It's a two-iron now."

Hogan stared at Cecil for what seemed to the caddie like a year. Then Ben reluctantly took the two-iron out of the bag, moved to the ball, took a stance, addressed the shot, waggled the club.

But paused—and looked at Cecil again.

"If this goes *through* the green," Hogan said to the caddie, "I'm going to bury this club in your damn forehead."

Whereupon Hogan took the biggest, hardest, most vicious swing at a shot he'd taken in the entire championship, almost as if he was *trying* to prove his caddie wrong.

But the shot turned out perfect. The ball wound up ten feet behind the flag, from where Hogan easily two-putted for his par.

"And that's how I won the Open," Cecil Timms would say, permitting someone in his audience to buy another round.

My drive at the 10th was embarrassingly void of lore. I thin-pulled it and the ball found its way into the rough on the left. I was lucky with the lie. The rough wasn't high in that spot. It had been trampled down by fans. I thought I could get a long iron through it and clear the burn, which was forty yards short of the green. I thought I might reach the front edge of the green.

I went with a three-iron but I knew at impact I hadn't gotten all of it. I watched the ball land short of the burn and take a bounce. I didn't see how it could stay out of the water.

Meantime, Alfie drove straight for a change and hit safely onto the green. My immediate job was to stop the bleeding. I was thinking, OK, two in the burn, drop out in three, pitch on in four, one putt for a bogey, or, worst case, two-putt for a double. Looks like he'll make four. Lot of holes left.

I spent a moment looking for my ball on my side of the burn, making sure there was no chance it might have stayed out, hung up in the grass.

As I walked along the edge of the burn, I noticed the blue blazers huddled in a group, Jarvis Phillip W. Burchcroft among them.

Alfie wandered past me and nodded in a friendly way as he headed toward the green. A moment later I was approached by Jarvis Phillip W. Burchcroft and the R&A's chairman of the championship committee, Sir Nigel Fox-Dudley.

Squadron leader? Group captain? Wing commander?

"Mr. Grooves, I must inform you of an infraction," Jarvis Phillip W. Burchcroft said. "If you're looking for your ball, it's lost."

I said, "I was making sure it didn't stay up."

"You were looking for it. The lost ball penalty applies."

"I wasn't *searching* for it. The ball obviously went in the burn."

"We watched you looking for your ball."

"I walked along the edge, yeah. Making certain it was in the water."

"The penalty for a lost ball is stroke and distance. I'm sure you are aware of the rule."

"Uh-uh, you can't strap that shit on me. My ball wasn't lost and you know it! My ball went in the hazard. There's nowhere else it could be."

Jarvis Phillip W. Burchcroft said, "I repeat . . . if you're looking for the ball, it's lost."

Sir Nigel Fox-Dudley said, "Burchy is quite right."

" '*Burchy*'?" I said.

Sir Nigel's pocket-size R&A rule book was open. He said, "We do *not* have a twenty-six–one. I'm thinking . . . yes . . . should be twenty-seven–one, no exceptions. Local rule. Ball search. Twenty-seven . . . parenthesis, letter *b*, as in boy, not letter *z*, as in zed . . . easy to confuse . . . ignore letter *c* . . . dash, seven, paren, asterisk, see below, paren closed . . . footnote . . . smaller type . . . I should think official has discretion . . . twenty-four–three not applicable . . . ah, yes, there we have it. Return to spot, please."

He closed the book and marched away sharply.

I said to Jarvis Phillip W. Burchcroft, "You're telling me I have to play it as a lost ball? I have to go back two hundred and thirty fucking yards, drop in the fucking rough, and I'm shooting four? That's what you're telling me?"

"I am enforcing the rule."

"If you're looking for it, it's lost. That's what you said? *If you're looking for it, it's lost*. That's not the fucking rule. That's *your* fucking rule, you fucking asshole."

"Mr. Grooves, you may wish to know that I can report your foul language to the commissioner of your Tour and request a minimum fine of five hundred dollars."

"Oh, yeah?" I said. I took out my money clip, peeled off a wad of bills, folded them, and stuck them in the lapel pocket of Jarvis Phillip W. Burchcroft's blazer.

"Here's a thousand," I said. "That ought to cover me calling you the sorriest, weak-chin, flabby-ass piece-of-shit son of a bitch I've ever known in my whole goddamn life."

I spun around and trudged back up the fairway to replay the shot. Mitch walked along beside me, knowing not to speak, letting me sizzle.

Reaching for the seven-iron in the bag, I said, "Guess I'll do now what I should have done in the first place—something *smart*—instead of thinking I was Arnold Tiger Fucking Nicklaus."

I punched out of the rough well short of the burn. I pitched my fifth shot onto the green about thirty feet from the cup, and—small wonder, considering my frame of mind—I three-putted for a quadruple-bogey 8. Since Alfie made an easy 4, I was suddenly three strokes behind him instead of one stroke ahead.

Then another surprising thing happened. Alfie kept on playing well.

We both parred the next seven holes, and Alfie found himself on the 18th tee, the 72nd hole, with a three-shot lead to win the first golf tournament of his life, which happened to be the British Open.

There are three opportunities to hit a ball into the water on number 18, a 487-yard par-4. The burn crosses the fairway in three dangerous places. But Alfie Crangburn cautiously played the hole with three five-irons. He went layup, layup, layup, chipped on the green, and calmly two-putted for a double-bogey 6—and the championship.

# 44

Thousands of British fans went full nutso. They rushed onto the green, lifted Alfie on their shoulders, bounced him up and down, carried him around in a circle, and sang those incoherent songs like they do at soccer matches before the stands collapse and kill three dozen people.

The drunks fell about, joining the other early-day drunks who'd long since hit the dirt outside the Famous Grouse and the Bollinger tent and the other bars in the tented village.

Gwen was waiting when I came out of the scorer's hut. We hugged, kissed, and stood there holding each other and as we watched Alfie's fans march, sing, stumble, and crawl. Even though Alfie Crangburn was an Englishman, the Scots would take it.

The Scots had always baffled me. I knew one or two with a sense of humor, but most of the ones I knew were relentlessly stubborn and seemed to enjoy their dislike of England as much as their dislike of the United States—England for historic reasons and America for improving their economy. I avoided arguments about it. Wrote it off to the fact that they eat haggis.

Gwen said, "You played so well. I was so proud all day."

"Except for one hole."

"Everybody around me said you got a bum ruling at ten."

"Fate don't have a head."

"It wasn't fair."

"Alfie was in a coma, that's the basic story."

"Alfie's a terrible golfer. He's hopeless."

I chuckled. "The guy can't play a lick. But he held it together the last five or six holes. You have to give him that. Now I know how Hogan must have felt when he lost to Jack Fleck."

"You should have been permitted to play the tenth as a hazard, not a lost ball. It would have saved you two strokes."

"I should have, that's right. But the wizards ruled it a lost ball. Your only option on a lost ball is to go back."

"It wasn't a lost ball. I saw it go in the creek! Everybody did!"

"I mentioned that to them—in a matter of words."

"A *lost ball*? That's nonsense."

"That wasn't the whole ball game. I had some birdie chances coming in. I just didn't make anything."

"I can't *believe* some of the putts Alfie made. Scotty played a guy like that in the semifinals of the Amateur at Oakmont. It was a miracle he ever beat him."

"It's over, babe," I said, managing a smile. "And, hey . . . I'm not a loser. No man's a loser when he can walk off the last green and find you waiting for him."

"You're going to make me cry," she said, hugging me tighter.

I said, "You know, I started thinking back there on the last hole. All I've done my whole life is play golf, work at golf, study golf, listen to golf, read about golf. I've worked to build a game I can rely on, make a living with. Find a 'repeating swing,' as Hogan called it. I've experimented with all the equipment—graphite, metal, titanium. I've found what works best for me, for my body, my swing. This year I come up with some solid chances to win a big one. After all the years and all the hard work out here, my game's ready to win a major. But what happens? I get a lousy ruling at Augusta . . . I get a lousy ruling at Pinehurst . . . and I get another one here. Each time I let it beat me. I really let it beat me. So I'm thinking my hard-headed ass has finally learned something. Golf's not about equipment . . . technique . . . distance . . . practice . . . saving shots . . . the putting stroke . . . any of that. Once you know how to hold the damn club, golf is only about one thing. How you handle bad breaks."

# PART FOUR

# ANOTHER ROMANTIC COMEDY

# 45

We got ourselves back to America by way of London, where I'd promised to take Gwen for a week after the British Open and the bundle I won at Carnoustie for losing a golf tournament almost covered it.

Just joking. London wasn't that expensive. It wasn't any more expensive than it had been the previous year, but of course I didn't have juice with my breakfast every morning.

We stayed at Dukes, a cozy little hotel in a sneaky courtyard off St. James's Street, which connects Piccadilly at one end to Pall Mall at the other. The people who know Dukes are loyal, and the people who discover Dukes become loyal.

Sometimes, if you're a dummy like me, it takes years to discover you can walk almost anywhere you want to go in London. Often you can get there quicker if you walk than you can in a taxi. There are so many one-way streets and no-turn restrictions in London, it's somewhat amazing that anyone can go anywhere in a car.

For example, you can leave your hotel and grab a taxi and tell the driver where you want to go but find yourself crossing bridges, going around monuments, circling cathedrals, and passing Harrods three times before you reach your destination. Then you eventually find out that the destination was only three blocks from your hotel.

What I mostly did in London was eat, sleep, read papers, and talk to myself when I watched cricket on TV, usually saying, "Well, somebody's gonna have to explain *that* shit to me."

I did take strolls with Gwen. Through parks and around statues. We explored various pubs for lunch, hitting the Grenadier in Belgravia more than once. We awarded Best Pub.

The London I was fondest of was the one where it was no problem finding roast beef and Yorkshire pudding for dinner.

Not any more. Every joint where Gwen insisted we dine—thanks to her lethal restaurant guide—I would ask for roast beef and Yorkshire pudding, and the zipper-grabber we'd have for a waiter would burst out laughing, then bring me an entrée that wasn't dead yet.

Gwen dragged me to the theater twice. One singing, one talking.

In the singer, the all-male cast danced around ladders and stools and sang songs about geraniums and apples.

In the talker, men and women walked back and forth and sat on furniture and discussed life and fucking.

I accompanied Gwen to fly her plastic proudly at all of the mandatory shopping arenas—Fortnum and Mason, Harvey Nichols, the Burlington Arcade, Jermyn Street, Sloane Street, Beauchamp Place, New Bond Street, Knightsbridge.

I warned her about trying to shop in Harrods during the summer sales in what had become a hot July. For some reason hot in London seems twice as hot as it is anywhere else. Years ago I'd done it and sworn I'd never go into Harrods again when it was even warm and the summer sales were on. See the food court once, I said. But Gwen ignored me.

So I sat by the window in a tea room on Knightsbridge directly across from Harrods and put the clock on her. She staggered out in a little over twenty minutes, limped across the street, plopped down in a chair at my table, dabbed at her glistening forehead with a Kleenex, and said: "Dear God, I almost couldn't get out of there!"

Gwen stayed over four days in Fort Worth on her way back to California. One thing she wanted to do was check out office space to rent or lease that would be suitable for International Sports Talent. This was in case she got around to making the decision on whether or not to take the job with her ex-husband's company.

I suggested she rent, lease, or buy something within a block of Railhead barbecue. My idea didn't carry much weight.

Gwen wasn't sure how much space she'd need. Three or four rooms to start. Office for herself, and space for a secretary–girl Friday, a receptionist, and possibly a computer nerd. She knew from experience with her kid that pro golfers, if not all professional athletes, were helpless when it comes to anything other than what they do in the games they play.

Helpless about travel, lodging, homes, insurance, savings, investments, taxes, expenses, doctors, repairs. All the things normal people deal with are a big mystery as well as an irritable interruption to professional athletes.

"I can vouch for that," I said.

"Otherwise, agents wouldn't exist," she said.

"Come to think of it," I said, "I don't believe Smokey Barwood is aware that it's easier to fly Air Somalia than Delta now."

She said, "Perhaps I haven't mentioned it. If I take this job, we'll *buy* Smokey Barwood."

"He may well be for sale."

Gwen restricted her browsing to the downtown area. It would make the trip to D-FW about thirty minutes—except on those days when the tailgating pickups might decide to have an airport freeway scrimmage with the books-on-tape people and the cell phone people.

There were two possibilities she liked. One was in the twelve-story Fort Worth Club building in the heart of downtown. The other was a floor in one of the two striking black modern Bass towers that rise more than thirty floors over Sundance Square. Oneski and Twoski, as they were known to Grady Don Maples, the architecture critic.

The first media wizard to nab me after I was back in town was Skip Rucker, the local golf writer for the *Light & Shopper*. I took him to lunch at Joe T.'s so I could watch him get on the outside of eight cheese enchiladas and three jumbo margaritas.

The paper hadn't sent him to the British Open, and he was still mad about it. The reason the paper hadn't sent him was because the British Open had been played in the middle of July, which meant that the Dallas Cowboys would be off to training camp almost any minute, and God knows, Skip said, that was the most important thing in the world to the ignorant slugs who edited the paper.

He said, "A hurricane could wipe out Florida, but it wouldn't be the lead story in our paper if a Dallas Cowboy suffered a hangnail."

Skip wrote the same feature story about me that he'd been writing for the past four years. Hometown guy is still one of the game's top players and money winners. This time he was able to add the part about my two runner-up finishes in the majors.

I wasn't thrilled with the headline somebody put on the piece: "Bobby Joe Does No. 2 Twice."

It sounded like I was the one who ate the eight enchiladas.

That girl golf writer from the *Houston Chronicle*, Ellen Wheeler, was the media wizard who called to tell me about Anne Marie Sprinkle's press release, and ask for a reaction.

This was how I found out that the chairwoman of the National Assembly of Women Commandos was threatening to commit suicide on the golf course at Oakland Hills during the PGA Championship unless the club changed its membership policy.

"What's Anne Marie's complaint?" I asked. "Ben Hogan wasn't a woman when he won the Open there?"

"That's good," Ellen Wheeler said. "That's in."

"What *is* her complaint? Surely she knows it's not an all-male club."

"The club has too many married women."

"I'm assuming that's a joke."

"It is. She says the club has too many white Christian members."

I laughed.

"I'm afraid that's not a joke. She says it's criminal how many white Christians the club has in it. That's her protest."

"Does she know Oakland Hills Country Club is in Bloomfield Hills, Michigan—not Sumatra?"

"She doesn't even know she's a fool. She says every woman in this country owes her career to the things she's done for women. She said I owe *my* career to what she's done for women. Me."

"You talked to her?"

"I called her about the press release. I said while she was being so concerned about my career, I wish she'd given some thought to *Sports Illustrated* or the *New York Times* hiring me."

"Did she say what round of the PGA she'll kill herself in?"

"No. Does this news crank you up for the tournament?"

"It does, but I could prepare better if I knew whether she was going to kill herself on the front nine or the back nine."

Like Skip Rucker, Ellen Wheeler hadn't been sent to cover the

British Open. The reason was, the Houston Texans of the AFC South were poised to go to training camp, and all hands at the paper were needed.

"It's over a month till their first game," Ellen Wheeler said, "and we're still running five stories a day on the Texans. I wrote one today. They made it the lead. It's about a defensive back's favorite lunch meat."

"The NFL never sleeps," I said.

# 46

My folks invited us over for dinner while Gwen was still in town. Louise fixed smothered pork chops, scalloped potatoes, fresh corn buttered and scraped off the cob, asparagus casserole, a mixed green salad, and cornbread that by all means didn't have sugar in it—life was too short.

For dessert she served strawberry shortcake with the strawberries mashed up to make them juicy and poured over the homemade butter cake with a glob of whipped cream on top. My dad said to my mother, "You did good," and he said to us, "This is how my mama fixed it, and how her mama fixed it, and it's the only by-god way to fix it."

The other time we'd gone to dinner at their townhouse, I'd wanted my dad to show Gwen his den upstairs but the elevator I'd had put in for them was temporarily out of order, and since his battle cry in his retired years was, "Stairs go first," his hip didn't want to make the effort.

But now, since the elevator was working, he took her on the tour.

Gwen immediately gaped at the bicycle hanging down from the ceiling, one of George Grooves's prized possessions. He unhooked the bike from the contraption that held it, and applied the kick stand to station it upright on the floor. The bicycle was more than sixty years old but it gleamed like new, although it didn't resemble any bike you'd see today.

The frame was a sturdy bright green. A white sheepskin cover was over the seat. It had white sidewall balloon tires, chrome fenders, and a chrome chain guard. Front-wheel brakes on the handlebars. There were white rubber handlegrips with hotdog leather streamers coming out of the ends. Yellow and red reflector lights front and back, and a white rubber mud flap on the rear fender.

"This here is a Cromer's Ace with all the trimmings," my dad said. "It was my junior high school transportation. It would get me from 3105 College Avenue to E. M. Daggett Junior High, and anywhere else I wanted to go. His mother, Alma Louise Patterson, the woman downstairs, would sit right here side-saddle on this front bar, and get pumped to the Parkway Theater on Saturdays—that's when movies was worth going to—or to the Griddle for a hamburger, or to Whitley's Drugstore to see if the new *Photoplay* magazine had come in yet. I'm sure there's antique bicycle collectors who'd like to have this, but it ain't for sale."

The room was full of objects that wouldn't mean anything to anyone else. Sets of his old golf clubs that had once stormed the public layouts. MacGregor MT irons, Wilson Foremaster woods. Old and new putters standing in corners—the Cash-in, the Bullseye, the Armour Iron Master. Old letter sweaters and jackets from Paschal High and TCU. Autographed footballs and basketballs. Some of the golf trophies I'd won in my youth. Stacks of old *Life* magazines, old football magazines. The heavy old brass-trimmed cash register from the dry-cleaning business. Framed photos on the walls of my folks on vacation in Destin, Florida; Ruidoso, New Mexico; Yellowstone National Park; and on their Alaska cruise.

Gwen picked up an old steel army helmet off a table.

She grinned. "This what you wore when you killed gooks?"

Draped on the back of a chair at a table was a ragged olive drab jacket. On the shoulder sleeve was the blue-and-white diagonal-striped patch of the 3rd Infantry Division.

George Grooves said, "When I went to Korea I was supposed to be in supply or transportation—some such thing—but I wound up in a combat unit with an M1 in my hands. I'm proud to say I served under General James Van Fleet. He was a tough sumbitch, a field commander under Patton in World War Two. He'd have killed ever' gook in North Korea if our politicians had let him. Paved the place over and put 7-Elevens on every corner—and right now today you wouldn't see the goose-steppin' Commie bastards on CNN."

Gwen said, "Eisenhower must be your favorite president, huh?"

"Harry Truman."

"Really?" She looked surprised.

"He dropped the Big Mamoo on Tojo's ass."

"There is that. You *do* know Truman was a Democrat?"

"I do. But that's when Democrats was statesmen instead of hamheaded socialists and saboteurs."

"Interesting you don't pick Eisenhower."

"I liked Ike. But when he was in the office, my experience was that the banks wouldn't loan a man money unless he was rich to begin with."

"What did you think of Kennedy?"

"Cuber."

" '*Cuber*'? That's it?"

"Cuber and Marilyn Monroe."

"What about LBJ?"

"Biggest crook that never got caught."

"He was a Texan!"

"That was an unfortunate accident."

"Nixon?"

"Small-time crook. Deserved to get caught."

"Ford."

"Pardoned the small-time crook."

"Carter."

"Hostages . . . no Olympics . . . blamed America's problems on the two-martini lunch. He was a joke."

"Reagan."

"He outspent the Commies, sent 'em limpin' to the dugout, brought down the Wall."

"Bush."

"Most decent man ever sat in the office . . . spent a lifetime serving his country. Could have killed more ragheads, is all."

"Dare I mention Clinton?"

"I'm under doctor's orders not to discuss him."

"Little Bush."

"Went after the terrorist cruds, restored pride in the military, captured the Big Raghead."

"Feel good about the future, do you?"

"The future belongs to you, little lady. I've had mine. But my people will do what they can to see you don't wind up with that pretty face of yours hid behind a veil."

In general, I scored it another successful evening with my folks.

# 47

There's a scene I never grow tired of watching on the old-movie channel. It's the moment in every romantic comedy where two smart dames in a supper club lob wisecracks at each other over this nattily dressed guy with a pompadour who carries a cigarette case and doesn't work for a living even though it's the depth of the Depression.

When I was a younger movie nut, as opposed to the mature movie nut I am now, I used to think it would be fun to be that guy. Have Irene Dunne go to bat for you against the wealthy snob lady in the silly hat. Nothing to do but select your natty attire every day and go sit around somewhere and smoke cigarettes.

But I came to conclude that it might not have been that much fun after I listened more closely to my folks talking about how central air conditioning wasn't too plentiful back then, or even that reliable.

The thought crept into my mind again the day I finally arranged for my two favorite ladies to meet. I took Gwen and Alleene Simmons to lunch at Colonial Country Club. Gwen and Alleene were both Irene Dunne to me. There wasn't a Gail what's-her-name in the room. Gail Patrick, that's it.

Besides that, no man in Fort Worth would ever carry a cigarette case. Not unless he was a zipper-grabber who liked to eat dinner at the Greyhound bus station.

We lunched in the Cork Room at a smoking table where you can look out on the golf course. I nodded at people I knew at other tables—wives in exercise togs, tennis togs, men in business suits, men dressed for golf.

A member dropped by the table to tell me I'd made him proud at the

British Open. He said he couldn't understand how that lightweight Englishman ever won shit. Happy Pangburn. Whatever his name is.

When's the PGA, he asked?

Two weeks, I said.

Would I be there?

What a question. It was the year's last major. But maybe it went with the time of year. August. Hot and dreary. Football season arriving. Pennant races heating up. The PGA Championship ranks fourth in prestige compared to the other majors, which is unfortunate. The PGA at least is the championship of something—the Professional Golfers' Association of America. Just as our Open is the championship of the U.S. Golf Association. Just as the British Open is the championship of the Royal and Ancient Golf Club of St. Andrews, which is the governing body of golf everywhere but in the USA. Most people don't realize it but the year's other major, the Masters, isn't the championship of anything. The Masters has simply carved out a place for itself as a Grand Slam event through the beauty of the Augusta National course on TV and what Bobby Jones has meant to the history of the game.

The PGA began in 1916 and was unique because it was the only match-play major, and because of all the Walter Hagens, Byron Nelsons, Sam Sneads, and Ben Hogans who won it at match play. But then it lost favor with the press when it switched to stroke play in 1958 in order to get on network television, and it's been striving ever since to regain the stature it once held. Jack Nicklaus did his part by winning it five times, taking his first one in '63 and his last one in '80, and Lee Trevino, Gary Player, and Tiger Woods have helped by becoming multiple winners, but it still suffers in comparison to the other three majors because it's played in August.

Which doesn't mean I wouldn't choose to win just one PGA over a half dozen Bay Hill Invitationals presented by Cooper Tires.

No, I wasn't about to miss the year's last major, I told the member.

He told me to keep my head down.

I said I'd be endeavoring to feather my irons and nestle my wedges.

From elsewhere around the room I couldn't help sensing the unpleasant stares of members I didn't know. I figured they were thinking, "How can that guy be with those two beautiful women? He's not even an anchorman."

I was naturally proud to be with two beautiful women, but I didn't get to do much but watch them eat their salads for lunch, watch them smoke, and listen as they discussed workers comp, payroll taxes, health insurance, liability protection, operating overhead, and all the other things that add up to the fact that although they owned their own businesses, they spent most of their time working for the fucking government.

"This is your basic bonding," I said. "This is good."

They dismissed me with glances and plowed ahead with their thoughts on late deliveries, license renewals, expensive repairs, endless paperwork.

They traded horror stories about dealing with help.

Gwen said where she lived, if the surf was up, she'd lose another sales person. The girl might want to come back in the future, depending on how it was going with her suntan.

Alleene said the thing about the catering business, you never knew when a cook or a prep person was going to show up for work with Hepatitis B or a stab wound from a scuffle at home.

Gwen said, "In California, I'm better off with pale people. They won't have a beach volleyball game they want to be excused for."

Alleene said, "I'm partial to struggling students who want to be actors, singers, and dancers. They live four to an apartment, and they're total mercenaries—lot of energy."

Making an effort to contribute, I said, "California has more Gwyneth Paltrows than Fort Worth does."

They both squinted at me, and said, "What . . . ?"

A little later, when the babes were done with their bonding, it seemed safe for me to ask Alleene a question.

"What do you hear about Cheryl lately? I only inquire out of fear."

Gwen cut in. "She's the shit-fuck lady, right?"

"Hmm huh," Alleene replied with a glint.

Gwen explained that she'd listened to a message from Cheryl on my answering machine.

"I never hear from her," Alleene said. "She left me back on the trail a long time ago. I understand she's doing very well. Somebody told me she bought a million-plus home in that gated community over in River Crest. Or maybe it's Westover Hills—I never know where River Crest stops and Westover starts. I've been in one of those homes. They have great views. Off the back terrace you can see Omaha."

Alleene passed along a bit of gossip about Cheryl she'd heard from catering a luncheon for west side ladies. It seems Cheryl was now going out with Frody Latimer, a short, puffy sap in his sixties that nobody took seriously. Everybody knew Frody lived on a piddling inheritance. For years he'd traded on the fact that he was kin to Albert Hamilton Latimer, one of the original signers of Texas' declaration of independence in 1836. Frody liked to disappear on weekends and return wearing a neckbrace, a wrist bandage, or limping along with a cane. He'd claim he'd been injured in a polo match in San Antonio or Boca Raton. But everybody knew that if he'd been injured, it must have been from playing Ping-Pong with young boys. The west side ladies agreed that it would be fitting if this Cheryl person married Frody Latimer, thinking he was rich and socially important. Nor would they be surprised in the least if Frody Latimer tried to marry the Cheryl person—he'd always been looking for a meal ticket.

"Love a success story," I said.

Near the end of lunch, Alleene asked Gwen if she was going to the PGA in Detroit. Gwen said she hadn't decided. She'd been away from her business for three weeks and needed to get home and see if her partner had burned it down.

"I'm sure I'll wind up at the PGA," Gwen said. "I'll have two guys in it. This one and my son."

"That must be exciting for you," Alleene said. "Having a talented son and watching him do good stuff."

"I'm a nervous wreck watching, but it *is* fun, yes."

Alleene said, "Gwen, I feel like I've met a new friend, so . . . I hope you don't mind if I ask you a personal question?"

"Not at all," Gwen said. "I feel like I've met a new friend too."

"What exactly are your intentions toward my ex-husband?"

Gwen laughed. "I'm crazy about him."

"I'm glad," Alleene said. "He's never had a good lady."

"He had you."

"We were both too young at the time—and after me, of course, came the cur dogs."

"I have to tell you," Gwen said. "This is so amazing. You guys staying close friends after you were divorced. I mean, I think it's great. But it doesn't happen everywhere. Believe me, it doesn't happen in California. I may go to work for my ex-husband one of these days, but if I do, it will be for my son . . . my future . . . and a grotesque amount of money. It won't mean I like the devious asshole."

"It *is* unusual, I suppose," Alleene said. "Maybe it's just Fort Worth. People seem to hang on tighter to their memories around here."

"May I say something?" I said.

*"No."*

They said it at the same time.

# 48

The book from Irv Klar came with the last batch of junk mail that arrived before I left to have my ankles taped, put on the pads, and don my cleats for the PGA Championship, at Oakland Hills in Detroit.

A note from Irv was included in the package:

"I hammered this one out pretty quick. I wanted to reach the stores in time for pigskin season. Timing is vital in my business. By the way, it's opening third on the bestseller list. Best wishes."

Nothing about tough luck at the British Open, but nice going, you finished second, old buddy. I'm sure if I'd won the thing, Irv would have said something about a book proposal while the stove's hot. British Open winner tells all and cures your slice once and for all—by B. J. Grooves with Irving Klar. Not that I'd be interested.

Irv's latest effort was called *Hike It to the Hebe*.

I did stare at the title for a moment.

The subtitle was *The Story of Norman "Noodgie" Goldstein, America's Greatest Jewish Running Back*.

The book jacket informed me that Norman "Noodgie" Goldstein had toted the leather for Pitt in the early '30s, then for the Green Bay Packers, and then for Alcatraz after he was sent to prison for income tax evasion.

That was all I needed to know. But before I tossed it, I glanced at the photographs inside. The one I liked best was Noodgie at a night club wearing a tuxedo, chewing on a cigar, and flashing a big grin with his arm around a platinum blonde, who was identified as Sally Rand, the fan dancer. Noodgie was also wearing a leather football helmet.

---

When the call came from the Schlosshotel Vier Jahreszeiten in Hamburg, Germany, Cynthia did all the talking—Buddy was in his blue silk robe in the middle of his room-service dinner.

Cynthia first explained why they were in Germany. She'd wanted to revisit one of her old haunts from her flight-attendant days with Delta. Her route had actually been from Atlanta to Munich, not Hamburg, but that was another story, she said.

She allowed that as much as they liked Hamburg, a very chic city, they'd soon be going to the Villa d'Este in Cernobbio, Italy, where they had reserved one of the most desirable suites in all of Europe—their balcony would practically hang over Lake Como—but if they were disappointed with the frescoes and the Persian carpets at the Villa d'Este, they'd simply move to the Grand Hotel Villa Serbelloni, which was close by and practically sat *in* Lake Como.

"Frescoes," I said. "You worked with a lot of those at Delta."

Ignoring me, she said Buddy was sure I'd understand that he didn't want to be interrupted during his dinner of pork shanks with sauerkraut, green beans, and new potatoes—and lately he'd been trying to remember how many holes were on a golf course. Was it twelve, fourteen, or sixteen?

Funny old Buddy and Cynthia.

She did have important news, which was why they called.

It seems that Sven and Matt, her sons by Knut Thorssun, once known as the unruly little shits, had gotten into trouble again, and right on the brink of entering college. It had happened while I was in London or I might have read about it.

Knut had rushed to Vermont to handle the situation, and apparently he had taken care of it. The boys would not have to go to jail, and they would still be allowed to enroll at Mt. Gidley.

"I'm sorry the little shits don't have to do time," Cynthia said. "I think it would have done Sven and Matt some good—and Lord knows it would have been a good thing for society at large."

Smoothing things over with the Mt. Gidley police and the university and the families, she said, had cost Knut something like $3 million, but the asshole could afford it.

I said I wondered if she could put her glass of wine down long enough to tell me what had happened?

Well, what happened was, Sven and Matt had gone to Mt. Gidley to look around before they enrolled, and while they were looking around the town and the campus they came upon two unoccupied electric golf carts. The golf carts, it was later learned, belonged to the workers at an apartment complex that was undergoing repairs.

Naturally, Sven and Matt stole the carts and decided to have a race.

It may or may not have been anyone's fault that when they reached the top of a steep hill and started down, going full speed, they both lost control. Suddenly, the carts were going about fifty miles an hour toward a two-story building.

The boys were alert enough to leap to safety only seconds before the two carts crashed through the big plate-glass window on the ground floor of Mrs. Tate's Fully Licensed Day-Care Center.

Well, six children, ages seven through ten, and two adults, wound up in the hospital with injuries. It was those two adults and the families of the six children and Mrs. Tate that Knut had been forced to money-whip in order to stop their cussing, screeching, and threats of legal action.

Doing a reasonably good imitation of the dumb-ass Swede she'd once been married to, Cynthia said, "Those two boys, Sven and Matt, by golly darn. To be sure, they are a couple of ring-tailed tooters."

It was good to know Sven and Matt hadn't yet killed anyone in this life, but I considered it bigger and better news that Grady Don Maples had finally scooped a victory on our Tour, his first.

I rooted him home on TV before catching an early evening flight to Detroit for the PGA.

Grady Don won by four strokes at Firestone Country Club in Akron, Ohio, in a tournament that had been known for over three decades as the World Series of Golf but for the past seven or eight years had been known as the WGC-NEC Invitational.

He called it "the alphabet classic." Grady Don confessed to me when he arrived at Oakland Hills that he understood WGC stood for World Golf Championships, which evidently meant something to somebody somewhere, but he still didn't know what NEC stood for. Neither did I, to be honest.

He was a million-two richer after shooting a last-round 67 on Firestone South for a 268, 12 under. Sponsorships on our Tour shift with the winds of the economy.

I said to Grady Don he should think of it as having won the World Series of Golf, a name that once meant something to the public. He said he'd probably think of it as paying off the house in Southlake.

There must have been those watching TV who thought Grady Don's crowning moment came on the 17th green. That's where he rapped a thirty-foot birdie putt too softly for it to ever reach the cup, and eight or ten inches off line to the right. Grady Don had slowly followed the putt on its path, giving it the finger every step of the way.

"I wasn't giving that putt the finger," he said on the practice range at Oakland Hills Monday when I kidded him about it. "I was thinking about our football team this season. I was sayin' we're number one."

Grady Don and Jerry Grimes and I, and dozens of the other players, including Scott Pritchard, were staying at a Marriott near Oakland Hills. I'd reserved a suite—Gwen was coming Wednesday and I knew how much she liked comfort. It turned out to be the bridal suite. I found this interesting because Gwen and I weren't the ones getting married at the PGA that week.

Knut Thorssun and Vashtine Ulberg were.

# 49

Here was my question: Would you take your chick to one of those Las Vegas chapels and have the wedding ceremony conducted by a guy in an orange suit with hair that looks like cumulus clouds, or would you and the chick rather make up your own vows, invite the public, and get married on an outdoor soundstage at a golf tournament?

"Those are two swell choices," Grady Don said.

Knut and Vashtine voted for the soundstage.

The soundstage was in the PGA's tented village. The tented village was spread out on part of the other eighteen-hole golf course at Oakland Hills, the North, the "sister course" to the tougher and better known South, which is always used when the club plays host to a major. The South was originally designed by Donald Ross in 1917, but it was Robert Trent Jones who doctored it into the "monster" Ben Hogan brought to its knees in 1951.

I'd never heard the North course at Oakland Hills accused of being a challenging layout. In my travels I'd played all of the best sister courses at one time or another—Winged Foot East, Pinehurst No. 4, Baltusrol Upper, Olympic Club Ocean, Medinah No. 1, Oak Hill West—and I can tell you they work better as golf courses than they do as parking lots.

The soundstage was erected for evening concerts during the PGA—entertainment for the public patrons, the no-clubhouse throngs. It was next door to the merchandise tent—the Golf Shop, they called it—and a large outdoor picnic area with tables and benches, and across a broad spectator walkway from the private hospitality tents.

The wedding took place at twilight on Wednesday, the day before the PGA started.

The amplifying system was of such excellent quality, we stood off to the side and on the last row among the two thousand people who attended the wedding, most of them soggy with sweat from having been on the course all day following practice rounds. It was decidedly August.

I was standing with Gwen, Grady Don, and Jerry. I noticed some of the other contestants in the crowd—Cheetah Farmer, Chance Minter, Hugh McAllister, even Phil Mickelson. A scattering of wives of other players were in evidence.

Gwen had arrived that afternoon from Orlando, where she'd spent some time doing mom-decorates-the-townhouse things for Scott. The kid had been practicing at the PGA like the rest of us.

Scott wasn't at the wedding. At this moment he was dining in downtown Detroit with Dad the Agent and Tricia Hurt, Dad the Agent's newest client, the fifteen-year-old savior of women's golf.

Rick Pritchard was a shrewd operator, I'd give him that. One of the first deals he'd lined up for Tricia Hurt, space-alien teen bitch, was for her to be a broadcaster, a foot soldier, for CBS on the PGA telecast.

What did it matter to CBS that Tricia couldn't possibly know anything about the PGA Championship or Oakland Hills? She was young and attractive and had "name recognition."

Anne Marie Sprinkle wasn't present. If she'd been there with Pocahontas and the Kodiak bears, everybody would have known it. I commented that it was good of her not to intrude on the wedding.

Gwen said, "If she's serious about the 'white Christian' business, she'll lose credibility. I don't like to see her go off-message."

"Off-message," I said. "Is that far from here?"

You could safely say that curiosity seekers far outnumbered wedding fans at the Knut-Vashtine ceremony.

There were two warmup groups. This was a rock concert? If my vote had been the only one that counted, I would have left the minute the first warmup group came on stage, but Gwen and the guys insisted on staying to listen to the four pathetic skeletons who called themselves Stepping in Shit.

They played two devastating thunderstorms and got off.

Next came the other warmup group. Three chalk-white, diseased-looking punks on guitars and a skinny vampire girl clanging cymbals.

They wore white chef's hats and aprons, and the name of the group was the same as the title of their big hit, "Spit in the Food."

Their big hit may well have been the number they played, although it sounded more like a tornado ripping through small towns in Kansas.

Knut and Vashtine finally appeared, coming out of separate wings of the soundstage. Knut was in black tie and tails, Vashtine in a flowing white virginal wedding gown. They met at the center of the stage, joined hands, and bowed to the crowd. They were greeted by whoops and applause.

Vashtine took the mike and said she first wanted to thank her good friends, Stepping in Shit and Spit in the Food, for providing the entertainment for the occasion. "Vasn't dey vunnerfull? Ein fockin tell you for sure!"

The bride said she wanted to thank her other celebrity friends for their presence today. Up there in the Met Life blimp right now, overhead, looking down on us, were Rocky Stunner and Spicey Gates, stars of the new CBS drama *Yesterday's Tomorrow*. And soon, if not any moment now, she said, there would be a fly-by of a private jet in which a very close friend from the entertainment world, the talented rapper Snot Fishy Poot Stain, would interrupt his busy schedule to glance down on us and smile as the plane passed over.

We caught Jerry Grimes looking up.

Vashtine's own musicians slouched onto the stage, and she went about introducing them and giving a short thumbnail. I don't believe anyone listened any closer than we did.

Gwen said, "This wedding ranks high on the list of bad ideas."

"Worse than Vanilla Coca-Cola?" I said.

"Maybe not that bad."

Suggestions were batted back and forth among us.

The wedding didn't come close to making our final list of bad ideas. In no particular order, the results were:

Vanilla Coca-Cola
Fish tacos
Rap
Synchronized swimming
Foam-rubber pillows
Miniskirts with white boots

Long sideburns on guys
The Bowl Championship Series
Modern art
Green pasta
Designated hitter
Low carb
Talk radio
Belly putter
Globalization

As Knut nodded in agreement, Vashtine announced to the crowd that they had spoken to God and had learned they did not require the services of a minister to be married. God had told them they could make up their own vows, which they had done, by golly, to be sure.

As best I recall, their ceremony went like this:

Vashty: "Noots, my lovey dovey, you have winnen my heart, and Ein bam committink to you, mine bliffsul trothen."

Noots: "Vashty, I pledge to you the faithfulness of my skin and fibers, and I say let us romp over the peaks and valleys of our bodies, golly darn."

Vashty: "To be sure, Cupid has smitten us head over heels, and I say to you, Noots, we vill go stompin' through the berries and leaves and not mindin' dat rainin vit storms of life—praise dem apostle fockers."

Noots: "It is so, my beloved Vashty, as you can see, I too am the passionate one, and it is for the dirt and flowers and trees of the world that I say to you I must drink all the juices of your path, praise the Jesus guy."

Vashty: "My complete ladylove is what I dumpen on you, Noots. May you sleepin on mine doorsteppen forever. You have wipen away der sadness of my life, which vas empty as trees in Svenska vinter."

It went on like that for a half hour, I'm guessing. Maybe longer. I know it was still going on—we could hear it in the distance—as we drifted away with the rest of the crowd.

# 50

All through the first round of the PGA when I was shooting the speed limit, your basic 70, and parking myself on the scoreboard at even par, three off the lead, I occasionally thought about how Oakland Hills had suffered from acute schizophrenia—to haul out a word I wouldn't try to spell by myself.

Eight majors had been played there before this one. Six U.S. Opens and two PGAs. Dating back to 1924. Four of those winners made sense at the time. They were giants. I refer to Ralph Guldahl in '37, Ben Hogan in '51, Gene Littler in '61, and Gary Player in '72. But Oakland Hills had produced just as many off-brand winners. Flukes. I refer to Cyril Walker in '24, David Graham in '79, Andy North in '85, and Steve Jones in '96. Andy North did save the world from T. C. Chen, who wasn't even well known in Taiwan. You had to give Andy that.

There was no logical explanation for the layout's split personality. All I knew was, I wouldn't have been embarrassed to join the fluke parade.

Ralph Guldahl deserved to be ranked with the giants. I explained why to Grady Don and Jerry.

Guldahl was a tall, stoop-shouldered, slow-playing Texan from Dallas who swung at the ball with a caddie-dip. Kind of hurled his body at the ball. He claimed he didn't know what he was doing—"I just play golf." But during a stretch of four years, from '36 through '39, he was the greatest player in the world. He climbed out of the box ahead of his fellow Texans and onetime high school rivals from Fort Worth. Couple of guys named Byron Nelson and Ben Hogan.

Guldahl, whose hair was long and dark—he often combed it between shots—won three straight Western Opens from '36 through '38 (that's when the Western was considered a major), two straight U.S. Opens, in

'37 and '38, and the Masters in '39 after finishing second the two previous years. Six majors in four years, is what it was.

But Guldahl made the mistake of writing an instruction book, *Groove Your Golf*. Bobby Jones wrote the foreword for it. Guldahl then made the bigger mistake of studying the sequence photos in the book.

Flipping those pages made him start to "think" about his swing. The result was, his game completely disappeared. And so did Ralph Guldahl at the age of only thirty—off the Tour, into the insurance business, and eventually into the obscurity of a club pro's job in Tarzana, California.

"What's the moral?" Grady Don said. "Don't read or write?"

When I shot the speed limit again in Friday's second round, thanks to an old Wilson 8802 putter that believed it was an Armour, my even-par 140 put me in fifth place, still two off the lead. But I was a presence.

You couldn't say the same for Knut Thorssun, the newlywed. The day after his wedding night, which was the first round, he shot a 79. Then Vashtine left town for a gig, and I observed Knut standing by the gallery rope on the putting green having an intimate chat with Pookie Steekley, Claude's adventurous wife. Knut then withdrew, pleading illness, and he and Pookie hadn't been seen since.

But back to me, the presence. The trick was to try to be a presence late Sunday afternoon when there was little doubt in my mind that the last four holes at Oakland Hills would decide the PGA Championship.

The last four holes at Oakland Hills were flat-out tough. They didn't have a nickname, like Amen Corner in Augusta, or Abalone Corner at Pebble Beach, but Grady Don tried to come up with one.

He and Jerry Grimes barely made the cut at 148 and blamed 15 through 18 for making their lives hell. After the second round, Grady Don said, "I don't want to brag, but I parred two of the ho bitches today."

My best guess was that Ho Bitches might not stick as a nickname with the Oakland Hills members.

The 15th is a tree-lined 400-yard par-4, dogleg left, with a bunker in the awkward middle of the fairway, right at the bend of it. The green is well bunkered and shaped like an upside-down saucer. For two days, I'd Hogan'd up short of the fairway bunker off the tee, and jumped on a six-iron to the green, and gotten away with it for two pars.

The next hole is one of America's finest. It's a 406-yard par-4, sharp dogleg right, with a big pond you have to deal with on your tee ball as well as your approach. Drive it a little too far right and you're in the rough behind two big willow trees or in the pond. On the second shot, you can be short of the green and in the water or a tad wide to the right and in the water. I'd been creeping the drive into the fairway and going with an eight-iron to the green, and so far I'd stayed dry.

The 200-yard par-3 17th has six bunkers guarding the green, and two of them are so deep, you can't see the flag if you're standing in the bottom. From the tee, you're looking at a green sitting considerably higher up than where you are, and a long ridge divides the putting surface into two bowls. If you wind up in the wrong bowl, just take your three-putt bogey and move on. That's what I did in the first two rounds.

The 18th hole is an absolute killer par-4, a long dogleg right. The Oakland Hills members still play it as a par-5.

Back in 1924, at the National Open, where the obscure Cyril Walker stole the trophy from Bobby Jones, the 18th played as a 465-yard par-5, hickory being what it was. In the '37 U.S. Open, where Ralph Guldahl nipped Sam Snead at the finish, the hole had been lengthened to a 537-yard par-5, the steel shaft being what it was. It became a narrow par-4 of 460 yards for Hogan's Open, and it's been a par-4 for the pros ever since, but it had now been lengthened to 497 yards, titanium and the two-piece ball being what they are.

William Ben Hogan, not Benjamin—iceman, hawk, bantam, club designer, near-fatal-car-wreck survivor, oilman, Texas icon—went about experiencing a flood of emotions on the last four holes at Oakland Hills in the notorious '51 U.S. Open.

That Open was, by all accounts, the major that presented the competitors with the tightest fairways, deepest rough, and speediest greens ever conceived. Hogan got to know the four holes intimately.

He double-bogeyed the 18th in the first round when he drove in the rough then three-putted, and he double-bogeyed the 15th in the third round when he tried to skirt the fairway bunker and wound up in the trees on the left. But he managed some revenge on both holes in the last round.

In the last round he drove short of the bunker in the fairway on 15, then slow-faded a three-iron in there five feet from the flag for a birdie. And on the last hole, he nailed a solid drive, positioning himself for the perfect six-iron and the twenty-foot birdie putt he coaxed into the cup for the newsreels.

Hogan's three-under 67 that afternoon is still regarded as the greatest last round in a major ever, and for two large reasons. One, he did it on a day when the average score of the field was 78, and two, he did it on the toughest track ever devised by man, ghoul, or Robert Trent Jones.

The two pars I saved there on Thursday and Friday by getting up and down out of the front left bunker weren't likely to be discussed at length in any of the history books.

It had occurred to me that one of the reasons I might have been playing well at the ripe old age of forty-four in the last major of the year was because I hadn't seen Jarvis Phillip W. Burchcroft around anywhere among the rules wizards.

I was relaxing in the locker room on Friday after my round with Grady Don, having a beer, when I found out why Mr. Rules wasn't anywhere to be seen.

Dace Fackle, the executive director of the U.S. Golf Association, came wandering in and dropped the news on us.

It so happened that Jarvis Phillip W. Burchcroft was in the hospital and badly in need of a liver transplant or he would be departing this life in a matter of weeks, if not days.

His wife, Dalilla, the refrigerator heiress, had rushed him to the Mayo Clinic in Jacksonville, Florida, where he was now waiting for a suitable liver to be donated.

Dace Fackle was carrying a big greeting card, two feet by two feet. He was in the process of asking as many contestants as he could round up to sign the card and offer words of encouragement if they wished. He would see that the card reached Jarvis.

"Jarvis has meant a lot to the game," he said.

"He's certainly meant a lot to my game," I said.

Well, I didn't want Jarvis Phillip W. Burchcroft to die, for Christ sake, no matter how much he'd screwed me. I signed the card.

Grady Don wouldn't sign it, however.

"I don't even know the guy," Grady Don said.

Dace Fackle shrugged, started to move on.

"He's waiting for somebody to die so he can have the liver?" Grady Don said to Dace Fackle.

"That is the situation, yes."

Grady Don said, "Tell him this is a hell of a coincidence. I'm waiting for a black guy to die so I can have his dick."

# 51

My swing kept me on the practice range longer than I'd expected and this caused us to be a little late for the festivities Friday night, but Anne Marie Sprinkle was still at the microphone on the soundstage in the tented village when we arrived, and she was shouting, "My friends, I ask you this: How many Oriental transvestites are members of private clubs in America today where the corporate pigs play golf?"

"None!" the crowd responded.

"Correct! And how many repressed and dominated Muslims would you say are members of private country clubs in the United States of Corporate-Pig America?"

"None!" the crowd hollered.

Crowd might be too generous a word. I estimated there were maybe thirty people you'd consider to be part of Anne Marie Sprinkle's group, and this included the two beat-up old drag queens, Sister Janelle and Sister Emajean. Even so, the protestors were greatly outnumbered by the police, the security staff, and the press.

Sister Janelle and Sister Emajean's names were printed in blue letters on their orange shirts. Their faces were painted blue and orange. They wore orange tights, blue capes, and black patent-leather boots, and they mingled among everyone, offering pieces of candy from a box of Godiva chocolates.

We immediately ran into Ellen Wheeler, the Houston writer. After I introduced her to Gwen, she brought us up to speed.

"She's not going to commit suicide," Ellen said. "She opened up with that announcement."

"Well, heck, why are we here?" I said.

Gwen elbowed me.

Ellen Wheeler said Annie Marie Sprinkle told the crowd she had given it careful thought and concluded that a knife or a gun would have left too messy a photo-op. Even trying to drown herself in the pond on 16 might not have worked. One of the despicable "white Christians" would probably have jumped in and saved her. It would have been futile. So she'd talked it over at length with the voice of her inner self, and decided that she should continue fighting the war on behalf of oppressed minorities as a living person instead of a martyr.

"So I swear to you now," Anne Marie was saying—Pocahontas on one side of her and two Kodiak bears on the other—"when you see the poor immigrant laborer, the laborer who mows lawns for white evangelical Christians, and he's looking despondent because he's denied the right to play a round of golf at Los Angeles Country Club . . . I'll be there!"

"Yes!" Crowd deal.

"And when you see the illegal alien from Mozambique, who has only come here for a better life but can't find work because he doesn't speak English—let me finish—when you see this humble person refused a chance to play a mere nine holes at Dallas Country Club, I'll be there!"

"All right!"

"And when you see the Cuban drug dealer fresh out of prison, who was only incarcerated for trying to feed his family, a man who only wants to learn how to play the game that Tiger Woods plays, but white corporate-pig Christians refuse him the right to play a round of golf at the Seminole Club in Palm Beach, Florida, I'll be there!"

"Go, Anne Marie!"

"And when you see the two disenfranchised lesbians humbled and in tears because they've been denied the right to enter the Pro-Am at Pebble Beach, I'll be there!"

I squeezed on Gwen. "Is this off-message enough for you?"

"I believe so."

"Tom Joad," I said.

"Who?"

"Henry Fonda."

"What—?"

"It's *The Grapes of Golf.*"

"What are you talking about?"

"I'll explain later," I said, and we left.

# 52

As most people who dwell in the land of golfdom were aware, the crowd-pleasing stud-bubba cupcake after two rounds of the PGA was Scott Pritchard, he of the innocent good looks and the tee ball that looks like it's brought to you by NASA.

The awesome sight of Scott launching a drive has often urged Grady Don Maples to say, "Houston, there ain't no problem."

Scott's rounds of 70 and 68 had given him the lead by one stroke over Cheetah Farmer, Dunn Matson, and Stump Bowen, and by two over me and Madonna Els. Among other things, this meant that my gallery would be shy one female in the third round, and maybe for the rest of the PGA.

I assured Gwen that I understood. She was free to follow, cheer, and kick her kid's ball out of the rough with her foot if no marshal was looking.

"I have no intention of trying to hide my excitement," she said.

"I don't expect you to," I said. "Family comes first in time of war and majors. A mother's work is never done when it comes to golf."

"I should write those down," she said, with lip.

How to get her back to my gallery?

Well, how about I strap a light-running Flagstaff, Arizona, on the joint? Don't forget Winona . . . Kingman, Barstow, San Bernardino.

Talking about a Route 66. Double sizzicks. The wheelchairs.

I didn't look at anything but fairways and greens all day. One or two fringes. Must have been that secret I'd learned on the practice range the night before. Get comfortable and hit it. I was two under by the time I reached the Ho Bitches, and when I routine-parred the 15th, birdied the 16th and 17th, and drained a ten-footer to save par at the 18th, Mitch bent over, slapped his knee, and started laughing.

He said, "B.J., you done whip this place like a fishin'-pole lawyer from Texas whip a tall-building lawyer from New York City."

Ellen Wheeler grabbed me as I emerged from the scorer's tent. She'd been inside the ropes with some other writers over the last three holes.

"Quick," she said breathlessly. "Something for me, all mine, before you go to the interview. Today's round."

Smiling, I said, "Oh, I just went out there today to try to nurture myself and achieve harmony in this hectic world."

*"All right!"* She screamed with laughter, and ran off through the trees toward the press tent.

Scott Pritchard, possible future son-in-law, hadn't done badly himself. He shot a handy 69 for his adoring gallery of 20,000, plus mom, but it left him one behind his mom's boyfriend.

History tells us there once were big souvenir buttons to be seen in the galleries that said, "Arnie's Army," for Palmer, and "Lee's Fleas," for Trevino, and "Ben's Wrens," for Crenshaw, when he was single.

Now there were suddenly buttons to be seen on young girls at Oakland Hills that said, "Scott's Bods."

The top 10 on the scoreboard after fifty-four holes at the PGA read:

| | |
|---|---|
| Bobby Joe Grooves | 70-70-66–206 |
| Scott Pritchard | 70-68-69–207 |
| Cheetah Farmer | 69-70-70–209 |
| Dunn Matson | 70-69-71–210 |
| Stump Bowen | 70-69-72–211 |
| Ernie Els | 70-70-71–211 |
| Chance Minter | 71-70-70–211 |
| Claude Steekley | 72-70-70–212 |
| Phil Mickelson | 73-70-69–212 |
| Rainey Walters | 72-71-71–214 |

. . . . . . .

The golf fans who might have been wondering where Alfie Crangburn's name was in the list of scores for three days must have been disappointed to learn that the British Open champion hadn't entered. I'd read where he was still celebrating and could be found at the Hotel

Splendido in Portofino, Italy. I wondered if he had run across my friends Buddy and Cynthia.

I'd cleaned up and was selecting a frock for dinner when Smokey Barwood, live-wire agent, called to wish me luck and apologize for the fact that he couldn't be at Oakland Hills tomorrow—there was another pressing problem with Trapeze Cobb, his NBA client.

Trapeze Cobb was the Laker who'd beaten the rap on two rape charges back in April. But now he was in jail again and had been charged with kidnapping and raping Rachel Stafford, the good-looking criminal attorney, often seen on *Court TV*, who'd represented him in the first trial.

Rachel Stafford was going to testify that Trapeze came to her office and kidnapped her at gunpoint, kept her chained up for three days in the bedroom of his suite at the Beverly Royal Hotel, where he lived, and repeatedly raped her.

Further, Trapeze Cobb permitted a teammate, Smithsonian Wilson, to come over and have his way with her. Rachel said she wouldn't swear on a Bible that Smithsonian Wilson raped her—she kept passing out—but who else could the other dick have belonged to?

Rachel had been rescued by police after they'd found Trapeze drunk, stoned, and wandering around Rodeo Drive with nothing on but a pair of jockey shorts, dark glasses, and a straw hat.

Smokey said, "Trapeze says it wasn't rape because it was 'consexual.' That's what he thinks the word is. Listen, Bobby Joe. You watch cable TV. I hear there are lawyers on there all the time. I can use a name. Preferably a woman. And, just to be on the safe side, I'd rather she wasn't too good-looking . . . you know?"

"Good thinking," I said.

"Tempo, tomorrow," he said.

I said I'd take it under advisement.

# 53

The "family" dinner on Saturday night was Rick Pritchard's idea, and that's how he referred to it. He arranged it in a private room at a restaurant called Christopher & Gregory's that was next door to our hotel. I didn't want to go. Gwen didn't want to go. Scott didn't want to go. I don't believe Tricia Hurt wanted to go. So naturally we all went.

Rick showed up in a black suit, light blue shirt, silver tie—and makeup. He'd done a spot on local TV, discussing Tricia Hurt and the "bomberoo" impact she was going to have on the game of golf.

Tricia arrived with him. She wore tight jeans and a sleeveless blouse. She looked fresh and cute in that girl-who-plays-sports kind of way.

Tricia and I hadn't seen each other or spoken since Pinehurst. She seemed embarrassed for us to be in the same room. At first she acted like she wasn't sure whether to say hello to me or duck behind furniture.

I smiled at her to put her at ease and offered a handshake. What the hell. She hadn't hit the golf ball for me that day in the Open. And why make an enemy of somebody who was going to be president of CBS News before she graduated from high school?

She took my hand. "You're playing really good this week."

"It's the equipment. How do you like doing TV?"

She said, "I haven't done anything but walk around. I mean, like, there's this guy who talks to you on the headset and tells you to be ready, we're coming to you in five, but nothing ever happens. I couldn't have said more than two things on the air today."

"What two things did you tell the world?"

"I said, uh, 'He doesn't have a very good lie, Lanny.' I remember saying that . . . and I said something to Mr. Nantz, like, 'It's a five-iron.' I think that's what I said. I'll be with your group tomorrow. You and Scott."

"We'll be pleased to have you, Tricia. If I may ask, won't it be a comedown for you, going on the LPGA Tour after playing against the guys? Pardon me for sounding like a reporter."

"It was so cool, playing in your Open," she said. "But, like, I can't wait to go on our tour. I love to practice, I love to play golf, I love to compete. It's what I've been training for, working for. What I *don't* want to do is be something I'm *not*. Like, I don't want to have to wake up every morning and think, oh, my God, now I have to go out in public and be this person everybody wants me to be."

I said, "Just play golf and win, Tricia. All that other stuff will take care of itself. It's amazing how much personality and charm the press can attach to somebody because they win golf tournaments."

Tricia didn't act too happy to be with Rick Pritchard, and it was easy to see why after a while.

He couldn't keep his hands off of her. Squeezing, patting, touching, rubbing. Wherever there was bare skin. Forearm, upper arm, neck. But acting casual about it. Like it was harmless. Like Gwen and I were fools and wouldn't notice. It was sickening to watch. The asshole was in his forties, same as me, and to a fifteen-year-old girl that meant he might as well be eighty, but he was too dense to realize it, or too taken with himself to consider it.

Rick's second sin of the night was pre-ordering dinner for us.

I didn't know he'd done it until the first course was served. It was two patties of puffed rice crust—they looked like English muffins—with an overdose of wet spinach between them and warm maple syrup poured over everything. There was a name for whatever the deal was. Sounded like flute.

Rick said, "I inquired and discovered the chef here cooks cutting-edge French with Asian flavors."

I handed the dish back to the waiter, and said, "Pal, I don't go near maple syrup unless there's a waffle underneath it. Just bring me another martini rocks with four olives."

Tricia Hurt giggled, picked around at her plate. Gwen smiled to herself. Scott said, "Geeeahh, I'm so hungry, I'll eat anything," and devoured it.

When the curious-looking main course was placed in front of me I learned it was a "skewered squid" and "simmered oyster" salad with watermelon, pineapple, and green mango remoulade sauce.

This promptly extracted a hundred-dollar bill from my pocket. I put it in the waiter's hand with instructions to bring me a goddamn cheeseburger with French fries and a glass of iced tea with lemon and keep the fucking change.

"Make that two," Gwen said.

"Three," said Tricia Hurt.

All through dinner and coffee, Rick buried us in the carpet with talk about International Sports Talent. Its future, its hopes, its dreams.

Scott left first. Yawning.

Tricia was next. Rick's limo took her to wherever CBS was staying.

Rick asked Gwen and me to stay and have another cup of coffee, or an after-dinner drink—there was a business matter he wanted to discuss.

"Big day tomorrow," Rick said.

Gwen said, "I'm too nervous to talk about it."

"Relax, Gwenny," Rick said. "You can't lose. You have two dogs in the fight."

"I know," she said. "But whatever happens, I'm going to be happy one way, sad another."

"This is ridiculous," I said. "Scott and I aren't the only two people in the tournament. Jesus, there are *nine* players within six shots! Two of 'em are Ernie Els and Phil Mickelson, in case nobody's noticed. Anybody can win this thing tomorrow. A guy can go out early, put up a number, swoop the whole pot. It happens all the time."

"I hate tomorrow," Gwen said, and smoked.

"Very true, Bobby Joe," said Rick. "Nevertheless, the odds favor it coming down to you and Scotto. You're both looking sharp. If that turns out to be the situation, I believe there's something we should discuss in all seriousness."

He gave me a long look.

"What do you think it would be worth to you—financially—to win the PGA?" he asked. "Aside from the winner's purse, the prize money? Which is what—a million-four?"

"I haven't noticed," I said truthfully.

"What else would it be worth?"

"It's impossible to make an estimate. A five-year exemption on the

Tour, that's the big thing. My career would be set till I'm fifty and hit the Senior tour. I suppose my fee for outings would go up, and there'd be endorsements. Why?"

"Do you know how much it would be worth to Scott Pritchard? Twenty mill."

I stared at him.

"And twenty mill is just for starters," he said. "Think about that."

"I'm not sure I want to."

"Twenty mill, Groovo."

"I hope you're not getting at what I think you're getting at."

"We're just skating here. Once around the rink, maybe twice. You don't like the ice, we don't do couples only."

I looked down at the carpet, slowly smiled cynically, and said to him in a low voice, "You . . . miserable . . . fucking . . . asshole."

"*Au contraire*, sir," Rick said. "Allow me to think of myself as a practical and realistic fellow when it comes to commerce."

"What am I missing here?" Gwen said.

"I'll tell you what you're missing," I said. "Your ex-husband is suggesting that if it comes down to a contest between your son and me tomorrow, I should lob a couple of three-putts on Oakland Hills to make sure Scott wins. Go in the tank, in other words. For the sake of—I'm fairly certain I have this right—International Sports Talent."

Gwen glared at Rick, and shook her head with disgust.

Rick shrugged. "I'm a businessman."

She said, "Let me ask you something, Rick. When you were our fullback at SC, what would you have done if someone had offered you money—any amount of money—to fumble away a touchdown in the Rose Bowl and let Ohio State win the game? What would you have said?"

"Altogether different hypothetical, Gwenny."

"Oh, really?" Gwen said. "I only have one more thing to say to you, Rick Pritchard. It's something I should have said a long time ago. If you ever call me Gwenny again, I'm going to kick you so hard in the fucking nuts, you'll cough up your dick!"

She turned to me. "Did I say that right?"

"Almost. I'll have to check with Grady Don on it."

"Take me home, please."

"With pleasure, madam."

Walking to our hotel across the parking lot, I said, "I have to say I liked your exit. May I assume it's now a 'no' on going to work for International Sports Talent?"

"You bet!"

"Sounds good to me. I couldn't handle too many more nights of watching a grown man sniff around on Shirley Temple. I seem to recall Rick was going to pay you a half million a year, babe. That was an expensive speech you just made. Was it worth it?"

"Every penny," she said.

# 54

At the rear of the number 1 tee on the South course at Oakland Hills, with the monstrous old white clubhouse furnishing a backdrop, the Wanamaker Trophy was displayed on a table. It's the prize awarded annually to the PGA champion. The trophy was donated in 1916 by Mr. Rodman Wanamaker, a golf-loving gentleman who owned a highly successful and popular department store in New York City at the time, a store named, as luck would have it, Wanamaker's.

Scott and I were on the tee waiting our turn to go in the final round. Thousands of fans stretched out in front of us on both sides of the 1st fairway, a par-4 that didn't break your back. There's no scrapbook quality to the front nine on the South course. A bunch of solid holes, is all. The back nine was where the thrills and serious trouble lurked.

I'd already done the good-luck-handshake thing with Scott.

"This is some sight," I said. "This tee and the clubhouse there—it's what a major's supposed to look like, isn't it?"

"I guess," he said, glancing around.

Now I was standing with Mitch.

I said, "That trophy there. It's the biggest one of the four majors. You may or may not know this, but it's two and a half feet high, over two feet wide—handle to handle—and weighs close to thirty pounds."

Mitch gave me a look that said I probably should be thinking about something else.

"Did you ever hear about the time the trophy got lost?" I asked.

"No, but you gonna tell me."

I told him about Walter Hagen and the trophy. How the trophy disappeared after Hagen won the PGA for the fourth year in a row at match play in 1927—at Cedar Crest Country Club in Dallas, which is now a public course. Hagen's story was that he handed the trophy to a taxi driver to deliver to his hotel, but the trophy never made it there.

This meant there was no trophy to present to Leo Diegel, who won the PGA in 1928 and 1929, or Tommy Armour, the winner in 1930.

But in the fall of '30, three years after the trophy had mysteriously vanished, it was found by accident. Workers were rummaging through a warehouse in Detroit—right here in this city—and when they opened a leather trunk, there was the Wanamaker trophy, unharmed, in beautiful condition.

"The warehouse?" I said. "It turns out the warehouse was owned by the Walter Hagen Golf Company."

Mitch said, "So Hagen a thief. We on the tee."

A younger man might have been embarrassed by Scott Pritchard outdriving him 50 to 100 yards on every hole, but I was bolstered by the knowledge that he might be long but he had no idea who Irene Dunne was.

We were both even par through the first eight holes. I'd been reaching the greens like a normal human. Scott had been getting there a little easier.

Good example. The second hole. It's a 523-yard par-5. Neither of us birdied it but I reached the greenside bunker on the right in two by coming out of my shoes with my driver, and coming out of my socks with the three-wood. Scott reached the same bunker with a one-iron off the tee and a sand wedge for his second.

Some people say length like Scott Pritchard possesses is not only criminal, it's immoral.

It was something of a relief—to me, anyhow—that the other contenders on the leaderboard, who were playing in front of us, weren't making the kind of moves that cause a gallery to go running over a cliff, leaving you lonely and in a bad mood. If anything, the other contenders were falling back, whether it was your Ernie, your Phil, or your Claude Steekley. They were all over par.

Players who say they don't look at the scoreboards on the course when they're in contention are either liars, stupid, or don't care about winning as long as they can collect a fat check.

I'm better off if I know what's going on around me. It keeps my mind from jacking with my swing when I haven't invited it to the shot.

Scott's length got the best of him at the 9th hole, a 220-yard par-3. The only thing unique about the hole is that it's a par-3.

Modern course designers never end up with a par-3 hole as the 9th. It's out of balance. But you often find it on the older courses. It most likely had something to do with the real estate they were given to work with.

While the length of the hole required me to put everything I had into a three-iron to reach the green, Scott hit an eight-iron. But the problem with the shot was, the ball wouldn't come down. His shot soared over the flag, over the green, and almost over the grandstand behind the green that was jammed with spectators.

"Get down!" Scott hollered.

"Hit a town!" his caddie hollered.

There were two rules officials going along with our pairing. They'd been introduced on the first tee. One was Haley Sprackling, the current president of the U.S. PGA. He was the director of golf at Whispering Silos Country Club in Sheboygan, Wisconsin. The "walking observer" was Barney Rivers, the director of golf at Dancing Fairways Country Club in Rancho Pronto Honcho, California. I might have the name of the town wrong.

They ruled that Scott should receive a free drop from the grandstand. One club length away, no closer to the hole. Anyone familiar with rule 24-2b(i) "immovable obstruction," would know that Scott obviously deserved relief.

Tricia Hurt, the foot soldier with our group, would know it. I imagined her saying on the air, "He's getting relief, Lanny, and he deserves it under twenty-four–two, of course."

The free drop didn't help Scott. He was left with an impossible pitch over a bunker to a pin that was back left. His pitch raced past the pin by fifty feet and he three-putted for a double-bogey 5.

When I gingerly two-putted from thirty feet for a par, I went to the back nine with a three-stroke lead on Scott, and everybody else.

As we left the 9th green and made our way to the 10th tee, I said to Scott, "Tough deal—that was a brutal pitch shot you had."

"My lob wedge sucks," he said. "Geeeahhh."

I'd scanned the crowd from time to time and I hadn't seen Gwen all day long. I figured she was staying out of sight on purpose.

"Have you seen your mother anywhere?" I asked Scott idly.

He said, "I didn't know I was supposed to be looking for her."

"You weren't," I said, and dropped the subject.

We both parred the first two holes on the back, then Scott made the 12th hole beg for mercy. While I scrapped around and made a par 5 on the 560-yard hole, playing it with a driver, five-wood, wedge, and two putts, Scott put it on the green with a 335-yard drive and a 225-yard seven-iron, and two-putted from twenty feet for a birdie.

This pulled him up to within two strokes of me again, and after we parred the 13th and 14th holes, that's how we stood when we came to the last four holes, the Ho Bitches.

Scott drove first at the 15th and took it over the trees on the left, ignoring the bunker in the center of the fairway, and left himself with nothing but a simple pitch to the green on the 400-yard hole. His drive rendered the "strategic" bunker in the fairway so out of date, the club might as well have ordered the bulldozer right then.

I had no choice but to play short of the bunker, which I did, and after I put a five-iron on the green but nowhere near birdie range, I could only wait to see what Scott would do with his easy pitch. Fortunately for me, his lob wedge sucked again. He failed to make a birdie.

The 16th hole put far too much trauma in my life.

First of all, I knew from the scoreboards that the best score in the clubhouse was Phil Mickelson's 280, even par for the 72 holes. Phil had caught fire on the back and closed with a 68. Everyone else had faded. But I'd started out six ahead of Phil, and I thanked Lucille for the fact that I still had him by four strokes. So by all that was logical it had come down to Scott and me, just the two of us now, and I had him by two strokes with three holes to play.

It was still his honor on 16 and he drove it into the future again, way past the dogleg, past the willows, leaving himself with another short pitch to the green.

I took the driver out of the bag, saying to Mitch, "I've been straight with this all day. What do you think?"

"You feel confident with it, go ahead on," he said.

Confident didn't swing the club. Unfortunately, I did.

I pushed the drive too far right, and for a moment I thought for sure it was in the water. It's impossible to describe that feeling. Food poisoning comes close.

But the marshal down the fairway, right at the willows near the edge of the pond, signaled that the ball stayed up. Heart-pound deal.

Mitch and I didn't speak as we walked to the ball. He knew I wasn't done with the hole yet, and knew my confidence had been shaken.

When I reached my ball, I was happy I could see part of it in the tall grass. But it rested between the water and a marked-off red line. It was in a hazard. I wouldn't be able to ground my club.

My lie wasn't that bad. I thought I could get an eight-iron up. Try to reach the green with it, but keep it left, away from the pond if it landed short. And I didn't want to think about the shot too long.

Maybe I should have thought about it longer, however.

I did the stupidest thing in my whole life—aside from marrying Terri Adams and Cheryl Haney.

I didn't swing hard enough and my clubface hung up in the twisted grass. As a result, I scuffed the ball into the pond.

There were gasps, groans, and shrieks from the gallery.

I stood there and looked at Mitch. He stood there and looked at me.

All I could think of was two in the water, out in three, shooting four, probably make a 7—congratulations, you pissed away another major, you spineless, no-talent, give-up shit-ass.

That's when I heard Tricia Hurt's voice.

"Bobby Joe, I think this is your ball here," she said. "This is where I saw it go into the grass."

She was three yards behind me, pointing down to a ball.

"What—?"

"Are you playing a Titleist Two?" She bent over to have a closer look at the ball. "There's a red star on this one. Isn't this yours?"

I said, "Yeah, I guess that *is* mine. But I've already hit another one. I'm history, dear."

"No, you're not," Tricia said. "There's no penalty for playing the wrong ball in a hazard."

I almost laughed. "Since when?"

"I'm not kidding, Bobby Joe. *There is no penalty for hitting the wrong ball in a hazard*. It's in the rules."

I looked at the PGA officials, Haley Sprackling and Barney Rivers, who were standing nearby.

"Is she right?" I said. "I don't know the damn rule. I've never had a situation like this come up."

Tricia said, "It's under 'provisional ball'—twenty-seven–two."

Haley Sprackling removed a thick book from his jacket pocket—*Decisions on the Rules of Golf*—and consulted it. After a long moment, he raised his eyebrows at Tricia Hurt and me.

"You're right, missy," the official said. "You dang sure are. Bobby Joe, you can play this 'un here without penalty. You're a lucky gunch."

With a grateful nod at Tricia Hurt, I took the eight-iron out of the bag again and quickly punched a shot safely out into the fairway before anybody could change his mind.

Thanks to a fifteen-year-old girl, I'd gone from dead in the water, slim and none, to alive and well in a matter of two minutes.

I was ninety yards from the green for my third shot. I wedged it up there to ten feet from the pin and somehow holed the putt for an All-American 4 after Scott missed another birdie chance from fifteen feet.

We made pars at the 17th, me with a 200-yard five-iron shot and two putts, Scott with a 200-yard nine-iron and two putts.

I must tell you that with a two-shot lead and only one hole to go, I wasn't embarrassed or humiliated in the least to play the 18th for a bogey 5. I did it with a sick little tee ball, a sick little layup, a sick little pitch, and two putts from twelve feet. The last putt would have even been a gimme in a Texas gambling game.

I always said happiness was a six-inch putt to win a major.

# 55

The moment was a basic blur. I was aware of people rushing out on the green and hugging on me, lifting me up. Mitch, Grady Don, Jerry, a couple of strangers. Finally Gwen, out of nowhere, leaping into my arms.

"Well, where have you been?" I said, as she strapped a big kiss on me. "I've been looking for you all day."

I was conscious of applause from the crowd, but I knew it would have been louder and longer if the stud-bubba cupcake had won.

Speaking of which, Scott's mother and I edged our way over to him, and he put out a hand to me. Good sport.

We gave him a hug together, and I said, "Scott, my man, you're gonna win a scary bunch of these before you're done—try not to hold this one against me."

"Geeeahhh," he said. "You got a big break on sixteen, but I gotta say, that four you made was awesome."

I grinned. "I've always said the zebras do a good job."

Gwen wanted to go wash Oakland Hills off of her. She assumed I'd be in the press center a good while. She'd see me back at the hotel, she said, and don't forget to bring the trophy home.

The first thing I did was give the press a sound bite. I said I was so exhausted, I felt like I'd tried to fight a war with France for an ally.

The ruling at the 16th hole was discussed at length. I said I'd be glad to saw off part of the Wanamaker Trophy and give it to Tricia Hurt.

Some of the writers wanted to know why I wasn't better versed in the rules of the game?

"Like you people are?" I said, smiling politely.

I explained how most of us on the Tour aren't rules junkies. We've all read the little book called *The Rules of Golf* you can buy in any pro shop, but most of us had never read or studied the bigger and thicker book called *Decisions on the Rules of Golf*.

I said, "The decisions book is where you have to go to find the law of the land. Tricia Hurt was familiar with it. I'd only seen it on a shelf."

A writer wanted to know if I was ashamed of playing for a bogey 5 on the final hole?

"Why would I be ashamed of using my head?" I said.

I reminded the writers that I wasn't the first guy who played for a bogey on the last hole to win a major. I rattled off the names of some of those who'd done it in the past—Olin Dutra at Merion, Sam Parks at Oakmont, Hubert Green at Southern Hills, Andy North at Cherry Hills and here at Oakland Hills, Curtis Strange at Oak Hill.

I said, "Maybe you'd think more highly of me if I'd played a banjo and tap-danced up the last fairway and blown the deal."

Ellen Wheeler, the Houston poetess, followed me out of the press center and waited to corner me alone after I did radio stuff. She wanted the usual exclusive.

What I shared with her was, I couldn't help thinking about Clayton Heafner while I stood on the 18th green waiting to tap in the six-inch putt for the win. She wanted to know who Clayton Heafner was, how to spell it, and why he would come to mind. I spelled it for her and explained that Heafner was a big, gruff Carolinian who played the Tour from the late thirties through the fifties. Jimmy Demaret liked to joke that Heafner was known for his "even temper"—he was mad all the time. Heafner hated the majors, I said. One reason may have been because he never won any of them. Anyhow, Heafner used to say his ambition was to have a one-foot putt to win a major so he could walk up to the ball with his putter, say "Fuck it," and backhand it into the trees. That's what I was thinking to myself on the last green. I was thinking about Clayton Heafner. If she'd been close enough, I said, she might have noticed my grin.

"Thanks," she said. "There has to be a way I can use that."

" 'Screw it'?"

"Maybe. Probably wouldn't make the cut."

" 'Forget it'?"

"Sold!" she yelped, and scampered away.

---

There was a smattering of applause from the hotel staff when I carried the trophy through the lobby on the way to the elevator. I waved thank-yous to one and all.

I put the trophy on a table in the living room of the suite and went to the bar where I was pleased to find a bottle of Junior, a bucket of ice, and tall glasses. I was making myself a cocktail when Gwen came out of the bedroom. She was fresh from a long bath. She wore a pair of snug khaki denim pants and a light purple linen tank top.

"Hi, champ," she said, grinning. "I've colored my hair and had a body wrap for the occasion."

I said, "You may notice how smart I look. I've won a major championship, so I must be a lot smarter."

"You definitely look smarter than you did this morning."

"I'll have to change my life around now that I'm so smart. I'll have to get a whole new set of friends. I'll probably have to get rid of you and find a smarter woman. One who wears glasses maybe."

"Bobby Joe."

"Yeah . . . ?"

"To get rid of me?" she said, coming toward me with a look I'd always remember.

"Yeah . . . ?"

"You've got two chances."